Victoria Williamson

'Brilliant, lyrical and portrayed with a nuance that captures the beauty, history and contradictions of present day Africa'
Adamma Oti Obonbuo

532 024 61 6

'A complex and lyrical adventure that's part ghost story, part thriller, part love story. Compelling atmospheric and beautifully written'
WRD About Books

'A powerful novel transporting the reader to a richly observed setting . . . stays with you long after closing the last page'
Ipswich Children's Book Group

'A fascinating richly-layered novel asking big questions about how we explore and understand the past as well as deftly building to a thrilling climax. Highly recommended'
Cath Howe

'Beautiful, intense and atmospheric book. Intricately drawn characters in a rich, vibrant setting, and is packed with mystery and action'
Mo O'Hara

'Beautifully written, compelling, magical and with powerful historical and political information elegantly woven into the mix'
Judy Allen

'Perfectly woven together, I lived it, heard it, smelt it, touched it as I was transported to the forest and beach to Shanza and . . . Kisiri. And underneath it all a deep, knowing current anchored in factual history and oral traditional tales giving it depth and resonance'
Margaret Bateson-Hill

'Set on the idyllic Kenyan coast, in luminously beautiful writing, it combines a poignant ghost story, modern day love and a serious political message'
Patricia Elliott

Song Beneath The Tides

GUPPY
BOOKS

SONG BENEATH THE TIDES
is a GUPPY BOOK

First published in 2020 by
Guppy Books,
Bracken Hill,
Cotswold Road,
Oxford OX2 9JG
This edition published in 2021

978 1 913101 09 1

1 3 5 7 9 10 8 6 4 2

Papers used by Guppy Books are from well-managed
forests and other responsible sources.

GUPPY PUBLISHING LTD Reg. No. 11565833

A CIP catalogue record for this book is available from the British Library.

Typeset in Sabon by Falcon Oast Graphic Art Ltd www.falcon.uk.com
Printed and bound by CPI Group (UK) Ltd, Croydon, CR0 4YY

Song Beneath The Tides

Beverley Birch

GUPPY
BOOKS

To IRIS and OLIVE and all the adventures
and explorations ahead of them

The winds call our names
We hear, we hear
And the drum takes up our song
Our song
flies on the seas
soars on the winds
swells on the great tides
They hear, they hear

from *Songs of Zawati*

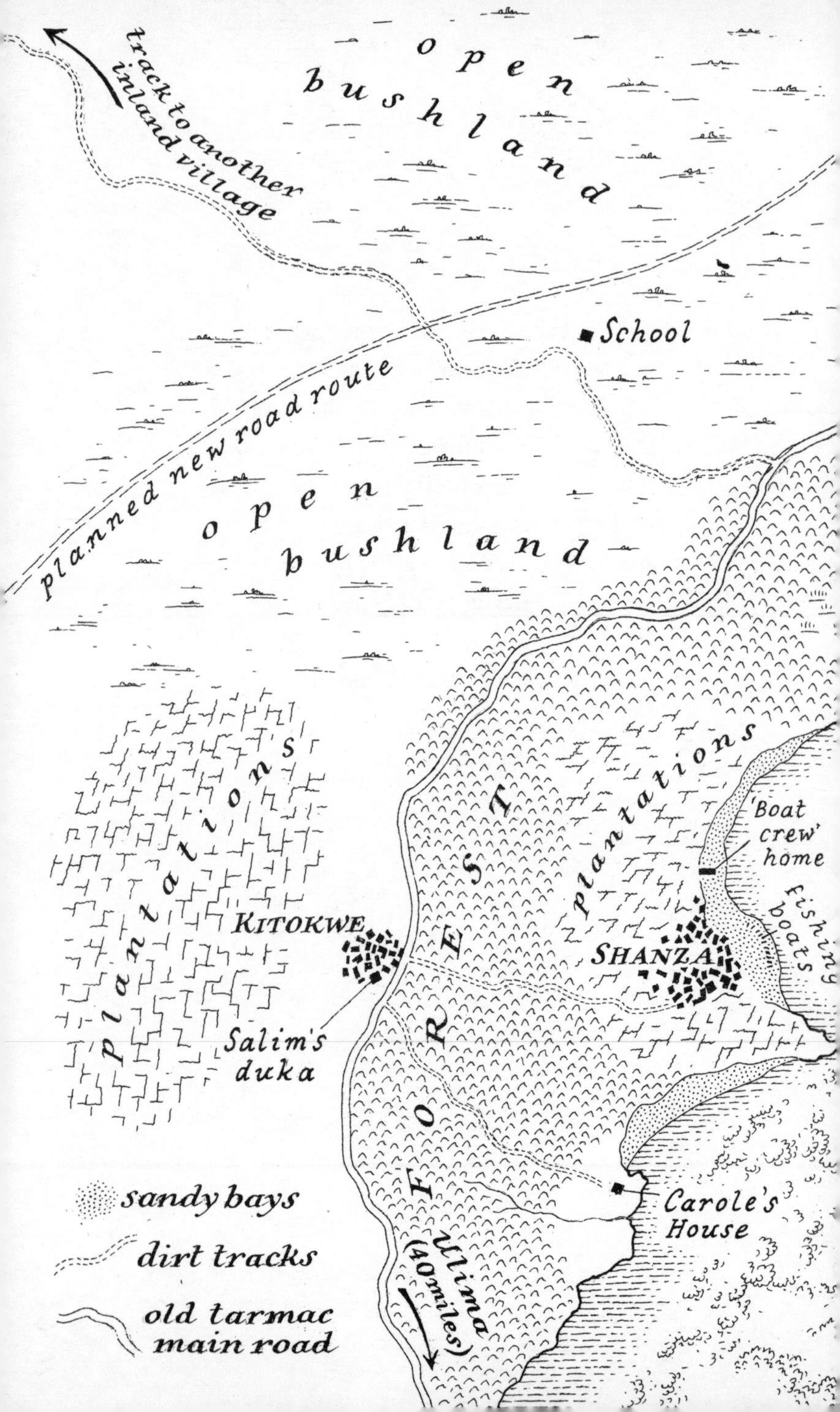
track to another inland village
open bushland
School
planned new road route
open bushland
plantations
FOREST
plantations
'Boat crew' home
fishing boats
KITOKWE
SHANZA
Salim's duka
Carole's House
Ulima (40 miles)
sandy bays
dirt tracks
old tarmac main road

Ruined Arch (7 miles)

Tundani (15 miles)

buried coral reefs

N

MANGROVES

INDIAN OCEAN

deep water bay

very deep channel

Fumo + Zawati burial grove

hidden coral reefs

KISIRI

Ras Chui

high rocks

coral reefs (exposed at low tide)

One mile

N·G

first day – *whispers*

second day – *warnings*

third day – *invaders*

fourth day – *secrets*

fifth day – *warriors*

sixth day – *vultures*

seventh day – *attack*

eighth day – *storm*

one month later, London – *dancing*

first day
whispers

One

It begins with a forest, and with Ally.

Light slants green through a high, leafy canopy. Hanging creepers sway and rustle. Everywhere, chirrups and cheeps and whistles and trills, and the flit of small, busy wings . . .

She spins round, braced to run.

No one there: the path empty. Sunlight dapples the scuffed sand so that it seems to move, but it's just a track, curling back to a dark outcrop of coral rock, then turning out of sight.

The hair on the back of her neck prickles. Something's about to appear. Between the curtains of leaves. Or the bushes. Or from behind that rock.

She watches. She shifts her gaze to a claw of roots from a tumbled tree. Arches of shadow like a vast skeleton, sheltering – *what*?

The forest stirs. Ripples of light speed towards her. She fights the urge to back away. A rush of sound. Birds whirl in fright.

Common sense says a ripe coconut has fallen.

It takes all her nerve to hold still, listen, then turn away, present her back to the path and resume her trek towards the sea. She should yell for her brothers – moments ago she'd seen them against the sheen of water beyond the trees ahead, Jack's tall silhouette beside Ben's stocky little shape.

She's reluctant to probe the forest with her voice.

She walks faster. And at once has the same unnerving sensation of *nearness*, of brushing the warm contours of something live, of eyes following her, of a soft breath exhaled.

This time she runs, breaking through the last trees into the blinding brilliance of the open bay. She clears the mounds of drying seaweed in a single bound, kicks off her shoes, grabs them and leaps down through the soft powdery sand towards the reef, putting distance as fast as she can between herself and that menace – that *terror* of the forest.

*

I dream . . . I dream . . .

I flee the festering walls of our prison.

I walk the paths of the forest.

I seek Hope, a flame of life in the dark.

In my dream I find Her. In my dream I speak to Her.

She gives no answer.

Is it the poison that dreams?

Is the sickness in me now?

*

'It's a leopard! It's stalking you!' Ben said. '*Pad, pad, pad,* just behind you! Bet it *is* – cos that rock's called Ras Chui an' that means Leopard Rock.' He waved a hand along the beach towards a coral promontory like a knobbly finger pointing to sea.

'No, really!' Ally protested. 'It felt . . .' She trailed off. *Spooky* sounded too ordinary.

'Well, it's a forest, so there's animals all over.' Jack shrugged off her alarm. 'No *leopard*,' he pretended to whack Ben over the head, 'you can see people use this path a lot. Leopards'd keep clear.'

He said it with a tone of certainty that made Ally grind her teeth. Jack had taken on this all-seeing, all-knowing air since they'd stepped off the plane from London.

'How can you see? You've only been here five minutes like me!'

Jack pulled a face, then grinned. 'Yeah, well, sure. But you heard Carole say it's a track used by people from that village along there. You know, she showed us on the map – *Shanza*, it's called.'

'Well don't walk so fast,' Ally finished lamely.

In this bright air, way out on the open reef where she'd caught up with them, with the tang of coral pools and warm salty seas carried on a light breeze, the menace of the forest walk was fading fast.

'Didn't mean to leave you behind, Ally,' he waved a hand at the sweep of wide white sands, 'but look – no one for miles— Hey, Benjy!' He set off at a run towards their brother splashing gleefully across the coral towards the seaward edge of the reef. 'Benjy! That's deep sea out there!'

A tickle brushed Ally's toes – a cavalcade of tiny crabs

5

scuttling to a rock pool. She crouched, tracking the pale shadows along the sandy bottom. Then she stood, looking round, only now taking in how far the tide had ebbed to expose the honeycomb landscape of miniature coral mountains and lakes, forested with seaweed, crusted with shells, popping and crackling in the warming sun.

A month ahead, a *whole month* here. Africa! Ever since that morning at home, her mother opening the email from their aunt, Carole, she'd felt this spiking thrill.

'*Send Jack and Ally for as long as they can come. Benjy too, if you trust those two to keep track of him. And make him promise to OBEY them! I'm being posted to work in a hospital in Ulima on the coast for a while . . . so NOW'S THE TIME.*'

Ally'd printed out the photos Carole sent, pinned them all over the walls in her room, debated every one with Zoe – Zoe wailing, 'I'm coming too! I wish my mum'd let me! Ally, you owe me an email every single day! Promise! Everything, every-thing, everything, you got to tell me, yeah?'

Ally inhaled the salty, tangy air. How? *How can I make Zoe feel this?* Green forest, creamy sands, the rainbow reef glittering as if it moved, restless in the sunlight. A dream! She'd only ever seen this in adverts and films. Never, ever, did she believe she'd see it for real!

A ripple of shadow passed overhead. Just a wisp of cloud crossing the sun, the thread of its darkness travelling up the beach; she found herself watching till it merged with the forest.

That weird feeling in there! It flowed through her again, a thread of a sigh, a longing, like an emptiness deep in her centre.

She was oddly cold. She scanned the trees. They stared back – an impenetrable barricade along the summit of the sands, the path invisible.

'It *is* someone,' she whispered. 'It is!'

*

I have been to their deaths, and returned.

The fever brings this horror! Does my own death draw near?

I dream – I dream, that I have been to all their deaths. Before the monsoon breaks they will be lost.

I have been to their deaths, and beyond.

Even as I write these words am I dreaming, still?

It is the first hour of the first day of my sixteenth year, and I have a terrible dread. Vultures gather. Our ships rot on their moorings. Two more men have died, and three begin to fail. We dig more graves in the court below and soon there will be no square of ground to take more dead.

We should have burned the corpses, burned every man, woman and child who died. So my father said even as he died. But we have no firewood.

We have not eaten these seven days. Only the children had the scraps of food we had saved, and now there is nothing.

Where is Hope? In the secret paths of the forest, I fly to find Her.

Amid the green trees, I see Her.

Her face is fierce. Her hair flames like the rising sun.

The fever conjures Her to me, it is the poison in me!

I speak; I beg.

She turns from me.

Is there no hope left for any of us?

Leli paused on the spiny ridge of Ras Chui for his friend to catch up. He surveyed the reef below with satisfaction.

'You are right, Huru,' he announced. 'These strangers are the expected ones. There, you see! Two cross the reef. These are the brothers. That one, alone, is the sister. She has the strange red hair, like the doctor auntie. Red hair, like a fire!'

'Why do you speak to me in English?' Huru demanded, in English, puffing from the short, steep climb up the rocks from the village. 'This language sits like a stone on my head.'

'We practise! So that they will know our words and hear that our greeting is good!'

Huru snorted. 'You are mad, Leli. Very mad! These tourists will not want to be our friends. They will not want to hear our bad English. This red-hair girl—'

'Afraid, always!' retorted Leli, but with a grin. He was watching the third figure with interest, how she trailed the others, stopped to look at something at her feet, how she turned, how her hair caught the glow of the sun, how she looked back at the shore, and stood watching, as if she saw something.

'How can we know if we will not try?' Nudging his friend forward, together they scrambled down the rocks, still arguing, and veered in long, easy strides across the reef towards the three distant figures.

Two

Deep green water lapped the edge of the reef.

'Too far to swim,' Ben said, crestfallen. 'I thought we could swim to your island!'

He directed this at Ally. She'd been first onto the beach at dawn. And there was the little hillock of land, stark against the pink dawn sky. It rode the tide like a ship. Surf creamed from its high bluff like the wake of a boat, mists wreathed its summit, a drift of birds coiled above the trees.

Then the rising sun tipped the island's rim. Fire flooded its slopes, streamed towards Ally across the waves. She was drenched in sunlight. She gasped in the startling delight of it – like the thrilling soar of a song.

Now, she scrambled up onto a ridge of coral to get a better view over the rippling stretch of sea. 'It's a mile away, more, maybe,' she echoed her little brother's disappointment.

'So, we'll find a boat, then,' Jack insisted. 'That's if we want to get out there. We do, agreed?'

'*It is forbidden.*'

The voice came so unexpectedly that Ally whirled to look, slithering on seaweed, nearly falling.

Two boys stood lightly balanced on a nobble of coral, tall and black against the sky's hard glare.

'The island is forbidden to strangers!' The speaker jumped down and advanced towards them, hand out for shaking. 'I see you are the family of Dr Carole, the children of her sister, from England. This is my good friend Huru. We come to say a big, big welcome!'

He turned, bright-eyed, to Ally. His gaze seemed to envelop her, and, unexpectedly, brought a flush to her face.

'You will visit our place?' he said – more a demand than a question, leaving her no time to answer. 'You will stay how many days? I am Leli! Come to Shanza for welcome, now, now!' And off he charged, signalling them all to follow, drawing them into a stumbling run behind him, across coral ridges and rockpools towards Ras Chui, Ally struggling to keep up.

'Jack!' she hissed at her brother's back. 'You *know* what Carole said about strangers!'

'Not strangers,' he hissed back. 'They're from Shanza village.'

'So, what about Carole's rules?'

'Here's the deal,' their aunt had said last night, leading them up to the breezy flat roof of her house to recover from the scorching drive up the coast from the airport, 'you know I don't usually make rules, but—'

Ben had groaned and crossed his eyes. She'd crossed her eyes back, 'Listen, *you*, I've rented this house specially for your visit. Punished myself – eighty miles driving every day, down the coast to Ulima Hospital and back – *just* for you. What a sacrifice!' Laughing, sweeping a hand at the coastline's lazy curves – long white bays, mangrove creeks, soft dunes and sandflats, on and on as far as they could see in the waning dusk.

'But, the point is,' she gave a mock glare at Ben, 'I can't get holiday for the first two days you're here, we've several doctors ill. So, *Rules of Engagement*, you hear? I'm trusting you, Benjy, you in particular, or I'll haul you to the hospital with me to watch me work, and that's no picnic! And by the way, put your phones away – no signal here. The nearest landline's a mile away, so *Rule One*: for help, go to Shanza along the shore. I've only been here three days, but the Elders invited me to tea, so everyone knows you're coming and staying in this house – they call it the Old Fisheries House for some reason. *Rule Two*: no wandering off with strangers . . .'

There'd been several more, but nothing about talkative boys from the village hijacking them for obscure reasons. Nor anything about boats, and Ally could hear Jack and Ben eagerly negotiating a boat-trip now as the two Shanza boys led them all up the rocky slope of Ras Chui and down into the bay beyond.

'My cousin Saka will help,' the boy called Huru assured them. 'He has a boat. We can take you everywhere!' Airily he flapped a hand towards thatch roofs and brown walls in the mottled shade of palms. There was a buzz of activity along the shore below, their scramble down the rocks met by a torrent of small children, yelling, jiggling round them, plucking at their clothes, leaping to touch Ally's hair.

11

'It is the colour.' The taller boy – Leli – turned back to wait for her. 'They are curious. They have not before seen this colour hair. They say it is like the sun! And they are always happy for guests. I, too!' Again that eager, warm gaze: she felt it flood over her, heating her cheeks.

In fact curious glances came from all sides. Two girls kept pace with them, making some remark to Leli in what Ally guessed was Swahili.

'We greet you!' One switched to English, addressing Ally. 'But we leave you to Leli, for now.' Linking arms with the other girl and strolling away, giving a backwards, mischievous glance.

Leli sternly ignored her. 'Eshe and Koffi being foolish,' he told Ally. 'Jokes, always!'

'What's the joke about?'

He tossed his head to throw the question off, steering her along the shore between boats unloading their catch. A few still sculled inwards with a raucous escort of gulls. A small dhow dropped sail and ran at full tilt up the sands. Baskets of fish, hoisted past, vanished into shady spaces between the homes. And all along the ribbon of seaweed and shells at the highwater mark, gulls and crows strutted and squabbled over fish scraps.

Now two tiny girls were attached like limpets to Ally's hands. She allowed them to haul her further along the beach and station her for a view of a mushroom-shaped rock offshore.

'They want to show good swimming,' Leli said. 'Specially they make a show for you.'

Ally glanced up at him, startled, then at the splashing

12

cavalcade of little bodies heading for the rock, clambering up, somersaulting back into the water shrieking.

For her? Like she was someone important, famous!

She laughed. He laughed happily back. 'For guests – always special things! Every person enjoys guests! Me – I am specially, specially happy for you to come to Shanza!'

But I must not talk too much, he thought. *I must close my mouth, or this English girl will be very bored.*

He stole a sideways look at her. Eshe and Koffi's little sisters had run from the water and were swinging from her hands, lifting their feet off the ground, almost pulling her over, and she was giggling with them.

She does not look bored. But she is not saying much. He studied how she looked around and listened.

He scanned the fishing beach, scattered nets, ropes, baskets, screeching gulls, seeing it as she would. To his eye, suddenly, it was noisy and messy. And the fish smell was strong. A girl from a city in England would not like the fish smell. And the grandfathers were cackling like old crows where they sat to watch the boats. The girl would not know that Eshe's grandfather told very funny jokes. No one could stop laughing at his stories. The girl would just think the grandfathers were madmen.

A wobble of nerves went through him. *Is her place in England shiny and everything modern? She will not like Shanza! Her brothers will not like Shanza. It is a mistake to bring these tourists to my place.*

Huru is right, she will not like my bad English, either.

13

He watched her watching the children dive from the rock. Her brothers were in a knot of boys steered by Huru to the boats, and Huru's voice carried clearly.

'My cousin Saka's *ngalawa*—'

'Is that what this kind of boat's called?' The little brother's voice, excited and shrill.

'*Ngalawa*, so,' Huru pronounced it slowly, and the English boy copied. 'We make it together, from a tree, we take out the inside, so.' You could see Huru's pride, patting the strong sides of the boat, the logs fixed as side-floats to balance it, the big curved rudder, the lobster traps and nets, the patched yellow sail. 'The sail is put away, so it is not broken. It must always be ready again to go to fishing.' Huru frowned at it dropped in a heap in the boat. 'Why has Saka not done this? And he is not here! We must find him.'

It *was* strange. Leli reflected on it. The fishermen always stayed till everyone's boat was unloaded, tidied away, and safe on the shore.

Huru hauled up the sail and dropped it again tidily, furled and tied it, instructed the small brother to stow the paddles. The big brother sat on the prow listening to everyone talking to practise their English.

Huru is clever to offer Saka's boat, Leli thought. *It is a suitable thing to offer the visitors. Saka will be happy to help. The visitors will like the sea. And the mangrove creeks.*

Suddenly, he felt lighter. He contemplated the girl again, how her hair glowed in the sun, how she felt his look and turned to him and gave him a joyful smile. The thought entered his head that he found her beautiful. With it came a

14

new knot of nerves. He considered how to arrange his words to make no stupid mistakes in her language. Teacher said his words were good, but his grammar was terrible.

'They're like little fish,' the girl murmured, meaning the children, just a flash of bottoms and feet tumbling from the rock.

His prepared words took flight, like startled birds. 'Fisher children,' he said in a rush of need for her to understand everything. 'And *boriti* cutters' children—'

'*Boriti*?' She repeated it carefully.

The English name – 'mangrove poles' – came to him and he beckoned her towards the new house at the end of the village, showing her the roof – still just a lattice of *boriti* to take the *makuti* ('palm thatch' in English, he remembered), and the walls just the *boriti* frame. 'They will put the mud on,' he demonstrated the plastering with his hands. 'In Saka's boat we can go to the mangroves where the *boriti* is cut. It is my father's work—'

Ally peered up through the skeleton of the roof. 'Ben'll like this *so* much,' she began, 'he loves to figure things out—' Leli was frowning at her in concentration, and she halted.

'Figure things out – what is this?' he asked.

'Oh, sorry – I mean find out how things work? He's always taking things apart.'

'Ah!' Leli nodded. 'Me, I will figure out sickness. I will be a doctor, like your auntie-doctor Carole. But not in the city. I think perhaps the city is interesting, but I have heard there are too many people. It is good to be where there are great seas – to breathe in air. And forests – you can find medicines in forests—'

'Your forest's so strange!' Ally told him, without thinking.

It took her a moment to understand that the look on his face was one of terrible disappointment.

'Oh! No, look, Leli, your forest is beautiful, it's just – it's – well, I just find it a bit . . . well, scary . . . But I really like your place, I . . . I feel . . . I mean, I'm *lucky,* I'm *really, really* lucky to be here!'

He rewarded her with a beam of delight, as if she'd handed him a priceless gift.

Walking back along the sands, he questioned, 'What is this *scary* in the forest?'

'Oh, well . . . nothing—' Again, it ambushes her – a warmth, close by. Unheard words. She glances back.

He looked behind too. 'You are troubled?' He examined her face so intently that she had to look away. '*Haya*, OK,' he declared. 'I have not seen strangeness in the forest. But I tell you, there, on Kisiri . . .'

'Where's that? *Kisiri*?' She pronounced it carefully, learning it, liking the sound.

'Our island there. Kisiri is its name. It is . . .' He screwed up his face with concentration. 'It is a hidden thing, it is . . .' He put his finger across his lips.

'Secret?'

'*Secret*. Yes, *secret*. Secret! Kisiri means this – secret. Some of my friends, they swim to Kisiri in the night and they come back yelling! Phaw, if the Elders saw they were going . . .' His tone signified something beyond description. 'I think my friends are joking, but I see truly they do not go again. Not Eshe, who is very brave, not Koffi, who always follows

16

Eshe, not even the one, Lumbwi, who is a bit mad and will do forbidden things *because* they are forbidden! But he will not go there in the night! They tell that a cold wind is there, going round, and round, and the tide is fierce by the island, but it is calm on our beach! I tell you, no one will go again after the sun is gone!'

'But why would your Elders be angry? Why's it forbidden?'

'*Sababu . . . sababu . . .* because Kisiri is for special times, for Shanza only.'

She thought about that. 'You mean private – like, someone owns it?'

'Everyone owns it! It is Shanza's place!'

'Then can't we just ask? You know, get permission from the Elders?'

He chewed his lip as if it helped him sort out answers. 'They will not allow. We go in special times only. It is the burial place of—'

'Oh,' she said, 'it's *sacred*!'

'Sacred.' He nodded. 'The place there is very sacred, in Kisiri's forest.'

He pronounced the word so that it sounded like secret, if you didn't listen carefully. *Secret* and *sacred*. A tingle went up her spine. *Secret* and *sacred*. She looked at Kisiri, from this angle a curl of white shore, leaning palms, the green swell of the tide round it.

After a minute, she resumed, 'So who's buried? Can't we go if we're very, very careful – and . . . you know . . . respectful?'

'It is the burial place of Bwana Fumo and Mwana Zawati. They are the great founders of Shanza – many many many

17

hundreds of years ago. They are young people. They do brave things. Kisiri is where they lie, for ever. For the *Sherehe ya Kwazi* . . . so . . .' He puckered his face, searching for the translation. 'So when we are together, everyone, we eat, tell stories, there is dancing, singing . . .'

'A party?'

'*Ndiyo*! I mean '*yes*'! We go round Kisiri – everyone in the boats. We go on Kisiri and we stay for a night. Mzee Kitwana tells us the stories of Bwana Fumo and Mwana Zawati, how they came from far dangers to be safe on our island. We are joyful! We come away when the sun is high. But sometimes, it makes the skin go cold, this place, even when the sun is hot—'

'Eh, Leli, you are the storyteller now!' a voice broke in. 'So now you let old Kitwana rest from his duties!' A deep, warm chuckle followed, and a kind of lilting sigh.

Ally looked for the speaker, and spotted him at the top of the beach – very old, very stooped, his frail frame a shock to her against the musical strength of his voice.

He brandished a walking stick at Leli. 'You have time for stories, still, Leli? Or you are too busy with the world that cannot keep up with itself?'

He squinted, head on one side. Ally saw the hint of a smile in the twist of his mouth. 'When I was your age, young ones did not have to go to distant places to search for wonder! Leli, Leli, will you remember to tell your English friend of the big dhows?' He pointed his stick at the open waters beyond the island. 'Just there – just there. Flying over the ocean like great birds. And men from many places rested their tall ships and traded good things and told us tales.' For a minute he stared pensively into the distance and Ally found herself turning to try and see what he saw: fleets of ships? Billowing sails?

'It is calm, calm, now.' The old man's voice dropped to a slow lilt. 'Now it is the birds that come every year to our warm place from the cold places of the world. But in the old, old time of our Bwana Fumo – who was just a boy like you, Leli, and Mwana Zawati, who was just a girl like your friend . . . Ah, when, together, they came to deeds of great bravery – in that long ago time, other ships and other men wandered this sea. Such ships! Such men! To fill people with fear and hatred and many other feelings it is terrible to have in your heart.'

He turned a sudden sharp gaze on Leli. 'It is in my mind that it is like this Tundani place you must go to see, Leli. So that you will understand. So that it will be *remembered*.' He tapped his head and sighed, a gusty, wheezing, wistful sound, and plodded away through the soft dry sand, muttering.

'What's he mean?' Ally whispered, reluctant to have the old man hear.

Leli frowned. 'Tundani is the place of the big new hotel they make for the rich tourists, many, many miles away . . . But *remembering*? I do not know what he means.'

'Eh-eh, Leli!' The old man had stopped at the top of the beach and was contemplating them again. 'Leli, Leli, my son of the night, I have in my mind,' he chortled, 'I have in my mind that you have found your Zawati!' He waggled his head and went on his way again, enjoying his own joke.

Ally glanced at Leli. She could see his embarrassment.

'He is old,' he said. 'It is nothing. He is talking about

19

Bwana Fumo's friend, Zawati. She is a great warrior, a great leader. They lie there together on the island. Bwana Fumo and Mwana Zawati. Warriors and leaders.' He sniffed. 'Mzee Kitwana is making a big joke. Everyone is joking today—'

'It's a nice joke! I quite like being called a warrior and a leader!'

He narrowed his eyes at her suspiciously. She was tempted to narrow her eyes back, except he'd definitely think she was mocking him.

Instead she asked, 'So why did he call you "son of the night"? Is that a joke too?'

Warily he regarded her. After a pause, 'My name, Leli – this means night.'

'Oh, OK! I like that – *Leli, Son of the Night*. So not anything to do with this Bwana Fu—'

The blare of a car horn blasted through her words. Then the thrum of an approaching engine. Goats galloped furiously into view, scattering chickens and heralding the apparition of a large, very shiny red Land Rover.

The vehicle ground its way through soft sand, bumped to the top of the shore, halted, and the engine switched off.

As one, the small children abandoned the rock and streamed out of the water towards the newcomer. But then they stopped, gathered in a circle, waited.

The length of the bay, work ceased and a watchful silence descended.

For a moment, nothing happened. Then the door swung open and a ridiculously large white broad-brimmed hat emerged. But there was nothing ridiculous about the irritation with which its owner swept it off and used it to swat away the bolder children venturing close.

The man shoved the outsize hat back on his head, ignored everyone else, strolled to the water's edge, lifted binoculars to his eyes, and panned across the bay until he came to rest on the island.

Ally sensed Leli, close beside her, bristle with tension.

'Who's that?' she asked, low-voiced. 'He marches in like he owns the place!'

'This is no person we have seen before—'

An earsplitting roar cut him short, two powerboats screaming round the bulge of the mangrove swamps. They ploughed towards Shanza village as if to mount the shore, at the last moment skidding away in a vicious turn, bow waves surging towards the beach. Murmurs rippled through watching Shanza fishermen, grew to angry shouts.

'Idiots!' yelled Jack. 'They'll hit someone!'

The Land Rover man lowered the binoculars and turned to stare at him.

'Leli, I am thinking this is maybe the new hotel people from Tundani.' Huru kept his eyes glued to the speeding boats.

'So why're *they* going to your special island if no one's allowed?' Ben demanded in a tone of outrage.

The boats had cut their engines and were gliding silently towards Kisiri's shore, passing out of sight on the far side.

Agitation rippled along Shanza's beach, so sharp Ally could feel it.

'Oh, oh! There will be anger,' Leli said. 'This will bring big anger!'

Three

That evening, for their aunt, Ben eagerly reported the events in the village.

'Everyone argued, then someone fetched a man – *mizay* something—'

'Mzee Shaibu?' Carole asked. 'The headman, Benjy – leader of the Shanza Village Council. *Mzee*'s a respectful word for Elder. It means old man.'

'Yeah, him, and then they all shot off to that island, everyone in canoes like an army!'

'Those speedboats'll run someone down and not even know they've done it,' Jack put in, lazy in a hammock slung from iron pegs in the wall.

They were all on the roof of the house, digesting supper – fish, grilled by Carole on a tiny charcoal stove, or rather by Carole and Ben. He'd watched her, interrogated, then taken over.

Now the little stove glowed in the corner, heating water for tea, while they finished great, juicy slices of pawpaw.

After the long, hot day, Ally's eyes felt scorched. Up here, a strong sea breeze took the sting from her skin. Carole had doused the paraffin lamp, and the night filled with the breeze in the casuarina trees and surf sighing in the coral hollows below the house. A few points of flickering light from Shanza gave a hint of other human habitation. Otherwise, all was a dark expanse, fringed by a snow-gleam where moonlight touched the sands.

But Ally was having to force herself to listen to the chatter. A cocoon seemed to hold her at a distance from the others. Was it the heat? Or the newness of everything? Or a retreat from the hullabaloo in the village, the struggle to work out what was happening when everyone yelled incomprehensibly to each other in Swahili?

Other things kept swallowing her thoughts. Colours, sounds, faces – Leli's face – that look of pure happiness, the amazing way his eyes lit up and he'd given that slow smile when she'd said she was lucky to be here. It felt like the best present she'd ever given anyone.

I should've told him about the forest. Properly. He'd have listened. Like he told me about the island's strangeness.

Not telling him felt like betraying a trust.

In the darkness now the weirdness in the forest was real to her again, as if it rose on the trees' whisper and the restless swash of the ocean; as if the wind carried words she should be able to hear; the sensation prickled over her skin like a touch.

She forced herself to focus on Ben telling Carole, 'That Big-Hat Land Rover man was talking on this *big*, big satellite

23

phone, but he drove off really fast when everyone jumped in the water! And then the speedboats zoomed off too.'

'Thing is,' Carole mused, 'if the boats *are* from the new hotel at Tundani, they've really got no business this far down the coast.'

She poured tea and handed out cups. 'There, see if you like it – it's how Shanza people drink it. Spiced with ginger.' She leaned back in a ramshackle basket chair that creaked and squeaked as it settled. 'There's been a long-running argument over that hotel – still is, mind. People haven't been able to get a health clinic built here, and it's *so, so* badly needed – but suddenly a massive tourist thingy gets government approval, just like that!' snapping her fingers to emphasize the point.

She sipped her tea for a minute. 'But the hotel complex is supposed to be spreading *north* of Tundani, way north up the coast, not *south* to here. That's – what, fifteen miles away, I'd say, at least, maybe more.'

'Leli made us meet the Mzee headman,' Ben ploughed on, 'he was carrying this *cool* stick with snakes on it, and he shook our hands and said, *"it's an honour to meet the doctor's family—"*'

'There's people buried out there,' Ally said, because that was the other thought that kept shoving its way into her head. 'On the island, I mean. Leli told me—'

An elaborate groan from Ben. 'Now you'll never dare go there! You were really *spooked* in the forest!'

'You would be too!' Ally retorted. 'It felt like someone was – I don't know – following or something. Like, hiding—No,

24

it really did!' she insisted to Carole, ignoring Ben crossing his eyes at her.

'Kids teasing you, maybe,' Carole said. 'The people buried on the island, Ally, they're from centuries ago – way, way back, around the time the first ships from Europe reached this coast – oh, five hundred years ago, at least, I think. To be honest, I don't know much about it, keep meaning to find out. Maybe we should do that while you're here, what d'you think? It's a murky, nasty bit of history . . .'

'The storyteller in Shanza said something about it,' said Ally. 'I didn't really understand. I wished I did.'

'So we'll do that, we'll find out,' Carole confirmed. 'Anyway, whatever worried you in the forest wouldn't be anything criminal. There's some nasty stuff happening a long way up the coast, eighty miles at least: smuggling, trafficking. It's been in the newspapers. But not here. It's really peaceful here – the Elders are very proud to tell me there's no crime in this place, not like in the city.'

'No, I don't mean it was like a thief or anything—'

'Like what, then?' Her aunt scrutinized her.

Like what? They hadn't returned through the forest, instead taking the longer route by shore and climbing the coral bluff to reach Carole's house on the headland. All the way, though, Ally *felt* the forest marching to her right, at first hugging the shore, then giving way to the scattered, feathery casuarina trees with their carpets of piny needles and cones. All the way that sensation of nearness travelled with her, echoes, whispers, a voice she couldn't hear. Her mind circled what Leli'd said about Kisiri, about sacred places and warrior-leaders.

25

She didn't try to explain.

'Monkeys, probably,' concluded her aunt. 'They can be scarily mischievous. Plenty of Sykes around – sometimes you only spot their tails dangling just above your head, like a big question mark.'

'Monkeys!' Ben shrieked gleefully. But Ally's stomach gave an inexplicable flutter. As if she'd reached the edge of something, about to step over.

She got up hurriedly and went to sit astride the low stone wall surrounding the roof. She turned her face to the dark, to the night chorus of frogs coming and going on the wind. A bat flitted low overhead; she followed its flight against the glint of the sea, looping and twisting back towards her, until, to her relief, behind her, she heard her aunt change the subject.

'Listen now, all of you, round the village, keep to paths near crops, greet everyone, ask permission even when you think you don't need to. And swimming gear – don't offend people. A bikini's fine, Ally, just – when you're not swimming – wrap something extra round you – a *kikoi* or *kanga*. I've got some for you all. And listen, wear shoes on the reef – or at least watch out for sea urchins. Nasty spines, hideously painful. And should I be worrying about you all in a boat? When're you going, tomorrow afternoon? D'you have *any* idea how to sail one? Or paddle, row – whatever?'

'No worries!' Jack murmured sleepily. 'Leli and Huru'll sort us out.'

'Yeah, we can hire Huru's big cousin's boat when they're back from school.' Ben rocked forward and back, pretending to row. 'His name's Saka, an' he didn't tidy his boat properly, just lying in his house cos he's cut his foot on coral, so he can't fish an' get money, an' he's all sick and worried.'

Jack added, 'His wife Hasina got *really* upset when Leli said Saka had to see a doctor.'

Their aunt didn't reply, as if she hadn't heard him. Then she put her cup down. 'Because he can't walk a mile to the bus stop, and they haven't got the money anyway, not for the thirty-mile fare to the nearest clinic *or* for medicines.' She got up and stretched. 'So, anyone for a drive?'

'Me, me, me!' Ben jumped to his feet.

'If Saka's foot's infected, it shouldn't wait till morning. Coral's vicious stuff. You can be lazy slugs and not come,' Carole was already halfway down the stairs, 'or you can be sweetiepies and keep me company. I'll get my stuff.'

Jack settled deeper into the hammock and closed his eyes.

'Slug,' Ally poked him, and headed for the car with Ben.

*

Why have I not died, as others?

A hundred and fifty souls have perished here. Their spirits inhabit the tides that wash our shores and lick at the hulls of our ships. We have cut every name into the stones of the seaward bastions.

Thirty-seven still cling to life, and our enemies circle, ever beyond range of our guns – birds of prey to pick our bones when sickness and starvation have triumphed and they can slaughter anyone still alive. They rake the island's shores with cannon-fire if we try to reach our ships.

My body burns. Such pain! Dreams stalk me. Horrors imprison me. I dream again, again, again, that the poison takes Fernando and

Theresa, that I see their deaths, these two who are father and mother to me since the fever took my father. Before the monsoon breaks, they will be lost! I wake, and tremble that my dream is truth. I fall to my knees and beg my Spirit to come.

I cannot draw Her face to me! Does She abandon us? Is Her flame of life lost again? Did we ever have true friends?

Twenty days have gone since on a moonless night we lowered a messenger by rope from the sea-wall of the north-east bastion. We saw his shadow slip across the shore far below. I imagined him entering the water, swimming the deep channel to the mainland, hiding from the craft of our enemy. I imagined him coming ashore in some distant place to seek help.

The tides of the deep channel are fierce. That night, a high wind was blowing, and the seas were restless. Did the waves take him? Did he perish? Or did he reach the mainland shore, yet abandon us?

I cannot blame a man for fleeing the certain death of this dread island.

The sun's scorch bakes the walls long after night falls. The fever's stench shrouds all. Children wail their misery. Men and women still strong yesterday stagger now in agony. They bleed. They swell. Skin cracks. Their eyes stare blindly.

We dare not use our water to rinse the blood and vomit from the court. Hour by hour our water dwindles. One well is not yet poisoned by our enemy. We guard it closely, share it out in sips each hour.

The women's voices trying to soothe the children haunt me. The baby Jorge is so weak he cannot crawl. With her cloth, Goma binds his coldness against her warm skin. She croons in her language to him, day and night.

Little Caterina lies vacant. She has been so since her mother died still cradling her, and Neema has appointed herself new mother, though she has skin coal black as all slaves of this fort, and the child so pale, milk-pale, as if no veins carry blood within and she already a corpse.

Day and night Neema softly coaxes her to live.

Only little Sefi has the light of life in his eyes and remains strong. I pray that hunger torments them, not fever, for these women keep them far from the fever chambers. And there is Winda – how fiercely she guards the doors against the sickness daring to enter there and touch the children!

Seven men died tonight. Another sickens fast.

Thirty now remain. Twenty-two men, four women, three children, and I.

In the world of my visions I do not see my own death. I tremble at its mystery.

Where is Hope? I call, I call, but I hear no answer.

*

In the night cool of the village, everyone was out. Families sat round cooking stoves, children bowled hoops in and out of pools of light, groups of men hooted with laughter and argued over games of draughts.

Carole parked the car. 'Stay around, you two. I'll call if I need you.' She headed off to find Saka.

Ally threw open the car door. She could hear fast, pounding music coming from the shore below, and laughter. Yells of welcome greeted Ben, sprinting ahead of her towards the noise, eager signalling for them both to come and join the group. A radio propped on a boat; several people dancing, others sitting or lying on the sands. Ally looked for Leli, but could only pick out the girls, Eshe and Koffi, and then Huru, running to her, pointing along the bay to the edge of the village.

'*Angalia*! I mean, look! Look there! Stranger children – little ones in our broken boat!'

Flames flickered in the distance near an upturned hull; small figures crossed in their glow. Splashing offshore, excited shrieks. High, young voices.

'Before dark they are not there!' Huru said. 'Then we see the fire come!'

'Who—?' Ally began, giving a start at Leli materializing from the darkness beside her.

'Street children from the city,' Leli told her. 'Some people say we must chase away quickly or they will steal. But many say we must give food and I think we must do this, for sure! Tomorrow there will be talk what to do.' He seized her arm. 'Come, Ally, there is another thing – Lumbwi has been to the Tundani hotel!' he pulled her to where a boy was brandishing a red baseball cap, putting it on, clowning a jaunty walk. 'He tells about Tundani Paradise Village! It is open now. There is a restaurant, and two coffee bars! And music playing every night. And there is dancing, much dancing! He heard this from Suleiman, who is working in the kitchen. He will get Lumbwi a job and he gave Lumbwi the hat.'

'Lumbwi, there is a big problem!' Eshe yelled, in English, with a wink at Ally. 'You must use your head for more than wearing a fancy hat. If you work in hotels, you must speak English. And the dancing will be for the beautiful tourists, not for the ugly kitchen boys! Not even the fine hat makes the chameleon beautiful—'

'Hah! Suleiman speaks everything!' Lumbwi answered loftily, in English. 'German. Italian. Every language! He teaches me. For sure, we will get work! People from everywhere are coming to this place. From Ulima! From the north! From the south! I will go to see him and get work for everyone!' he added grandly.

'And you must live in a broken boat, or a plastic bag, like street boys,' Eshe retorted.

For answer, Lumbwi tipped his cap at Eshe, did a whirling double spin, landed in front of Ally and grinned at her.

Ally laughed and clapped. 'Is that the boy you said would do things just because they're forbidden?' she asked Leli. 'He can really dance!'

'Hah! Lumbwi can do everything!' Leli snorted. 'Even when he shouldn't. He is just a little mad!' His voice softened. 'He is a good friend.'

'But why'd that girl say he was a chameleon?' Ben demanded.

'His name,' said Leli. '*Lumbwi* – chameleon, like the little beast that always changes its colour.'

'So everyone's name means something?'

'*Eshe* – Life! *Mosi* – First Born, *Pili* – Second Born,' Leli pointed at two boys, who did a thumbs-up, hearing their names.

'*Huru* – Freedom!' Huru's yell prompted a sing-song chorus from everyone, shouting names with translations.

Almost instantly, it quietened. The headman, Mzee Shaibu

was coming down the sands towards them, and from the direction of Saka's house, their aunt. The Mzee was waving the snake-carved stick he seemed always to carry but never to lean on, pointing it at the distant upturned boat with its beach fire and shrill voices.

'You have seen, Dr Carole? Children! *City* children with nowhere to live and no food!'

'Why've they come *here*?' Ally asked Leli, but Carole answered, dumping her medical bag at her feet and contemplating the scene, hands on hips. 'What do you think, Mzee Shaibu – a stop on the way to the new hotel? Restaurant scraps for food. Errands for rich tourists. Work for starving little pigeons, they hope.'

Mzee Shaibu tilted his head in agreement, and there was silence for a moment.

'And I hear you had unwelcome strangers on your beautiful Kisiri island, Mzee,' Carole added.

The old man grunted. 'Strangers, who run away quickly when we go near. This is not honest, I think. We must be watchful. We have fears, Dr Carole. These hotels are greedy to eat people's land, like a big monster.' He looked at Kisiri thoughtfully, before fixing Carole with an enquiring look. 'So – what news of our young man, Saka?'

'I've given antibiotics for the infection, Mzee, but he must go to Ulima Hospital for an x-ray in case his foot's broken. He'll come with me in the car tomorrow morning.'

'Eee-ee, Dr Carole! He cannot pay doctors! The fishing has been poor these weeks.' The headman pondered for a moment. 'We will all help.'

'No need, Mzee—'

'He will not take charity.'

'Of course. We agreed a price – a good fish, when he is well and can work again.'

The Mzee inclined his head. 'That is fair.'

His voice rang suddenly loud. The radio had been switched off. Lumbwi, Eshe, Koffi and the others were gathering, silent, along the water's edge, looking towards Kisiri.

Ally touched Leli's arm. 'What's everyone looking at?'

'Koffi sees lights on Kisiri. Now Mosi hears engines. There, I hear,' Leli looked at Mzee Shaibu, 'you can, Mzee?'

The Mzee stared to and fro into the dark around the island. A flare briefly streaked the water in luminous green. Then nothing. But the wind dropped a little, and quite clearly now, came the steady throb of an engine.

'Something big, isn't it?' Ben piped up.

'There,' Mzee Shaibu pointed, but to Ally's eye there was only the black smudge of Kisiri on the sea's shimmer.

The Mzee was turning his head, listening to left and right. Then he straightened decisively, hefting the snake-stick over his shoulder. 'I do not know what is ahead if these people come to misbehave in our place!'

He called something in Swahili, getting a chorus of response. Then he waved towards the houses. 'Dr Carole, I invite you to take refreshment. The Elders wish to greet you and thank you.' He moved off with her, sandals slapping on the sands and the loose folds of his *kikoi* billowing around his legs. Their voices drifted into the darkness.

'Leli,' Ally burst out, 'I wish I could understand Swahili!'

He looked startled. 'You are angry? I am sorry to make you angry!'

'No, no! Sorry! I mean, I just want to know—'

His face relaxed, and he gazed at her, holding her eyes, and she registered she had put her hand on his arm again, and it was still there. She took it away, suddenly self-conscious.

He gave that slow, warm smile. 'I teach you our language. I do a bargain. You teach me English good.'

'OK! Yes!'

'*Haya*, we begin! Like you say – "OK".'

'Oh, *haya*, then! So what did Mzee Shaibu say to everyone just now?'

Leli lost his smile. He looked away from her, at the island. 'That everyone must be watchful. That he must know at once if anyone sees strangers on Kisiri. That we must all keep Kisiri safe.'

Four

Leaving the village, their aunt was preoccupied. Ally sat forward, peering through the windscreen at the car lights tunnelling through the maize and banana plantations, jogging with the jolting of the vehicle on the narrow, rutted track. Wild eyes caught the beam, and something slipped across the pale ribbon of sand just in front. Carole stamped on the brakes and swore as the car slid in a sand-drift; she shifted gears hurriedly, rode the slither. The car whined its way out, wheels spinning till they bit firm ground again.

'*What* was that?' Ally asked.

'Mongoose, or . . .' Carole didn't finish, muttering instead, 'Why should Saka have to walk twenty miles to a doctor? Or forty to Ulima? The government gives licences for hotels, bars, restaurants, shops, hairdressers! You'd think *government* money for a health clinic wouldn't be too much to hope!' Fiercely she swung the wheel to avoid another flitting shape and they lurched out on to the narrow, potholed tarmac road south to Ulima, speeding up slightly till they reached a little shop and bus stop. Swinging lamps lit a cluster of people lazing round the roasted maize stall and Carole pressed the car horn in greeting, raising a hand as they went by, receiving waves in return.

'That's Kitokwe, where the nearest landline is, in the shop. People always just call it Salim's *duka*. And wouldn't you just know,' she declared a moment later, turning left onto the track to the house, 'the *brand new* tarmac road to the *new* hotel will run a mile inland from here. Nowhere near any villages. Wouldn't want riffraff local buses ruining it for tourists, now would we?'

'But *you'll* take Saka to the hospital. You said!' Ben insisted anxiously from the back seat.

'Course I'll take *him*. But what about all the other Sakas, Benjy?'

Ben considered this, frowning.

Already they were leaving the deeper gloom of the forest. Then they slowed to a walking pace as the track became little more than a sandy gap between casuarina trees. Finally they came to a halt behind the house on its rocky headland jutting into the bay.

Jack's head poked cautiously over the roof parapet, haloed in moonlight. Then he stood up.

'Am I glad it's you! Couldn't tell from the engine noise. Did you see that boat a while back? Came in right up close, shone a big searchlight all round, like they were checking out the house or something.'

Carole slammed the car door and stomped round the house to the veranda and up the stone steps to the roof. She looked out at the sea. 'These boat people must think there's no one along here. This old house hasn't been lived in for decades. And of course *local villagers* don't count! I'm not surprised Mzee Shaibu and all the Elders are worried. Even my alien bones tell me something odd's brewing.'

For a long time after the others had gone to bed, Ally sat in the dark on the roof. She was tired, but she couldn't contemplate sleep. Something churned away, spiked by the long, cackling cry of some forest animal. Not as complete as a thought, or as distinct as an emotion. It wasn't that she was picking up the unsettled mood of Shanza, or her aunt's unusual flare of anger. It wasn't that she was dwelling on the prickles of disquiet from the forest walk, though she considered all.

What's Leli doing now? She was imagining his house. Was it like Saka and Hasina's square two-room house under the deep palm-thatch roof? *Is he sitting there thinking, like me? What's he thinking? What would I be thinking if Kisiri was my island and those people were tramping over it, secretly?*

And the final thought, the one that stayed with her when she gave in and went to bed, and slowly, slowly, drifted towards sleep.

Is he thinking about the things we talked about, like I am? Is he maybe thinking about me?

Leli was looking out at Kisiri. The high moon caught the angles of the island, so that it seemed to grow out of the water as he watched.

He'd always had a fear of Kisiri, of its sudden winds and

37

mists, of its fierce tides, of the coldness he'd told Ally about.

But it was not fear he was feeling now. Just unease. Like Mzee Shaibu's worry, and Mzee Kitwana's. After everyone else had gone into their houses, the storyteller still stood and gazed at Kisiri, sucking his teeth.

'Leli!' came his mother's voice, interrupting his thoughts. 'Why do you not come in now?' She stood at the top of the beach.

'I am coming.'

He didn't move. She came and stood beside him.

'Do not be a worry to your father, Leli. Already there are troubles enough with your brother Shaaban – this going away and this terrible wait with no news. And now your father goes away to visit Shaaban, so we know what is happening with this boy!'

'I have done nothing to make worry!' He fought to keep his voice calm. 'And you should not worry about Shaaban. He is only going away to learn what he needs—'

'You are a good boy, Leli. Your brother is a good boy! But this foolishness—'

'No foolishness, my mother! My brother will be a mechanic. I will be a doctor. Shaaban is just going to Kinyangata to do something about it. There, at the garage, he can learn what he wants to know. I will learn at school.'

She sucked in her cheeks with disapproval as she always did when they had this conversation. 'And what will we do for money, to pay the school? And you tell me why you are interested in these English visitors, Leli? Why do you waste your time? You talk, talk, talk to this English girl! I see you!

38

I see you! What is wrong with the friends you have now? There is Eshe!' She clicked her tongue. 'Bad things will come, I tell you!'

She glared at him as he stiffened and turned angrily to protest.

'Do not give me this look, Leli! And that foolish Lumbwi with his nonsense about this hotel! That place will suck everything to it, like a whirlpool! Then it will swallow and spit out what it does not like. Everyone will run there to sell more fish and take the vegetables to market, and take visitors on the boats, and everyone will leave their own place and go to fight each other for *that* place under the eye of the rich tourists.' She sniffed. 'And then there will be another hotel and another, and all the bad people will come from Ulima, to sit like vultures and wild dogs to pick the people's bones when they have nothing else left. Oh!'

She turned her head, listening. 'I am hearing the owl. This bird is not comfortable. Nothing is comfortable today.'

He could hear it too, the *tink tink* of the little owl that roosted in the mango tree. It was just a noisy bird that liked to remind everyone it was still there. It was the same as always.

But it would be no good telling his mother that. Until his father returned from seeing his brother, his mother would stay worried.

He sighed. He felt annoyed with her, as always, these days. But he also felt sorry for her. He felt sorry for Shaaban too, who was just trying to learn to be a mechanic. He missed Shaaban. It would be good to ask his brother what he thought about their mother's worries about the big hotel. And about the motorboats and Kisiri. And about the visitors, this interesting Ally. *Learning about new people is good!* He imagined asking his brother, *Why is it so troubling to my mother?* allowing the irritation he felt at her words to fill him again.

On the threshold of his house, he glanced back, feeling the warmth of someone's presence nearby.

There was no one. But again a dream that had disturbed him last night enveloped him. A man stood tall, alone, in the surf of the high tide, looking at Kisiri. He turned his face towards Leli. He looked into Leli's eyes, and Leli could not look away. Leli's feet sank deep in the soft sand, and the water lapped high round him, but he could not move. The white of the man's cloth rippled round his body in the wind, a shifting glitter in the moonlight. Yet the figure was still, like a carving in black wood.

And Leli felt his eyes, searching, speaking silently.

With a jolt, Leli'd woken. He could not get his breath. He could not sleep for a very long time.

He wished he'd told Ally today. His heart told him something: this man was the great warrior, Bwana Fumo! *Ally will not think it is foolish. She will listen.*

He saw Mzee Kitwana walking slowly along the path now. He acknowledged Leli with that tilt of his head. It brought the old man's words to Leli again: *so that all will be remembered.* He was tempted to ask what he was supposed to remember.

But the storyteller passed on, shaking his head, as if talking with an invisible companion.

Leli turned to go in, before his mother had another chance to scold him.

Then he halted again, and looked towards the lamps of Dr Carole's house on the cliff.

'*Ally*,' he breathed into the darkness, a small, certain act of defiance.

second day
warnings

Five

Ally left the shade of the veranda. Heat thumped her like a sledgehammer. She'd slept late, woken with a headache, grouchy at Jack and Ben for wanting to just flop around at the house.

She wrapped a *kanga* over her bikini and pushed through scratchy bushes between the casuarinas, looking for the creek. Carole said it cut in below the headland to the right of the house. Rocks to dive from; deep, shaded water. Anything to escape the sultry, windless warmth hanging over the headland this morning.

Casuarina cones spiked her foot and she leapt clear of them. But the exposed sand burned, and she had to hop, over-balanced, dropping her towel, and had to disentangle it from the clutches of a thorny ground creeper.

She straightened up, selected a shadier channel through the trees, and set off.

Ahead, she caught a flash of colour. A sudden drum of wings made her duck, an earsplitting cry, something big and dark lifting past her and vanishing among high branches.

She laughed in relief. Then stiffened as there came an answering laugh. From near, a clump of dense bush ahead. Instantly she was back where she'd been yesterday, in the forest, frozen at what might be there.

A distinct, unmistakable, sustained rustling in the undergrowth. A tendril of creeper across her path twitched and snaked back, disappearing towards the laugh.

A giggle, the whisper of a light voice, a flash of red and blue within the shadow.

'I know it's you, Benjy!' she yelled. 'Stop trying to wind me up! Benjy!'

The bushes were mute.

She marched forward then, towards the creek, past a new snapping and crackling in the undergrowth, low, as if someone was crawling beneath the leaves.

A figure stepped out in front of her.

The boy was tiny, five or six at the most, dressed in an outsize blue-striped T-shirt and shorts so large they were trousers on him. He was grinning broadly. Pushing through behind, standing up breathlessly, was an even smaller girl. Grubby red dress, pocked with holes. Outsize green plastic sandals, like boats at the end of little stick legs.

Both so unlike the children of Shanza in their *kangas* and *kikois*, that it took her barely a moment to realize they were the new kids of the broken boat on Shanza's beach. The street kids, from the city.

'Hello, madam,' the boy said, in careful English. 'How is you?' His expression had become serious, formal.

'I am very well, thank you. How are you?' Remembering

the round of handshaking in the village when anyone was introduced, Ally offered her hand.

The boy stared at it in surprise. Then he shook it enthusiastically. 'I am very well, thank you. My name is Joseph. My . . .' screwing up his eyes with concentration, '. . . *rafiki yangu* . . .'

Leli'd taught her those words already. 'My friend?' she offered.

'My *fren*, yes! My *fren* is Grace.' The little girl thrust her hand out for shaking. 'What is you doing?' Joseph resumed.

'Swimming. I am going for a swim,' she corrected herself. 'I'm Ally.'

'Eh, Ally!' he repeated. There seemed no more to come. The girl tittered. He pulled a face at her. Then solemnly they both moved aside, and, accepting the signal, Ally walked past, feeling them fall into step behind her, whispering. She tried not to be unnerved by the fleeting thought, forcefully dismissed, that tiny and frail as they were, they were plotting something.

A few paces further and she could see the creek below. She scouted along the fringing bushes for the natural stairway of steep rock her aunt had described, finding it part-hidden below trees arching over the water. The children imitated every move, clambering down with her to a ledge at water level.

She threw off the *kanga* and pushed off thankfully, striking out for the middle. She submerged to let the cool surge over her head, swam down as deep as she could force herself, surfaced again just as two small figures slid off the rocks, fully dressed, and splashed excitedly towards her.

She rolled over and floated on her back. She stared up into the vast blue of the endless sky. With the soft lick of water, her headache was easing. *It's good to bump into the kids.* She came upright to ask them things – like where they'd come from, why to Shanza.

They weren't there. A flip of alarm went through her. Could they swim, *really*?

Then she saw them, backing towards the bank under a drooping branch and moving very, very slowly – as if trying not to make even the smallest ripple in the water. And the boy was signalling her with one hand, a movement she understood instantly was one of urgent warning.

In the same moment she heard the low, stuttering grumble. It came from the direction of the sea. But she couldn't see anything because jutting rocks hid the mouth of the creek.

Then the prow of a motorboat slid into view, sleek and white with a broad red stripe. Nosing in slowly. Two men in it, one white, one African. They were surveying the bank much further inland, where rocks gave way to a reedy mud slope. Their words were almost lost in that engine growl. Swahili; but she also caught a snatch of English: *it's the right place* – or something like that.

She sucked in breath and sank below the water till she was sure the engine rumble had passed. The men hadn't seen her. Instinct, and the rigid silence of the children, made her certain they shouldn't.

'But any boat could go along the creeks,' Jack insisted, 'there's nothing—'

'I know, just . . . the kids hid and they'd have good instincts.'

She looked down at Grace and Joseph standing warily below the veranda, observing her conversation with Jack; until now, since reaching the clifftop and spotting the motorboat leave the creek and push out from the coast, they'd been chattering loudly to her.

'Well, they're probably just used to being chased off, sleeping rough – all that,' Jack pointed out.

'But the boat was checking the place out, Jack! It felt – I don't know – *secret*. They had a map. One of them said it was the "right place", or something. Don't keep doing that big brother "don't-be-silly" stuff!'

He looked startled. 'I'm not, just . . .' He reflected for a moment. 'OK, we'll tell Leli and Huru later, if you want.'

But it was still a dismissal – he didn't really *see*, and, frustrated, she threw down her towel and went along the veranda to the kitchen at the far end. She poured three glasses of water from the bottles kept cold in a bucket, and took them to Joseph and Grace.

They sat together outside on the stone bench against the wall of the house, shaded by the canopy of bougainvillea. There was a long view of the shore towards Shanza, and beyond that, Kisiri. She thought of the boats screaming round the little island yesterday. The boat nosing about the creek here was a different one. Maybe a fleet of them was heading this way. *Why?*

'Ally, come and look,' Jack called from the veranda. He'd fetched a map and spread it on the floor, and had his finger on a long sliver of blue cutting into the coastline from the sea.

'See, there's our creek, going a long way inland beside this headland and the house – that's us there – and look, there's this track running close to the creek, and if you follow it up here . . .' he traced the line across the map with his finger, 'it goes right up to the main road, up beyond the forest. So maybe you could bring a car down close to here. What d'you think – maybe that's why they're looking along the creek?'

Joseph had come over to stand beside Ally, watching closely. He plucked at her arm. 'I clever at that,' he volunteered.

Jack squinted at him. 'At what?'

For answer, Joseph dropped to his knees and put his finger on the map.

'Oh – OK, well, we're here,' Jack tapped the headland.

Joseph pondered this. Then he followed the coast with his finger, from Ulima far in the south, through Shanza, on northwards. He paused, looking hard at the map. He stabbed a place some way north. 'We go there.'

Ally leaned forward and read the name, 'Tundani. Jack, that's the place they keep talking about in Shanza – where the big new hotel's going to be.'

'Yes, yes!' Joseph's voice squeaked in excitement. 'Collins do take us to Tundani for selling many things. Me and Grace and Dedan. Collins says we rest for one day. We come from Ulima, many days.' He held up the sole of one bare foot, blistered and battered, the scar of a deep cut on the heel. 'Our foots is sore—'

He broke off as Ben jumped down the roof steps, lugging Carole's little charcoal stove, shouting, 'Look, it's just a big tin can with holes!'

50

Joseph chuckled, and ran to take it, hoisting it high to show it off and doing a jubilant jig. 'Yes! Yes! We! We do take that and tins and small things and Collins' big *fren* does lamps and for cooking,' he elaborated confusingly.

Jack sat back on his heels, frowning. Then his face cleared. 'You get stuff from the rubbish. And make things?'

'I saying,' Joseph nodded energetically, 'and lamps and big things, and Collins' *fren* is getting rich and can make a house. He do make a house for Collins and we—'

A long, melodious, rising and falling whistle came from the beach; instantly Grace was on her feet yelling, 'Collins! Dedan!' and running, Joseph right behind her, the two of them vanishing down the cliff path.

'Wish I could whistle like that.' Ben put his lips together. A whispery breath trickled out.

'Better get lessons from this Collins or you'll shame us, Benjy,' Jack told him. He went back to studying the map.

Ally watched Joseph and Grace sprinting to join two boys on the sands below. She guessed the taller one, in front, was Collins, the other, Dedan. Grace pointed back up at the house, and all of them looked up towards her. Grace and Joseph waved. Ally waved back.

After a moment, Collins raised a hand slightly in what she took to be a greeting. But he began walking fast back along the shore, not waiting long enough to see her own hand raised in answer.

She turned back to Jack. 'So we should tell Shanza about the boat in the creek. In case it's important? At least tell Leli and Huru?'

'OK, deal – when they take us out on the boat this afternoon.'

She turned away, so he wouldn't see her check her watch. Five hours to wait!

There was the crunch of tyres beyond the house. A man's voice called.

Ally padded through from the veranda to the heavy old door on the inland side of the house. For a second, in the cool dark of the shuttered sitting room, she couldn't see how to open it. Then she found the large iron ring set among the intricate swirls of interlaced leaves and flowers carved on its panels. Beyond, the voice sounded again, louder, impatient. She grasped the old ring and heaved the great door open.

The man easing himself out of the car was large and jovial in style – or at least there was a wide, cheery smile on his face. Incongruously though, he wore a dark, thick suit, and from the beetroot face and the sweat-soaked armpits, he was suffering. He mopped his face with a handkerchief, ran fingers through a thatch of white-blond hair, loosened his tie and unbuttoned his shirt collar. He flashed the smile in Ally's direction.

'Hey, kid,' he called, 'anyone at home?'

'I am,' she said, annoyed.

The smile flickered, but stayed.

'Well, guess I can see that, honey. But how about you point me to someone a bit older? Got important stuff to talk about. Stuff that can't wait.'

His English had a trace of accent she couldn't place and

an odd fake-American drawl. The smile, on closer inspection, was a fixed toothy grin, without warmth. He was peering past her, trying to see through the open door into the house.

It struck her that she should make clear she wasn't alone here. He was ambling towards her, still smiling, and every instinct in her screamed alert: he was something to do with the boats, the one in the creek this morning and the one they'd heard last night, and the ones circling Kisiri yesterday. She saw the light behind the car window alter, there was a second person, in the driver's seat keeping the engine running, she was a fool to walk out to the car without Jack knowing – where was he now? Probably out of earshot! And Ben?

'There's my brothers.' She managed to sound nonchalant. 'My aunt in a bit – any moment, in fact,' she lied, pretending to check her watch.

'OK, Ally?' Miraculously Jack emerged from the house behind her and reached her side in a few quick strides. In a conversational tone he said, 'So are you the people messing about on Shanza's island?'

'Shanza? Who the hell's Shanza?' A genuine look of puzzlement crossed the man's face.

A woman's head poked out of the car. 'They mean those huts by the shore, dope,' she said. 'We're wasting time. Get in.'

The man hitched up his trousers. He was close enough for Ally to smell musty sweat and aftershave. And to see the massive animal claw on a plaited leather thong round his neck. She couldn't take her eyes off it. She had a sudden picture of it being wrenched from a paw.

Jack's arm pressed hers, shifting her behind him.

Unmistakably a warning, but she didn't need it. The man had changed, as if Jack squaring up to him had flicked a switch.

'*Pete*, I said get in.' The woman's voice carried its own warning.

The man focused on Jack. '*You* can tell whoever's minding you, that our island's *off limits*.'

'*Your* island!' Ally's voice came out as an astonished squeak.

'Pete!' The passenger door flung open and the engine revved.

'Uppity kids,' Pete growled. But he backed away and heaved himself into the car. He turned and glowered at Jack, flicked a sour look at Ally, snapped something inaudible.

They half-heard the woman's snarl, '. . . fool . . . kids . . . aunt can't refuse,' and before he'd even slammed the door, the car left with a crash of gears and a spatter of sand from the wheelspin.

Gently, Leli moved the tiller and Saka's *ngalawa* slid into the green tunnel through arching mangroves. Huru had dropped sail and was paddling the boat slowly, showing Ben and Jack how.

Leli glanced at Ally, savouring her obvious pleasure at being here and that flooding relief he'd felt, seeing her waiting in Shanza when he walked in from school. Now, she was kneeling, watching water ripple by, mangrove roots patterning the depths.

He said, 'Actually, Ally, I cannot tell Mzee Shaibu of this man who comes to your house this morning, because Mzee Shaibu goes to see the D.O. now to—'

'D.O?' she asked, without looking up. 'What's that?'

54

Leli digested this. Some time he must ask her how they organized things in her city. 'District Officer,' he explained. 'Mzee Shaibu goes to say about the strangers on Kisiri. But sometimes so many people from the villages wait to see the D.O. that it takes many days! So I tell Mzee Kitwana and Mzee Issa, for now.' The news troubled the two old men, he saw. 'The Elders are happy you tell them this news. They tell their thanks.'

She turned and smiled at him, then returned her gaze to the mangroves drifting by.

He imagined seeing mangroves for the first time: the great tangles of roots plunged into the water like giant claws studded with star shells and oysters. Now she was leaning over the side, turning her head to listen to the little squeaks, plops and splashes in the mesh of wood and plants and mud, noticing the fish crawling on fins in the mud, the green bee-eater bird twisting through the air to its nest in the high bank. She glanced back at him – her look shot a fire through him, as if every one of these things belonged to him, and he had given them to her, and she loved them.

He did not know the English names. Only 'kingfisher', the blue-green flash skimming the creek. And 'fish eagle'. Its dark wings spread shadow as it alighted above them.

'*Kwazi*.' Huru jutted his chin at it.

Jack shaded his eyes to squint up. The great bird sat there, still, silent, regarding them. The yellow beak curved to the black hooked tip. The white head and fiery red and black feathers caught the water-light and gleamed. Yellow talons gripped the low branch. It was close.

'Is that the one called the Sound of Africa?' he asked.

For answer Huru made the high harsh scream of its call, and the great bird shook its wings and glared at them.

'Wow!' Ben squealed. 'You should bring people from the hotels. You could sell them tickets and make pots of money – hey, Huru, don't tip us up!'

Huru was writhing to show how the fishermen swam down to catch squid, letting them wind round their arms, wrestling them on to the boat.

'Good idea!' he said, stopping. Meaning pots of money.

Leli thought about money. No more worry for his mother and father about school fees. Huru could pay for Saka to go to the doctor for his bad foot.

'*Haya* – Lumbwi and Mosi and Pili will help,' Huru added gleefully. 'Eh, Leli?'

'Lumbwi would have some too big idea, or know someone with a too big idea.' Leli spoke scornfully. Lumbwi knew boys from other villages who made Leli uneasy. They had brothers and cousins in the city and talked a lot about the money they earned, sending things home – radios, and clothes.

Now Huru was telling Jack about Bwana Fumo, that he was the *kwazi*, the fish eagle, the eagle of the sea. 'The big festival – *Sherehe ya Kwazi*, you see? This bird in the tree is Bwana Fumo guarding us— No, no, like this! *Weee-ah, hyo-hyo*!' he demonstrated the yodelling call to Ben, who was trying to make the eagle's cry.

'Stories for children!' Leli tried to sound unimpressed, not wanting to admit to Ally's brothers how Bwana Fumo was tickling his thoughts. That dream two nights ago – how strong that figure stood there on the shore! How real. How the look lingered, as if the man called Leli with his eyes.

And just this morning, waking early and lying in bed, considering the plan to go out in Saka's boat: a picture had taken hold – that same figure, but younger, a boy, his white cloth knotted over his shoulder. Beside him a girl holding a spear, moving silently in a canoe in the night through the mangroves towards Kisiri. *Bwana Fumo*, Leli'd whispered. *Mwana Zawati*.

'Leli, do not dream!' yelled Huru and rolled his eyes, copying Ben, who was always rolling his eyes, or crossing them. He signalled to turn the boat, and Leli moved the tiller so that the *ngalawa* slipped between the great roots into open water. Huru signalled again – across the deep channel. Towards Kisiri.

Very strong, very strange, Leli had the image of Bwana Fumo again, as if he was there, now, standing in the prow of Saka's boat, turning and looking at Leli. There – and then gone.

He glanced back at the mangroves. Ancient trees like that had once seen the people's canoes pass silently, secretly, in the dark, long, long ago.

Then the fish eagle threw back its head and rose up with that long, trailing shriek. And it felt as if the cry was just for him, and Leli shivered.

Ally trailed her hand in the silky water, feeling the *ngalawa* glide forward with every stroke of the paddles. Water rippled across the side-floats, slapped the hull. Mosaics of light and shade in the coral slid below.

'The island's two miles west to east, a mile north to south, roughly.' In the glare, Jack peered at the map.

They were already across the deep water from the mangroves, close enough to the island for Ally to see the small coves and fringing palms, the beach littered with fallen coconuts; scarlet-flowered creepers binding the sand; a lone baobab. Towards the open ocean, trees climbed a hill, became a denser spread of forest upward.

Closer still, she saw the hill was a great coral bluff, hunched forward over a space of darkness, that, as they drew level, she could see was a cave boring deep into the coral.

'We could land just for a while, couldn't we?' Jack said. 'I know it's forbidden for strangers, but we're with *you* – that counts for something, right? We're not really strangers any more. Shame to come all the way out and not even land for a minute!'

Huru flicked a look at Leli. 'True, Leli! They are not *strangers.*'

'Why do you look at me?' Leli demanded. 'It is not me that says yes or no!'

There was a long, taut silence. Leli looked at Huru and Huru looked at Leli. In a flash Ally understood. *The Elders'll be furious! It's really serious for them.*

'Leli—' she began, but Jack cut across her.

'Look, don't want to get you two into trouble!'

Leli gave a nod. He turned to look at the island. They were entering the shadow of the coral bluff and its cave, and he looked up, to where a lone bird soared from its heights. Ally saw how he followed its flight. The bird wheeled over them, veered towards the mangroves, and vanished.

Again, Leli looked back at Kisiri; then at Ally.

Abruptly he said, 'We tell Mzee Shaibu, so it is not secret. *Tutafika*, we must arrive quickly. Now the tide is gentle, but it will change. We must not be long, or it will be difficult to go against strong water.'

'*Haya*, yes, yes, we go!' Huru at once began to paddle the boat round. Ben eagerly followed his lead; within minutes the boat was skimming back along the island's northern shore.

Ally sounded the island's name under her breath. '*Kisiri.*' Secret. *Secret and sacred.*

As if he'd heard her, Leli caught her eye, for a moment held it.

The land sloped down again, trees thinned, the first of the small island coves reappeared. Swiftly they swung the boat inwards and pushed towards the beach, hitting the shallows, jumping out and hauling it high and dry up the sands.

A frisson passed through Ally, a prickle of chill. She glanced at Leli. This time he didn't return her gaze. But he moved to her side – she could feel the warmth of his arm against hers – and they turned to face the island.

Six

Purple lizards watched them from a fallen tree, the island full of sound, trills and warbles and hums and clicks. Clouds of yellow birds floated among the palms.

The sun was hot, the air fragrant.

Already Ben was running between the bushes gleefully, jumping back with a shriek at a frantic scrabbling and a long body sliding away.

'A crocodile!'

'Lizard!' Huru flung his arms wide. 'Bigger than this!'

'Wow, it's brilliant! We could live here! Why's no one here?'

'No good water to drink.'

'But if we *brought* water, we could camp. Here!' Ben tore round in a circle, arms wide, marking the camp out.

Huru shook his head. 'No, we come all together, just for *Sherehe ya Kwazi* festival, when we thank Bwana Fumo and Mwana Zawati, singing, dancing, dancing, the whole night like this! Come, I show you where . . .' He ushered Ben and Jack into the trees.

Ally trailed behind with Leli.

Across the powder sand of the upper beach, between palms, among feathery ferny bushes. Trembling blue butterflies greeted them, a chirrup of birdsong, a well of sunlight in a circle of trees.

'Leli, are we near their burial place?' Ally whispered. 'You haven't told me properly about Fumo, yet. And I want to know all about Zawati.'

He gazed at her with a strangely pensive expression, and she wondered why. But he didn't explain, as if thinking something over.

'They are the first people of Shanza,' he began, as she reached the centre of the sunny glade. 'They have lost their mothers and fathers in a terrible killing time before. They escape terrible things. The big tides carry them from their burning city to Kisiri. They bring many others with them, to hide away in the mists. They stay one night, and when the sun is up they go across the water into the forest of the land, and after many months, when it is safe, they build Shanza.'

'Safe from what?'

A gust of wind plucks at her. Then she's holding her breath, as if the world holds its breath. As if she's alone, Leli gone.

She looks for him. She sees the clearing around her thronged with movement – a shifting of texture and shape, dark, flickering like firelight. And murmuring sound, though is it just the wind stirring the palms?

She's held by the strangest idea: *if I move too fast, something will break, something will be lost.*

A touch on her shoulder – she's swayed slightly, almost a dizziness, and she turns to tell Leli it's all right, *I'm OK, really.*

Leli is too far away to have touched her.

That familiar coldness whispers over Leli's skin.

He's felt the strangeness of Kisiri before, but always in the higher places, among the forests and rocks.

Never in the warm spaces of the lower island.

Now the strangeness is here – stillness, no birdsong, no fluttering or rustling of animals. A darkness, growing to blot out the sun. Yet across its centre, fire.

Or the lowering sun. He turns to look at it, great and red, falling into the forest behind Shanza and throwing its long shadows at him.

Lower than it should be.

A butterfly quivers against his cheek; the wings brush the air; everything seems to move and take a new place, and Ally turns back to him, wide-eyed, a question and fear in her face.

Jack, walking fast out of the trees towards them, is white-faced.

'Feel that? The tremor? D'you get earthquakes here?' he asks Leli.

'Not earthquake,' Leli says.

'Well, so – waves hitting the coral below?' Getting no reply, 'Leli, could it be?'

Huru arrives, breathless, Ben running beside him. 'The sun is going fast! The mists are coming!' He's sharp. 'We go now! Leli, we are here too long!'

'We are here a short time, only a short time,' Leli answers.

But the sun is already lower than when he looked just now. As if an hour has passed. Sharp, cold fear spikes through him.

'Leli!' Huru's voice jerks him to movement. They heave the boat into the water, everyone springing to help and splashing in, and Huru pushes them off with a long pole, till the tide takes them, swings them into a strong current – but the wrong way, away from the mainland, out towards the open sea.

'The water is strong. Leli, the water should not be strong yet,' Huru mutters.

Leli looks back. Kisiri, moving away from them, is wrapped in a fierce orange glow.

Against the thrust of the running tide, they fought the boat round.

'It's not working,' Ally gasped, clumsy with the unfamiliar paddle, struggling to take the rhythm from Huru.

'Don't stop!' Jack said it through gritted teeth and she could tell he was frightened too. Ben looked terrified – even a moment's pause in the paddle-strokes let the current sweep them back with startling speed.

'We're getting even further away!' She tried not to show her panic.

'No, no. It is OK,' said Leli. 'Truly, OK,' he repeated, holding her gaze to make her calm.

'We just go, go,' Huru nodded. He paddled firmly, rhythmically, and pointed with his chin to the approaching bulge of the mangrove swamps. 'They make the water not so strong soon.'

But minute after minute stretched. Ten. Twenty. Thirty.

Only the rasp of their breathing, the rush of water, the mainland shore a pale white shimmer in the fast-gathering dusk, Ally's vision narrowing to the paddle in her hands, to stilling her terror, to holding on to the calm certainty of Huru and Leli.

Lights flared in the village, like a beacon. Ally fastened her eyes on them.

And abruptly the tide surge slackened, as if releasing them. Instantly the boat picked up speed, skimming past the glow of the city kids' fire, Grace and Joseph running to the water-line and waving as they slid by.

They swung the boat inwards, steering in utter relief for Shanza's shore.

Seven

Shanza was in uproar.

'Leli!' Eshe tugged him from the boat. 'Where were you? D.O. is here now!'

Leli could see him in a knot of people by Mzee Shaibu's house, listening to questions, waving his hands about. Koffi and Lumbwi were in the audience, and Lumbwi beckoned Leli urgently, announcing, 'The D.O. says at first he tells Mzee Shaibu not to worry about strangers, it is what tourists do, visit places, make noise! But Mzee Shaibu is fierce, fierce! He sits down in the D.O.'s office and will not go till the D.O. telephones someone to ask questions—'

'Lumbwi, *you* make all the noise so *we* hear nothing!' hissed Koffi.

The D.O. held up his hand for silence. Leli pressed in closer to hear.

'If something is happening in my area, if something is *going* to happen,' the D.O. proclaimed, 'I must know! How can I look after everything if I do not know? But when I ask questions about Kisiri island, quickly no one is in government offices to answer! Eh-eh, something is not right, I tell you! But we get to the bottom of this!'

Sudden commotion behind Mzee Shaibu. Leli pushed further forward and stood on his toes to see better.

Eshe pulled Ally close and whispered in English, 'It is your auntie coming from the hospital with Saka,' and Ally could just see someone half-hopping on one foot, being shunted forward by people and waving a scrap of paper. It was plucked away and delivered over the heads to Mzee Shaibu.

Her aunt materialized beside her. 'Good, you're all still here! What've you been up to? Everyone's fired up, aren't they? Like an alarm bell's ringing.'

'Just got back from the island,' Ally said, peculiarly relieved to see Carole. 'It was . . . weird,' she finished lamely, alert to Jack listening beside her.

'How d'you mean?' Carole quizzed, looking at them both.

Ally shook her head. *How can I possibly explain?* She changed the subject. 'Saka's jumping about, is his foot OK?'

'No bones broken, happily. He's more worried about the Land Rover we passed close to the village. A couple of men with it, marking a map. Saka wrote down their numberplate— Who's that?' She broke off, as two small boys squirmed past, pushing expertly through the forest of bodies up to the D.O. Ally recognized the pair who'd joined Joseph and Grace on the beach below the house that morning. The taller boy made an announcement in a high, excited voice. Then triumphantly he poked his companion, who closed his eyes and recited something.

66

'The city kids living in Shanza's boat,' Ally said. 'Collins and Dedan.'

Mzee Shaibu checked Saka's scrap of paper. He nodded. A babble of comment broke out.

'Well, *they're* saying they saw a car at the Tundani hotel with the same numberplate Saka just wrote down,' translated Carole. 'Now everyone's debating that the hotel people are bad, wandering about here where they shouldn't, not bothering to speak to the headman or anyone else.'

Reluctantly, the crowd began to disperse. Ally scanned for Leli, spied him in heated discussion with Eshe, Lumbwi and others.

Look this way, Leli! You can't forget what happened on Kisiri already! Talk to me, you felt it too, I know you did! she willed him.

He glanced at her. As if she'd spoken aloud.

But then simply went back to more passionate arm-waving discussion with the others. Even if she could hear it, she wouldn't understand a single word!

Frustrated, she turned back to Carole and Jack. He was recounting the story of the visitors to the house that morning.

'They said *what*?' her aunt interrupted him incredulously.

'Something about, you can't refuse! Right, Ally?'

'Yes, and they called Kisiri "our island" and—'

'Oh, did they?' Carole said grimly. 'Tell me the whole thing on the way home.'

Leli was turning away. *He's about to just go!* Ally started towards him.

Halted by Carole's hand on her arm. 'Hey, don't wander off, Ally. Jack, find Benjy, will you? We'll get back to the house. I for one need a shower – the drive back's a nightmare with those works splitting off the new road to Tundani. Longer, dustier by the day. Come on, let's leave Shanza to discuss all this – we're intruding,' ignoring Ally's protest, steering her purposefully to the car. 'I've got a really bad feeling about all these comings and goings. Not surprising people are worried. There's a report in the newspapers today that the government's selling off bits of coast for more hotels. I gave the paper to Mzee Shaibu to show the Elders' council. There's a sketch of the design. You can guess the type of place, gated, exclusive, expensive. From now on local people can go there by permission only. And *pay* for the privilege! *Pay* to put one toe on land that's been part of their lives as long as anyone can remember—'

'That couldn't happen here!'

'Couldn't it?' Carole eyed her quizzically. 'Ally, you keep looking round. *Who* are you searching for? Jack'll find Benjy . . .'

'No one!' Ally protested, for some reason.

Her aunt gazed at her for a moment. A sideways, unreadable look that nevertheless brought a flush to Ally's cheeks.

Leli, still talking animatedly, only looked up as the car engine kicked into life. She saw him start towards her, but the car was already moving away and she found herself watching him with a bleak fear of being without him blurring his dwindling figure.

*

'What did you feel, on the island?' she asked Jack later. They were cooled from a shower, sitting on the veranda, watching the last light fade from the sea.

He shrugged. 'A thump – vibration, maybe, like I said. Something to do with the tide turning. Bit stupid to let it spook me like that!' He half-grinned, sheepish.

'But didn't you feel . . . oh, I don't know . . . a jump – like everything jerked, and then it was dark and the sun going down much sooner than we expected?'

'What, like time jumped, you mean? Ally! Seriously! Huru and Leli probably just got the tide times wrong. It was a big tide, and we all wandered around on the island longer than we thought.'

'They wouldn't get the tides wrong! And Leli knew there was something strange—' She stopped. Jack was rolling his eyes, deliberately Ben-like.

'Don't do that!' She pulled a face back. 'I'm not being stupid.'

'There's something strange going on with these Land Rovers and maps and boats and stuff – that's for sure,' he conceded.

It wasn't what she meant. How could she say? Anything she tried would sound daft.

Her aunt, standing on the roof with her in the late evening, sniffed the air.

'It's a brooding night, isn't it? The rains'll break early.' She pulled her shirt away from her skin and flapped it, letting air in against the stickiness. 'Maybe that's really why we're all so bothered. Maybe there's nothing particularly going on and we should just ignore these rowdy boaty louts and the wandering cars, and after a while they'll push off and leave Shanza in peace. The Tundani hotel *will* bring changes, but maybe some'll be good.'

'No one seemed to think so today,' Ally pointed out. '*Everyone* was really upset.'

'True, but there'll be some jobs, a market for selling more fish, tourists spending money on the baskets and mats people make. It's all money for Shanza, isn't it? Till now there's been a fair amount of talk about that. People *need* the work. Easy enough for us to dismiss it, Ally, we're not struggling with almost nothing to live on—'

'But Shanza people *are* worried,' said Ally. 'Leli – I mean – everyone, they're all talking about it!'

Her aunt contemplated her; then, for some reason, shook her head with a small smile.

'What?' Ally demanded.

Carole just put her arm round Ally's shoulders, and they stood looking out at Kisiri riding the moonlit swell of the sea.

Then she kissed Ally's cheek. 'Don't be too late, you. Remember, I've got a day off tomorrow. Got something special lined up for you all.'

But Ally stayed where she was. She heard her aunt's bare feet pad down the roof stairs. She heard Ben chattering at Jack below. They'd dragged their mattresses out onto the veranda to catch the night breeze.

She didn't move, though. She was caught in a memory. Of Leli. Of the island. That suspended, breath-holding moment on Kisiri. The undertone in the return of the wind. Like a voice. Like words. As she closed her eyes and tried to draw the memory back – heard it, felt it, saw it, even smelt it, that heady fragrance of ferns and honey and flowers and salt-sea – it became the strangest sense of something – *someone* – beyond view drawing closer.

More than anything, she yearned to talk to Leli. In that peculiar moment, he had looked at her, that eye-holding glance of his that had the power to make her feel as if everything around her stood still.

It told her that in this strangeness, whatever it was, whatever it was going to become, she wasn't alone. He *was* there too.

Leli sat with his mother and father. The lamp was lit, and people drifted by outside, talking about unwelcome visitors in boats and cars, whether the D.O. would be brave or like the government people in Ulima, getting fat on doing nothing except being rich with other people's money.

His father had walked in from visiting Shaaban in Kinyangata. He had also passed the Land Rover that Saka talked about. In the dusk light the men had not known he was going by until he greeted them.

'Eh, they were troubled to see me! They did not like me hearing their words! It was about where to put something in the water. One man returned my greeting, but the other did not. I did not like this man's look.'

'He is not eating enough!' Leli's mother interrupted, meaning Shaaban. 'You hear, Leli? Your brother sleeps in a store room! He leaves a good bed in his home and goes away to do this! How can he be happy? You tell me!'

'Tabia,' his father intervened softly, 'I have told you and

told you. Shaaban is happy. He is learning. Many, many interesting things about engines. He—'

'How can he go where we cannot see how he is? Just a boy!' She got up and turned her back, crashing the cooking pots about.

His father rubbed his eyes with the heel of his hand. 'Soon Shaaban will be a young man. In time all young creatures leave the nest! Listen to me, my wife! I have been travelling since very early. Do not torment me with this temper. Read our son's letter to you. Let me sleep and tomorrow I will tell you everything. Our son has a good heart. He has friends. He is learning from a clever man—'

'Huh! Did you meet this person?'

'Of course! But also I trust what my son says. You must trust him, Tabia. We will go together to see him. Leli, read your brother's letter to you – do not listen to your mother's foolishness.'

Leli went into the room he shared with his brother. His mother's grumbling tones continued in the next room, and his father's answers. But growing quieter.

He sat on Shaaban's bed. From the thickness of the envelope, he could tell there were many pages in it. He savoured the feel of the stiff blue paper marked with his brother's square writing. It was the first letter he had ever had.

What would he write back to Shaaban? About the D.O.'s words. About Kisiri. About Ally. About his feelings about what happened there on the island today.

Yet he could not, now, be certain anything truly happened. There was the look Ally cast him as she left the village with her aunt, finding him with her eyes. But too late to speak, she was already in the car.

A look of enquiry, he decided. Perhaps of pleading. It was to do with the island. It was to do with more than the island. Part of him felt he knew this girl well. Thinking about her now gave him a knot in his stomach, like nerves.

How could he write to his brother about this? What could he say to someone who had not been on Kisiri to feel this strangeness, or met Ally? Shaaban only trusted what could be properly explained. Like an engine.

His brother's absence was suddenly a gap in the room. Ally saw that. 'You miss him,' she'd said, when he started telling her about Shaaban going away. She understood part of him envied Shaaban, the new places and people his brother was seeing; part of him just wished Shaaban was here now, to share everything.

Then he understood that he wanted *her* here now; her absence was also a gap; he wanted to share the pleasure of Shaaban's letter with her.

He peeled back the flap of the envelope, taking care not to tear it. Four pages inside, folded twice. Inside them, a crisp new five-hundred-shilling note.

Five hundred shillings!

He put it safely in the wooden box his father had made for him to store important things.

At the top of his letter, Shaaban had written:

Breezy Point Garage
P O Box 21007, Kinyangata
Coast Province

24 March 2019

My brother,

I greet you from afar! I hope it is well with you, as it is with me. Actually, at first I wished to be there, with you and our father and mother. But I cannot be a baby! Now I learn fast. My boss is a good teacher.

The other apprentice is John. He would like to do no work and be many hours lying in the sun. He tells jokes and makes me laugh when I should not. He is like Eshe's grandfather, I think, when that one was young! He comes from the hills near Kinyangata, where I am now.

Kinyangata is on a creek with a ferry to go across. To go north or south on the big road you must cross by this ferry. All buses pass through, many people from many places! We have a post office, market, places to drink and eat, a cashew nut factory to make oil for waterproofing and brake linings for cars.

But everyone here is very worried! There will be a new bridge to cross the creek. The government says the ferry is too slow for foreign tourists. The bridge is going to be three miles away with a new road to it. What will happen to Kinyangata? No one will come by our road or want our ferry! What will happen to everyone who works here? I tell you, it is a big problem for us.

Now, my brother, I send you money for when our mother and father cannot pay school fees. I will send more when I can. In one month, if my work is good, my boss will increase my wages. I will find a room to share with John. He has a good heart. People warn us of the sharks who swim in these *waters and grow fat on other people's money. These are the words of the widow Jane Ntula, who has the tea stall by the garage. Her husband worked in the city and was killed by a machine. She tries to be mother to us.*

Even today two men bring their lorry to the garage because they fall in a ditch and break an axle. Jane Ntula just looks at them and says, 'They are evil. I smell it. He who walks with a mangy dog becomes mangy.' These men tell John if he works with them he will make more money in one month than he earns in a whole year here! John pretends he is impressed, but he is too clever. He says they are soldiers or smugglers, or poachers. There are men in his village who help kill elephants to take the ivory, and suddenly they build a new house and buy shoes for everyone, and these men who come to our garage are like that.

Leli, I pray such people never come to our Shanza! I tell our father, so he knows that I hold my thoughts firm. Try to help him make our mother not be angry with me for coming to learn here.

I will write again, but stamps cost much money, so it will not be often. If our father or mother visits me, come with them. I will show you Kinyangata!

Write, Leli! Greet our friends. I will be happy to receive them here.

Shaaban

Leli examined every word again, and thought about it. He heard his father go to bed. He sensed his mother in the dark outside.

He went out.

She was looking into the trees, motionless in the hot, close night. 'It will storm soon. The bird is silent. The rains come early. We must do the work in the field quickly.'

'You have read your letter?' he responded.

'We will try to save money for the bus, and go to visit your brother,' was her only answer, turning to go into the house. At the door she paused. 'Be early for school tomorrow. Then you will learn to write a good letter like your brother.'

He could not help smiling at her retreating back. *Yes! I will ask Teacher for some paper. I will tell Shaaban everything – Ally, Dr Carole, Ben, Jack, the Land Rovers, the boats around Shanza and Kisiri—*

He paused. There were also the strange thoughts of Bwana Fumo since Ally came. The dreams. And again since going on the island today, as if Fumo's voice echoed in the eagle's cry and the running tides round the island.

Do I tell Shaaban?

Tomorrow, I will tell Ally.

*

Am I truly mad? I call for Hope and there, she comes among the souls of the island. Her footprints mark the shore. Her voice lifts on the wind. She speaks to me. I answer. Hope, give us life, give us life!

But then I am alone on empty shores. No ships anchor in deep waters, no cannons fire, no fort rises above the trees. Only the clamour of seabirds, the drum of waves in the cliff. I feel my spirit wander between life and death. This is the silence beyond hope.

Yet again, sand soft beneath my feet, leaves brush my skin, I look in the light of Her eyes, touch the warmth of Her life, and she is real, and I thirst for Her life to touch ours and save us.

And then I am suddenly within these death-stalked walls again and the soldier Diogo is speaking to me!

Fernando is, within the hour, become very ill. Theresa sickens with him.

Terror blinds me. I cannot see Diogo's face. My lost father seems to stand at Diogo's shoulder. I reach for him. He fades. The court fills with shadows and murmurs – everyone we have lost, all who have died. Fernando and Theresa are with them. I cannot look, I cannot.

They died before dawn, Fernando, and Theresa following him within hours. I stayed with Fernando as the darkness shadowed his skin. Coughing racked him so cruelly I feared he would die from that alone. He begged me to leave lest the illness take me too.

Diogo tried to bar me from Theresa. When I reached her, already she did not know me.

Seven other men died with them. We carried their bodies to the court and Diogo said the prayer. We mourned our friends as the earth took them. But I could think only that it is my dream! My dream is truth! Even the last moments of Fernando's life are as my vision. With his last breath, Fernando gave command of the fort to me. To me! I trembled! I protested. He said, so quietly I almost could not hear, 'My boy, you are next in rank. It is your duty now. For Portugal. Hold this fort for Portugal.' And he was gone. I am hollow, can think only of his love and wisdom lost to me, to all of us.

This fort and all who live – in my hands! Twenty-one lives weighed in my weak, ignorant useless hands! We fifteen men, three women and three children – all that is left of the fort's garrison and all who serve it, slaves and free.

No courage, only mad visions fill me! I flee to my visions and Hope. I will the glow of Her life to enter this dying world. Help us! I pray and pray. To Her, to God, to Her, I no longer know to whom I send my call!

third day
invaders

Eight

Ally looked across at the map propped on Jack's knees. 'Are we going round the mangrove swamps? To that hotel place – Tundani?'

Their aunt just smiled, eyeing them in the rear-view mirror, weaving the car cautiously between potholes on the crumbling tarmac. 'Heading north, yes. There's something I want to show you, something you should see,' was her only answer.

'Bet you *are* taking us to the hotel! Lumbwi says it's already looking like a palace!' declared Ben from the front seat.

'A palace, yes!' Carole slowed the car and turned onto a grassy track towards the sea. They bumped along till it petered out in drifts of sand. 'Everyone out,' she ordered. 'Picnic, drinks – bring everything.'

Each slung a bag over shoulders. Jack took charge of the binoculars. They left the car, walked on down soft paths, between high grassy dunes.

Then Carole halted. Banks of shining white sand masked

81

the sea, though Ally could hear surf breaking beyond the dune-ridge. A large hill climbed to their right, clothed in tall grasses and scattered trees, and topped by a massive, spreading baobab. Everywhere, the shrill of birdsong, the click of insects, the skim and whirr of small creatures. Sunlight burned, dazzled.

She pivoted. A full circle . . . turned on . . . and on . . .

Then she swung back, looked again. On the hill. Stone? Peeping through the arms of the baobab – she saw it just as Ben whooped and clambered up to it, Jack in pursuit. She chased after them, sidestepping with a yelp as something small and brown shot between her feet and chattered angrily from somewhere low and out of sight among bushes.

Closer, what she'd seen as a lone pillar became one leg of an arch, high and pointed, set in a vast facade of carved geometric patterns, mottled with russet lichen, golden in the midday light. Climbing plants veiled the other leg, giving it the false look of a tree trunk wound with leafy growth. Its feet were lost in blankets of yellow flowers. Adjacent walls had long since tumbled to hillocks of broken stone knitted with grasses, as if the land battled to reclaim them. Fingers of sunlight felt their way through the arch.

'Entrance to a palace, see?' Carole gasped, breathing hard from the short, sharp climb. 'Remnant of an ancient Swahili city. Well over six hundred years old.'

Ally peered through trailing creepers. Beyond, air glowed and shimmered. As if she'd step through the arch into another world.

'Close your eyes, Ally,' her aunt went on. 'Imagine! Courts, streets, houses, mosques, orchards, palm groves. Harbours packed with ships!' She picked her way through fallen stones. 'Watch for holes! There are hidden wells here and there . . . This wasn't just a city, these were city states, with their own kings or sultans – all along this coast, prosperous and powerful. Hundreds of dhows, thousands of merchants, trading up and down. From here across to the Red Sea, the Persian Gulf, Arabia, India. Back and forth, sailing here on the north-east winds, the *Kaskazi* monsoon, October to March; back on the south-west monsoon, *Kusi*, April to September. Picture the rainbow markets – gold, copper, ambergris, ivory, gum copal, silks, satins, pearls, silver, perfumes, spices – cloves, nutmeg, mace, cinnamon—' She broke off as a man's deep voice sounded below them.

'*Hodi! Hujambo, Daktari!*'

'Aha! The police on our trail, Ally!' Her aunt's voice held a distinct tone of pleasure. Curiously, Ally assessed the tall, uniformed man climbing the hill towards them, Carole greeting him, '*Sijambo*, inspector! *Karibu*. Is this your territory too? How is your sister now?'

'Oh, recovering fast, Dr Seaton, to escape a return to the dreaded hospital! I am grateful for your care of her!' The man removed his cap and shook Carole's hand enthusiastically. 'Yes, my little empire is enlarged! A new police station north in Tundani – just concrete dust and noise now, but rising fast. Protecting tourists' expensive belongings is Top Priority, my superiors instruct! But I am very happy to see *you*, Dr Seaton. These are your family?'

'My niece and nephews from London – Ally,' Carole

introduced her, 'Ben and Jack,' indicating them wandering among trees beyond the ruined arch.

The policeman offered Ally his hand. 'Inspector Rutere. You are in our land for long?'

'A month,' Ally said. 'But there's almost three days gone and—'

'Eh-eh, you are counting! You have good impressions? I am glad!' He swept a hand round to encompass the arch, the dunes beyond. 'People complain it is not excavated to find what is underneath. Me – I do not like cars and tramping feet that come too. Or pickpockets and gangs – all those who prey on others.' He gave an elaborate sigh, gazing along the coast where creamy dunes merged into a distant white haze. 'A special peace here, yes? A man becomes calm standing here. Of course it should not be peaceful if you listen to the spirit of the place! This may have been buried in a tidal wave. Like the terrible *tsunamis* of now. Maybe the souls of its people sleep beneath us!'

Goose pimples crept over Ally's skin. *Sleep beneath us.* She was tempted to lift her feet.

'Or perhaps,' the policeman continued, 'it is another sad victim of greedy explorers, wandering like pirates in their ships. My friend Makena the mad archaeologist from the university should tell you these stories! She sniffs about *somewhere.*'

He raised his voice. 'Makena, stop crawling among old stones and come here!'

An answering shout from a nearby dune: a woman appeared, half slid down the sandy slope towards them and came fast up the grassy hill. She arrived, mopping her forehead

84

with one sleeve. Unlike the neat-uniformed policeman, she was dishevelled, jeans stained from kneeling on soil, hair streaked with sand.

'You find what you hunt for, Makena?' the policeman interrogated. 'You storm the world with new discoveries?'

'Eh, you joke, Rutere, but one day . . .' Makena shook her head at the policeman and grinned at everyone else. 'You like our beautiful place?' She circled the arch, and looked back at them all. 'A fine arch, yes? But it tells a sad story. The same story is told by the old part of our city of Ulima. Go there and look! Find the marks of cannon-fire. You must! People know the old fort there, built by the invaders. But before those invaders built their fort, they bombarded and destroyed the ancient city of Ulima. Many, many thousands killed! Three times the invaders did this! As punishment. As this city beneath us was also punished. Oh, oh, the men of the ships and the forts were quick to punish!'

Her words struck Ally with a jolt. Those strange moments on Kisiri surfaced in her mind again. *Fumo and Zawati came to Kisiri and when it was safe they went into the forests of the land,* Leli'd said, and she'd asked, safe from what? Then that weirdness . . .

Were Fumo and Zawati escaping a 'punishment'?

The archaeologist had moved on, and was gazing down into the copse of trees clothing the hill on the inland side. Ally made her up her mind and pursued her, leaving the policeman and her aunt still talking.

'Miss Makena, was this Fumo and Zawati's town? I mean, did they go from here to Kisiri?'

'Ah-ha! The legend! The great warrior pair! You are interested? I will tell you! Fumo and Zawati's birth city is perhaps
here. Or there. Or there, or there.' She flapped her hand north,
south, west. 'Even, perhaps, east, over the sea! It is maybe a
mixture of here and there, a story woven of many threads.
Like all legends!' She regarded Ally keenly, head on one side.
'Do *you* feel their town here? Do you *hear* it?'

Is she teasing? But Ally listened. Faintly, Ben in the trees,
calling Jack. The surf boom beyond the dunes. Haunting
cries of sea birds. In the bushes near the arch, rustling and
snuffling. Behind that the soft whistle and trill of smaller
birds.

'No-o . . . it doesn't feel like a place you'd run from,' she
acknowledged. 'It's . . . peaceful.' *Not like the forest near
Carole's house* – she was tempted to tell Makena, but the
woman simply tilted her head at her answer, and moved on
again, and the moment was lost.

'*Are* you looking for something here, like Inspector Rutere
said?' Ally asked, following her.

'Always I look! It would be good to investigate this place
well. It is special for me. The first very *old, old* place I saw. I
was very young. I did not understand it. But it opened a little
door in my soul. Perhaps it will open a door in yours. Perhaps
our land will open many doors in your soul!' Her eyes smiled,
again that tilt of the head. 'When I was a student, much later,
that door was pushed wider by a teacher. He told about the
birth of these cities, many centuries ago. And their death,
when the Portuguese ships came.'

'Are they the explorers Inspector Rutere talked about?

Or are they the invaders? It's really confusing, I don't know anything about it,' Ally admitted.

'The Portuguese? You do not study their great voyages of discovery in your school? Truly, they were explorers *and* invaders! It is not said any more that the Europeans *discovered* Africa! Of course they did not! We were here before! Perhaps we all *began* here on this great continent! That is something the scientists are saying!' Makena chuckled. 'But I must not tease you! I see you are asking to know – I must not be cheeky! So . . .' She gestured Ally to walk with her. 'The history of these things is too often written from the viewpoint of the conqueror! But the voyages of these men are nevertheless interesting – truly audacious, dangerous ventures.'

'Was it like Columbus?' Ally asked. 'I had a book about him when I was little.'

Makena's head on one side again, like a curious bird. 'You wish to hear? Truly? I will not trap unwilling listeners!'

'Yes,' Ally said, surprising herself. *I must understand.* In case it was all to do with Leli's words about going to Kisiri to be safe, in case – an echo of the forest trees and the voice stirred . . .

She said, 'My aunt called it a murky history, and said we should find out more.'

Makena smiled as if Ally's answer was immensely pleasing, and wandered on, talking, and Ally wandered with her, circling the crown of the hill, weaving between the tumbled stones, and the trees and the great pillars of the arch.

'Vasco da Gama – you know of him? *No?* So, the lesson begins! He was the first Portuguese commander to reach this

87

coast. Six years after Columbus first landed on the Americas – so, a little more than five hundred years ago. *Everyone* in Europe wanted to find the sea route to the rich spice lands of the exotic East! They could make a fortune bringing spices to Europe! So this Portuguese commander – this Vasco da Gama – had four ships, one hundred and sixty men. Daring voyages across vast oceans, blown by the winds, pushed this way and that by treacherous sea currents. Two out of three died. Just fifty-five of those men lived to tell the tale, you know!'

Ally was trying to picture Portugal on a map, the shape of Africa below. *How long would that journey take?*

Makena seemed to hear her unspoken question. 'Endless months! No sight of land, no idea what waited ahead. *Will I ever see home again? Will I ever set foot on land again? Will I die in this little box floating on an ocean that never ends?* Imagine the spirit of adventure, the call of the Unknown that kept those men going! And dreams of riches! Now, think of this, Miss Curious – to sail to the bottom of Africa, down the west coast, they must take winds and currents that swept them far, far *away* from Africa to the south-west. See,' she picked up a stick and drew Africa small in the centre of a square patch of sandy soil, 'they must travel *right away* from Africa, down to the bottom *left* corner. Over three thousand miles – nearly two months, almost all the way across the Atlantic to South America.' She traced it on the sand. 'Then all the way *back* across the Atlantic, this time trying to sail south-east – towards the bottom *right* corner. Two more months to reach Africa's southern regions. Weeks and weeks and weeks later, round the south tip – the Cape of Good Hope. That name, you know, was given by the very first Portuguese expedition to reach it. You can see why reaching there gave them hope – *Good Hope* – if you contemplate this journey!'

She straightened up. 'But those first ships failed to go far up Africa's eastern coast. They sailed back to Portugal – months and months more – very disappointed! Vasco da Gama's fleet was the first to succeed. He went round the bottom of Africa and sailed all the way up to here, on this coast where we are.' She stabbed the stick in the sand. 'He reached here in 1498, over five hundred years ago. And now, Miss Curious, think of this – these explorers expected to find *primitive*, ignorant people locked away from the world. What astonishment to find instead rich stone cities! With ships that had been trading across the oceans for centuries, and people who looked out on the wide world and were part of it.'

'Like here,' Ally said, 'I mean, this city.'

'Like here, yes! Now, Miss Curious, face the sea. Close your eyes. You are in your busy town, people, ships, merchants, travellers, markets all around. One day – open your eyes – there, just *there*, surging in on the waves, are great ships. You have never seen such ships before! Three tall masts. Flags flying. Many sails, many guns, many soldiers.'

Ships that filled people with fear and hatred. Who said that? Carole? Not Carole's kind of words. The policeman? Ally cast around, and remembered – the old man who'd talked about the Fumo and Zawati legend. Mzee Kitwana.

'So that's when the legend comes from?' she guessed.

'Certainly the legend of Fumo and Zawati comes from that

time, or the years following. Yes, imagine you are the young girl, Zawati. You look at these ships. They come nearer. Now you see a large crucifix painted on each sail – the cross mark of the Christians.'

'I wouldn't think that means bad things coming, though, would I? I mean,' Ally pointed out, 'I'd be used to lots of ships coming, from all kinds of places.'

'True, true. You are thinking well, young friend! Your first thought "interesting new people, maybe good new things to buy. What can we sell to them?" But premonitions of disaster would not be far away? The guns, the soldiers . . . a horrible worm wriggles into your head. Not just traders, you think.' Makena sighed deeply. 'You are right. They do not come just to trade, but to *conquer*, with their big, powerful guns.'

She picked her way down the slope to a stone ledge jutting from the hill and sat down. Ally clambered beside her.

'The story is very sad,' Makena went on. 'These ancient Swahili cities – never subjected to foreign rule before! The Portuguese explorers arrive and plant their Portuguese flag wherever they land. Within ten years every city has fallen under their power!'

Again she fixed her eyes on Ally, as if to make sure she was listening. 'But more – the men of those ships hated the Muslims – and these coast places were all Muslim. In fact the men of the ships hated anyone who was not Christian, so they loathed the "heathen" inland Africans too. But not quite as much as they hated the Muslims. In truth, they proclaimed war with the "infidel" Muslim, and trade with the "heathen" African. And always there was the lure of immense wealth!

'And think of this: when the ships conquered a town, soldiers and sailors looted *everything*. Even by the standards of that long ago time, *these* Portuguese on *these* ships were very, very violent and cruel. Their own chroniclers wrote of them with great disgust. Complaint after complaint was sent to the King of Portugal! You can read them now, in the museum records, here, and in Portugal. One man's words are engraved in my mind, so often I have read them to my students! *Is this the vision that drove us to leave our homes and see the world? We are a breed of able sailors, undaunted, tough. Great oceans do not temper our courage. Has that vision become remorseless savagery? We hammer all men into our image, and snatch their wealth. We breed terrible revenge in those we conquer: thirty of our people in a southern settlement, even infants, massacred by native assailants. Yet more terrible punishment will be given to* them *by the next Portuguese vessel to pass. So the wheel of violence turns* . . . You see how it was, my young friend? These invaders were here, on this coast, for two hundred years, they left only destruction behind! And a few forts.'

'So there was a fort here?'

Makena shook her head. 'Nothing we have found.'

Questions queued up in Ally's head. 'You said *quick to punish*. Punish what?'

'Resistance.'

'What, rebellions?'

Makena snorted. 'Oh, much, much, much less. Refusing to pay a tax, refusing to celebrate the Portuguese king as your ruler. *Punish* if a town did not give in quickly. *Destroy*, to make an example to others.' She patted the stone underneath them. 'Many of the old cities have never been found – razed to the ground, sometimes just made poor and abandoned, their stones carried away to build other things, over hundreds of years. Sometimes, of course, other people – from other lands – laid them waste, not just these Portuguese! Oh, yes, there were others who came after . . . and some of these came as Muslim "friends" to these cities. When people realized their true purpose, it was too late. But those are other stories, for another time, I think! For now, Miss Curious, we see just a wall here, a tomb there, part of a mosque – near river estuaries, on islands, on beaches like this. Everything else just *vanished*.'

'And you will spend a lifetime searching for them, and be very happy,' the inspector's voice cut in behind them. With Carole and Jack, he was walking slantways down the hill towards them. 'This obsession of Makena's! She drags everyone in! I come to ask policeman's questions and when I am here, I forget them all!' He turned to Carole. 'So – I am the policeman again! Mzee Shaibu instructs me, "talk to the doctor and her young ones at the Old Fisheries House", but I did not see he means you, Dr Seaton. I did not know you lived so far from Ulima.'

'Oh, not usually, just for this month. Half a chance, though, I'd stay for ever!'

The policeman laughed. 'So – open the longed-for health clinic, and stay to work there! You and your colleagues from Ulima hospital, Dr Kuanga and Dr Ahmad – a first-class team! Eh, Makena, we capture these doctors for the people of the north coast?' He sobered and squared his shoulders. 'But, the D.O. telephones me early: "something strange is happening in Shanza, go and find out," he says. So, I ask, you too have seen these unknown men who worry the good Shanza people?'

Carole nodded. 'And someone nosing about at the Old Fisheries House.'

'And boats round there and in the creek,' Jack put in.

'Indeed,' the policeman responded, 'much unusual going up and down. And other troubling signs: the Wild Life Service detects new animal poaching gangs in the north and inland.'

Ben, just then crawling out of the undergrowth speckled with twigs and bark, wrinkled his nose in disgust. 'Killing animals? Lions and elephants and that?' he protested.

'A butchered elephant carcass found, yes . . . but a long way inland,' the policeman answered. 'Here, we are – how do you say – just poking about! I have a report of your car on this road, Dr Seaton, and so I am investigating, and Makena comes for the ride to search for buried somethings!' The policeman turned his cap in his hands and, with an air of reluctance, put it on. 'Makena, we go! The driver patiently waits at the car. He will think we have gone swimming!'

But as he turned away, he paused again. 'I am as concerned as any person in Shanza to know who is going where and why. And what these new business people building the hotel in Tundani are planning. Where will they plant their flag next? Be alert. This area is peaceful. I would not like you now to meet unpleasant people in our land.'

Ally wandered away from the chatter of her aunt and brothers. She struggled up the far dune ridge till she could feel the onshore breezes and see the sparkled blue of the water on the far side, the receding tide opening an arc of glistening sands thronged with wading birds. Beyond stretched open sea, on and on. *If I could see that far, I'd see India*, she thought, conversations flitting about her head in an interesting clutter.

Is Makena hunting for something special? What'll Leli think about everything she said? I'll get Carole to stop at Shanza on the way back so I can tell him and he can explain about Fumo and Zawati being safe . . .

Those strange moments on Kisiri with Leli rippled across her, like a wind ruffling the surface of water.

Nine

I stand alone, and do not know where, or how I came there.

A passageway looms. A door. My dead father's chamber, stained by my father's suffering!

I cannot enter. Diogo says it is ten days since, but I cannot count them. Days, nights join, only my father's last hours stay with me, Fernando forcing me away as my father dies.

Horrors seep from that room!

I lean against the passage wall. I force up courage. I push the door. Beyond, all calm and clear, each object as my father kept it.

It is Fernando's doing! Like a void about me, I feel the absence of that kind man who was my father's friend and became mine, and is now victim of the pestilence himself and dead.

I cross to the window. I stand as my father often stood, hands resting on the sill, gazing at sea and sky. As if the stones he touched might make me wise. Each night he sat here, writing. Each night he prepared reports for any ship to reach the fort. Each night, he hoped. Each night he refused despair. I see him lean over pages in dim light, writing, writing, pausing only to read his words, and then he writes again . . .

His papers and journal lie before me on a low stone ledge below the window, neatly piled and weighted with a blood-red shell of some spiked creature of the sea. I take up each page and in the light of the rising moon, see the neat hand for his writing of reports, the angry hand for his journal, his foretelling of the price we would all pay for the greed and savagery of the man whom Fate had made first captain of this fort and brought this horror on us.

That cursed, cursed name: Dom Alvaro.

My father's furious words: 'Ruthless. Greedy. His every act will cut friends from us. His actions will have one outcome – the deaths of men and women and their children.'

Memories rise like mist from the stones of the room, as if my father breathes them to me. Days, weeks, months, years, roll over me as the tides that carried us here.

I write it now: that journey here with my father. That icy February we left Portugal! My mother dead of fever, my father striving to hide his dread of life without her. We must cross oceans to new lands, he said. It would be our hope and our salvation.

How my five-year-old self shared his longing for escape from the places of my mother's suffering. For ever would they wrap our sorrow round us!

We boarded a ship in Lisbon, bound for Africa and India. It was in a fleet of eleven commanded by men of great repute for the brave, dangerous voyages into unknown seas they had made, to the glory of our nation.

My father travelled as ship's doctor. Our goal to reach the southernmost cape of Africa, named by our sailors 'The Cape of Good Hope'. Then to turn north along the far, eastern shores of that mysterious continent. Even the greatest commanders and explorers still knew little of it.

How eager we were then, my father and I, to begin our new life there!

And how our eagerness dimmed. Week followed week, followed week. Ocean currents drove us back. Cruel storms overtook us. We shipped much water and kept ourselves afloat by pumping day and night, every soul on board, even I, weak and small as I was. Then a hurricane struck and three ships were flung off course. We never saw them again.

Another two went down before our eyes, all hands drowned. Our ships pitched and plunged with such terrible force that our drinking jars were broken and many months' supplies of water spilled. Savage waves tossed us like corks, two hapless seamen swept overboard and swallowed in an instant.

Food dwindled. Fever raged. Almost dead with fatigue, my father tended the sick and dying night and day.

Not till the fifth month of our voyage, not till the first weeks of June, did we round that southern cape of Africa and turn north. Only eight men on our vessel still capable of working, even the navigator sore sick. No one else to plot our course in treacherous seas of hidden reefs and perilous currents.

July was well advanced before we chanced upon a welcoming harbour where people brought goat and fowl, eggs and fruit and honey to trade, and showed us where to find fresh water. There we took the sick ashore to recover under shelters on the beach. My father and I stayed with them, while the remnants of the fleet took on provisions and made repairs. Then the great ships hoisted sail and took the winds without us. We watched them dwindling to the north, thence to cross the ocean to India and its riches.

Years later my father admitted to me the terrible truth of that voyage. Full 2500 healthy men left Portugal with us. In the voyage and after, more than 1100 poor souls died.

For many more months my father ministered to those who lived, and buried those who died, until some few ships of the fleet returned from India and took up survivors.

So it was that my father and I were free at last to leave the fleet and travel with an Arab trading vessel bound for Mwitu, a town far to the north. There, the captain told us, Portuguese sailors who had escaped their ships had chosen to make a life among the towns-people, protected from the searching eye and punishment of passing Portuguese fleets. It was a town of many travellers: we might hear of some peaceful place for my father to find work.

So we arrived in Mwitu, and went to pay our respects to the king. I see us, again, haunted by all we had endured. And then I see the ruler's kingly splendour – the silken cushions and brass ornaments of his sumptuous chair, his crimson robe, the gold thread of his turban, the beaten silver of the ceremonial sword resting on a fold of satin at his side. He sat beneath a yellow silk umbrella held against the sun, and at his side, his son. No taller than me, no older: Jabari, Prince of Mwitu. I hear the king tell us it is the prince's Birth Day, and we are welcome to his celebrations. I hear my father tell him it is my Birth Day too, and so joyously does the prince whirl and caper! His green silk turban, the silver dagger in his sash, gleam and sparkle in the sun and he chatters at me merrily, though I understand no word.

All the while musicians played on ivory horns, great elephant tusks as tall as a man which had a hole for blowing in the middle.

I had never seen such splendid things! I could not drink the sights in fast enough. Such feasting for the prince's Birth Day! Meats and fruits and sweet confections of dates and honey and spices, and a wild, marvellous display of skill on horseback – that joyous day stretched on and on and on into the night, so far from the sickness and death I had seen on ship and land, that at last it began to sweep the darkness from me.

Now, I remember, too, that when the king asked my father about Portugal and its ruler, my father's anger showed – his shame at the barbarous deeds of our countrymen in distant places where they had savaged some city and few fled the killing. All in the name of Portugal and Christianity, yet only staining their names with blood, my father said.

Then, in my childishness, I did not know what he meant, and did not want to hear.

We roamed the port, Jabari and I, among merchants and seamen loading the riches that brought my countrymen to these shores. We drank sweet water in the wells, played among houses flanked by palm groves stroked by soft winds from the sea. We lived by each other's side, though we could not speak each other's language; gestures, smiles and frowns spoke for us till words came too.

He was my brother, until my father received word of a doctor needed in a Portuguese settlement to the south. A fort was being built there.

I howled with grief! Patiently my father insisted we must find our own way in this world and drew pictures of the journey we must make. The winds that ruled the sea blew now from the north-east, and we might freely travel southwards with them. But even a week's delay could bring the monsoon from the south-west with squalls and rough seas to trap us in port for months.

I prayed secretly for the monsoon to keep us in Jabari's house for ever. Before the week was out, we took a merchant ship bound for Zanzibar. The captain would leave us at the new settlement on the way.

'When I have my own ship,' Jabari whispered as we embarked, 'I will find you, brother, and together we will see the world!'

We swore eternal friendship. Brothers till death might part us.

Jabari. Prince. Friend, brother who lived in my heart until the memory grew dim behind all else in this place of poison.

Unable to rouse myself, filled with the memories, the voices of my father's room imprisoned me. The weakness spread anew, a creeping poison through my limbs, and a strangeness, half-dreaming, half-waking. I called again to Her.

I saw Her cross the water to this island's shore. I saw the world She inhabits filled with life, with talk and laughter – a promise She holds out to me in the sunlight of Her gaze.

Then Her image fractured, and I knew that I dreamed, only dreamed. This Spirit bringing Hope lives only in the turbulence of my fever. I tried to rise from the floor, but cold despair of trembling limbs bound me fast. Despair can kill; how often my father warned! First goes the will to live, then life itself. Even as he died, he murmured to us all, 'Hope! Hope may yet grant you life, my friends.'

I could not summon hope.

How long did I stay there? I do not know. Footsteps roused me. Diogo by the door. I searched his face, battle-scored, gaunt with starving.

I saw Fernando's death before it came, and Theresa's, and others besides. But I have not seen Diogo's. I have not seen my own.

I yearned to tell him. The horror and strangeness of these dreams!

Of death, of Her, this Spirit of Hope who haunts me and fires me as the rising sun.

I saw Diogo looking long and hard at me, for in my fever I had spoken all aloud. He raised me from the floor with hands strong on my arms.

I write his words: even now their meaning is a leaping spark of hope in me. 'I see no fever in you, my young friend! On my life, I do not! Your body's pain is hunger. Your soul's pain is grief. Ten nights you have wandered since your father died. Endlessly you roam and roam, as if you search. Endlessly you write, as if you search! This would make any soul a little mad. It is grief eats you! Take heart! Believe. Hope!'

My heart beats hard. Is there truly life still? For me? For us? Does Hope hear my plea?

I write this, I write this. So that our story is heard. So that our story is heard!

fourth day
secrets

Ten

The day dawned with a heavy, moist warmth. Ally woke early, into the shrill of birds in the bougainvillea and human voices somewhere near.

She stepped onto the veranda. She was edgy. As if she needed to be *ready*.

Ready for what? Nothing was happening. It felt like days and days since she'd seen Leli, not just one. They hadn't stopped at Shanza on the way back from the ruins yesterday, though she'd asked. Carole just brushed her off with, '*Tomorrow'll be soon enough, Ally*'.

Now she could hear Ben and Jack up on the roof, hatching a plot for a beach camp, wheedling a tent from their aunt.

'OK, OK!' she caught Carole's laughing reply. 'Condition one: you pitch it between Shanza and here. Two: no midnight boating expeditions! And listen, don't make any wild plans for the day after tomorrow. I managed to swap a day with another doctor, so – an unexpected day free! We could do another trip somewhere.'

Ally fetched a glass of juice. She couldn't face anything else, her stomach in a knot with this peculiar urgency to see Leli.

He's at school. He might not be around after. Even if she persuaded the others to go to Shanza, maybe he wouldn't be there. Maybe I won't get to see him ever again.

Carole's car drove off; Ben heaved an old green canvas tent out of the house. He struggled round, spreading it on the ground, untangling a spaghetti of guy ropes.

Ally downed her drink and went to help, holding an end of this or unwinding that, sorting out which pole fitted where. But he was plainly happier wrestling with it on his own, so she left him to it and went in to where Jack was shaking out sleeping bags.

'We can take what food's here, Carole said she'll bring in more later,' he said. 'Driftwood on the beach for fires.'

Grateful for purposeful activity, she offered, 'I'll do matches and torches and food.'

But then it was all piled ready, topped by a pan to cook in. And the heat beyond the veranda was a furnace, and no one could face carrying it anywhere. Ben flopped in a chair, and Jack insisted, 'Not moving till it's cooler.'

Ally wandered along the veranda, past open doors to the bedrooms used by Carole and her brothers, to the tiny one at the end she'd instantly claimed. She flopped on the narrow bed, shaded by half-closed window shutters. The little room, its view through the open veranda door to the curve of the headland and the glint of open sea, already felt like a place she'd known all her life.

Her eyes fell on the sill of the glassless opening that formed the window. Weighted with a twist of driftwood was the postcard she'd meant to write to Zoe. Days ago! She got up, picked it up, turned it over, put it down again: home, faithful promises to Zoe – *Everything, everything, everything, you've got to tell me . . .*

Guiltily distant, in another universe . . .

'*Hodi!*' Huru's call broke her thoughts. He strolled into sight up the cliff path from the beach.

Eagerly she ran out, jumping down from the veranda. No Leli appeared. Just Huru, gleefully announcing, 'School shut, school shut! Digging machines are there! The new hotel road is going just by. Not safe to pass to the school! Teacher is angry, angry that no one told her!' He inspected the camp supplies with interest. 'Good things! Very good! Everything to the beach!'

So then they were lugging it all down to the shore, and there was Leli after all, holding the dugout canoe in the surf, his smiling eyes welcoming her. Within minutes they were all ferrying supplies to the end of the long bay, below Ras Chui, Huru declaring, 'Ras Chui there, Shanza near – good for receiving visitors!' and skimming away again in the canoe with Leli to announce the event to everyone.

But there wasn't a single moment, not half a second's pause, for her to speak to Leli. The conversation wasn't for Jack or Ben to hear, not about what had happened – or not happened – on Kisiri, or the other things that jumped about in her head. Everything was for her and Leli, no one else.

She watched the canoe clear the long, rocky nose of Ras Chui. It turned shorewards and out of sight, steering for the

107

village. Beyond, Kisiri was sculpted in hard, angled shadows by the lowering sun, though the island rode a flat, dull sea in this windless, almost leaden afternoon, and she couldn't even see the birds that usually swirled like a smoke plume above it. For a moment it seemed almost to be a creature asleep, biding its time.

She turned back. Jack had been collecting firewood, and stopped. He was observing her watch the disappearing canoe. There was a question in his face, and she didn't want to answer. She set off, away from him, along the beach, finding chunks of driftwood and the husks of pods from the flotsam and jetsam along the high water line.

Only slowly, straightening up with a hank of dry seaweed in her hand, did she sense someone at the rim of the forest.

A stab of alarm: it was near the path, where she'd had that feeling, that *haunted* feeling – for the first time she named it honestly for herself.

The figure moved out of shadow. One hand lifted in greeting. With relief she recognized him – the slow, stiff walk, the stick. The old storyteller, Mzee Kitwana.

He was unsteady in the deep drifts of sand.

'*Hujambo*, Leli's English friend.' He halted, breathing heavily with effort. 'You work hard!'

'*Sijambo*, Mzee Kitwana.'

'Eh, you learn our language!'

'Leli's trying to teach me, but I'm bad at languages,' she volunteered. 'Did I get it right?'

'It is well.' He took a scrap of cloth from a pouch he wore round his neck and wiped his forehead, surveying the scene:

Ben, banging in tent pegs, Jack poking something at the water's edge. Then the old man turned a direct, unwavering stare on her. 'Leli is telling me you wish to hear Fumo and Zawati's story?'

'Yes!' she said, pleased. 'If—'

'Aha!' A gusty wheeze cut her off, and for a minute he said nothing more as if his mind had drifted off. He resumed suddenly, 'It was my father who told the tale before me. I learned it from my father. He learned it from his father. One passes it to the next, you see. I have heard it is not this way in your country.' He gave her another slow look. 'It is not this way in our country, in the cities that are always running to catch themselves.'

He considered her thoughtfully, folding the cloth and tucking it in the pouch. She felt herself flushing, tried not to look away, it would be impolite.

He said, 'There is the story of Fumo and Zawati's journey here. But it is part of a bigger tale that is not often told. I will tell you this . . . I see that you are old enough to know, and to *see*. It is a fine story, of Bwana Fumo, whose name means *Spear*, and his friend Mwana Zawati, whose name means *Gift* . . . It asks to be told!' He narrowed his eyes. That same disconcerting stare. 'You will hear. Wise leaders. Long ago. It must be told! It must be *heard*. You will come, Leli's friend, you will *hear*?' He looked hard into her face.

She held his gaze. 'I'll come to hear, Mzee Kitwana.'

'You will not forget.'

'I won't forget.'

'Leli's gift, like our great Zawati,' he murmured, and he

109

reached forward, making a circling gesture round her head. 'Daughter of Sunlight.' He let his hand rest lightly on her hair. 'Son of Night. Night and Day, Day and Night . . .'

She stared at him in surprise. Why say that? He couldn't know her name, her full name, she never used it! Did Carole say something to him – oddly, Carole had asked only yesterday – why Ally, not Elly? And Ally had answered, *Mum told me I just said it wrong when I was little, and it stuck . . .*

Kitwana sighed deeply. 'You will be a loyal friend to Leli. He will be a loyal friend to you.'

And she saw then he was only talking about the colour of her hair and the gift of friendship, and it was a coincidence, no more, nothing about her name, only Zawati's name, and already he was turning away, shutting her out.

Yet his words, *gift*, and *daughter of sunlight,* were a lingering chorus as the lengthening shadow of the trees absorbed him.

The darkness of the forest was suddenly very close. The memory of its strangeness stirred again, fresh: and with it came that moment on Kisiri: the throng of movement, that half-heard voice – now it seemed to thread among the cries of the wading birds distant on the reef. She almost expected to see someone walking there. The two experiences – forest and island – were mixing unnervingly in her mind; but they'd happened miles apart, separate, no reasons to think they were the same, were there?

She made an effort to push the silly, frightening thoughts from her head. The old man had gone. She stooped and collected up the bundle of firewood. She threw a last glance at the forest.

Then she went down to where Ben had managed to peg the tent, secure though lopsided, in the soft dry sand beyond reach of a rising tide.

'I'll try to get a fire going,' she called to Jack, dumping her armful of driftwood and kneeling to sort the twigs from the larger chunks.

Grace stepped so silently that only her shadow on the sand alerted Ally. The little girl crouched down to watch intently as Ally laid the wigwam of small sticks around dry seaweed, put chunks of driftwood nearby, and sat back on her heels.

'You do make your fire,' Grace remarked.

'OK, d'you think?' Ally asked. 'Will it light?'

Grace poked the seaweed tighter into the middle, considering the arrangement with a small, determined frown. She picked up a dry mangrove pod from the beach beside her, and dropped it on. Then, 'It is good.'

She was nursing a small leaf-wrapped bundle in her lap, and now she peeled back the covering and held it out for Ally's inspection. A ring of small shells lay there, creamy inside, a mottling of brown and ivory on the smooth, curved backs.

'Pretty.' Ally stroked one.

'Collins and Dedan do take them to the hotel. They do get money and go to market for eat,' Grace's voice dropped to a whisper, 'but I give you.'

'I haven't got money here, but I'll buy one tomorrow, promise,' said Ally, meaning it, because she'd understood that Grace was saying that if they sold the shells they could buy food.

'No!' Grace retorted hotly. 'I *give*.' She held one out insistently.

'Tourists like you'll get the reef stripped bare,' Jack murmured to Ally, bending to drop another armful of wood. 'I hope they're not picking up *everything*—'

'They're just trying to live,' Ally said quickly, not wanting Grace to hear his disapproval. 'What else can they do?' She took the little girl's offered shell and cupped it in her hands, smiling at her.

Jack grunted, and straightened to look at Joseph tearing along the beach towards the tent. Two older boys followed.

'Dedan!' Grace leapt up and danced about as the first one neared at a steady, bent-kneed jog across the sand, also going straight for Ben and the tent.

Collins, on the other hand, was trailing warily. *He's like a little fox*, Ally decided. Close up, he was surprisingly young. Older than Joseph, but a bit younger than Ben – six, seven at the most. Young, bonily thin, with a hard, bright stare that was difficult to look away from.

She held her ground. 'Hi,' she said.

'Hello, madam,' he answered.

'I'm not madam, I'm Ally.'

He made a twisting movement with his mouth – was it dismissal, disapproval, or just acknowledgement? He said, 'I am Collins Karanga. I am leader of the Boat Crew.'

At his name for the group, invented no doubt since their occupation of Shanza's old boat, she had to stop herself from smiling. He'd think she was laughing at him, and she wasn't. To mask it, she stood up, brushing powdery sand from her knees, more than a little thrown by his continuing, deliberate scrutiny. *Is he really much older than he looks? Just masked by his tiny, half-starved skinny body?*

To break the silence, she said, 'You're going to Tundani? Grace told me.' Now Grace was running to where Joseph and Dedan were rolling back tent doors and lifting flaps to reveal netting windows. With a yelp of glee, she squirmed in, her face appearing dimly through the netting.

'We will go to Tundani. We will come back.' This too was a kind of challenge. 'I ask Mzee Shaibu for work here, in his place. We are very good at many works. Mzee Shaibu is thinking. I am thinking.' He stared away. Turned back – that look again – tone changing, 'Why are *you* here? It is not your place! Tourists!'

'Well, yes, but . . .' *Is it a good thing if we are, or a bad thing?* 'We're staying with our aunt—'

'Hospital, I *know* this. Two years working!'

'How? I mean, how d'you know *two*?'

'Easy to know,' with scorn. He changed tack. 'I see you go there,' pointing at Kisiri. 'What is there?' He ducked as a missile shot past. It fell in the sand and rolled to a stop.

'Hey, sorry, sorry.' Ben ran past, retrieved it, glanced apologetically at Collins.

'It is our football,' Collins told him.

'Look,' Ben showed Ally, 'they made it themselves!' It was plastic bags wrapped round each other like onion skins, hundreds of them, the whole shape firm and round and the size of a football, though lumpy on one side.

'Is a good ball!' Collins stepped forward and snatched it away.

113

'Didn't say it wasn't, just saying how you did it!' retorted Ben, aggrieved.

Collins eyed him. Then abruptly he threw the makeshift ball, and Ben caught it and hurled it back, Collins tossed it to Dedan, Dedan kicked it down the beach, Joseph hared after it, and within minutes a chaotic, noisy game had spread, numbers swelling with the first arrivals from the village scrambling down Ras Chui. Collins, abandoning his interrogation of Ally, pelted loudly through the thick of it.

Ally scanned the arriving faces for Leli's, failed to find it. She made herself busy arranging things near the fire.

Eshe and Koffi took charge, one by one welcoming each new girl or boy arriving for the camp feast, presenting them with a flourish to Ally. Each ceremoniously delivered their donation to her: hard-boiled eggs, cassava, fruit, small sweet coconut cakes, goat's milk in a large metal jug, another with richly sweetened lime juice, everything added to the growing pile. Lumbwi sauntered in, with the brothers Pili and Mosi, pairs of fish slung over poles on their shoulders. Then, to Ally's relief, Huru and Leli topped the crest of Raz Chui, and ran down the rock path. They dropped maize cobs, fresh coconut, a bundle of driftwood onto the food pile.

But Leli was instantly caught up in the ball game with everyone else, even Grace, who skipped about on the edge, streaking to kidnap the ball when she could and having to be cajoled and bribed to return it.

Ally took refuge in watching over the cooking, seeing how Eshe and Koffi set the fish to grill on sticks over the flames, how they arranged the maize, cassava, papaya roasting below.

The talk was of the school, closed for days, even a week.

'The D.O. came,' Eshe remarked. 'To see the digging machines and the field next door. He is angry!'

'Yesterday – maize and bananas grow there,' Koffi expanded for Ally. 'Today, big holes and earth. Growing things – *poof*! All gone! No one tells the D.O. the road is coming there. Who changes it? When? How can this happen and not even tell the teacher of the school in the middle? Oh-oh, she is angry!'

'And listen, listen,' Eshe interrupted, 'strangers ask Teacher about places to bring cars to the sea, but not any place near a village! They want to hide away, everyone is saying this!'

'You should tell the policeman,' Ally suggested. 'Inspector Rutere. He's investigating. Everything.' She reported his comments yesterday about poaching and big gangs in the north.

Koffi shook her head. 'It is not that. No big animals anywhere here.'

'The hotel people, for sure.' Eshe made a clicking sound with her tongue against her teeth. 'They want to bring tourists everywhere! My sister sees the man with the stupid big hat again – that one who comes here in the shiny red car.' She sniffed disparagingly. 'This man marches about in Tundani hotel as if he is Big Man there. My sister walks to see the hotel because she wants to work as receptionist. If she cannot work there in Tundani, she will go far away like Leli's brother Shaaban. She does not tell my mother, because my mother remembers Uzuri, and is afraid.'

'Why afraid?' Ally asked, confused. 'What's *uzuri*?'

Eshe didn't answer. Koffi reached over and took her friend's hand, cradling it for a moment. 'Uzuri – our good, good friend. Beautiful like her name!' she informed Ally. 'She went to the city to live with her auntie and go to a big school. Then police came to tell us she was walking on the road and a lorry killed her. They have not found the person who did this. Now all the mothers and fathers fear these places with fast cars and too many people who are just strangers to each other.'

A gloomy silence descended. The fire hissed and settled with a shower of little sparks, and Eshe inspected the cooking fiercely, poking with a long stick. Then she sat back on her heels, wiping her eyes with the back of her hand. 'But you know, Pili's big sister is learning to be a nurse at Kipungani College. And Halima's brother is earning good money in the post office over there in Marafa.' In an instant the talk turned to those who had escaped Shanza or another village, and would not be coming back.

'Why?' Ally questioned. 'I mean, why's everyone trying to leave?'

'To go where we can do things!' Koffi said.

'But you don't have to *leave*? For good, I mean? It's beautiful here.'

'It is just our houses. You look with the eye of a tourist.' Koffi turned the corners of her mouth down.

It was not said rudely, but Ally felt it as a slap. She looked away. *No one wants to stay?* Even in this sultry evening, in the waning light, it was beautiful – olive green sea, gulls drifting above the incoming tide and flickering with final sunbeams through the palms.

Well, it's true. I am a tourist! I am just seeing it for a holiday. But then Leli filled her head, eager, telling her about everything, showing, explaining, *proud*—

'Me,' Eshe's voice cut in, 'I am not like my sister.' She patted Ally's hand as if recognizing her discomfort. 'I will not work in these rich hotels. No, no, no! I will be a lawyer and put a notice on people's islands and special places to stop those ones who should not go there! I will have a friend who is a good policeman, a powerful policeman, more than Inspector Rutere, and he will arrest them!'

'Ho! You are full of big stories,' retorted Koffi.

'You! I will get the higher examinations, you see. And I will come back to live in our beautiful place and defend it from people like you who just want to get rich quick!' Eshe leaned and gave her friend a pinch, which produced the desired squawk and shrieking laughter. Satisfied, she turned to Ally. 'And you, what will you do?'

'Oh! I . . . I don't know.' Her vagueness struck her as pathetic, and Makena's words about the ruin came to mind: *it opened a little door in my soul.* She thought: *everything – Shanza, Carole's house, Makena's stories, Mzee Kitwana, Kisiri, Leli – opens a little door in my soul.* She tried the words out again, liking them. *Leli opens a door in my soul.*

Is he ever going to talk to me? Not a word, properly, yet.

Eshe had caught her looking at Leli. He was running after Pili, who had the ball now. With a chuckle, she tapped Ally's hand.

'Leli will be your slave for ever if you let him tell you about this place!'

117

Ally felt her cheeks flush.

'Oh, oh! Do not let Leli's mother see you look at him too much or make him your slave.' Koffi rolled her eyes at Ally. 'Oh, no! The mother wants Eshe to marry him!'

Eshe snorted. 'Koffi, nonsense! You talk nonsense, you hear me, Koffi? You have no thoughts in your brain except marrying. We leave Leli to be Ally's good friend without this stupid story!'

Ally reddened. Koffi ignored Eshe and went on seamlessly, 'And your little brother and your big brother? What do *they* like?' No doubt, though, that Koffi was looking only at Jack. He'd subsided near the fire, and was learning a drumbeat on the bottom of a pan from Lumbwi and Collins.

'Ask him,' Ally said mischievously, relieved to have the focus taken from her. She'd spoken loudly, and Jack heard. He glanced up, met Koffi's gaze, flicked his eyes away again, bristled with self-consciousness.

'I will do this, I will ask him!' answered Koffi. 'Most definitely I will go and ask him.'

'I will travel in the air to Europe!' Another girl sprawled on the sand and gazed up at a plane rumbling by, lights winking through the dusk. 'I will visit you in England. But not stay. England is too cold, and you fight about football, I see it in the newspapers.' She waved a limp hand at the remnants of the game, now involving dives into the rising tide to retrieve the ball before it bobbed out of sight, or sank.

'We all visit you, Eshe, Jina and me. And we will be very sure to visit your brother!' declared Koffi, and all three roared with laughter, Jack now very much aware of every word, his discomfort intensifying as Koffi hauled her two friends to their feet, the three linked arms and strolled towards him.

Left alone by the fire, Ally felt suddenly and strangely bleak. *Is Eshe Leli's girlfriend, really? Stupid to be bothered! I've only known him four days. Three weeks till I go again. Four thousand miles away.*

She couldn't imagine it.

Eshe shouted something at a knot of boys running from the water, Leli among them. Leli shouted back. Swahili.

Now everyone was leaving the water, fetching food, flopping on the sands, chattering. Eshe's arms were round Leli and Mosi's shoulders. Koffi and Jina were sprawled on the beach, listening to Jack as he tried to look cool and unaffected, and went on drumming over their chatter and laughter.

Ally was hot and cramped and stupidly miserable. Not even a whisper of a breeze, moonrise blotched by a mosaic of cloud thickening ominously towards the horizon. Maybe rain would break and everyone would rush away and she'd never ever talk to Leli—

He's avoiding me. I've got it all wrong. He doesn't really want to talk to me, not specially. He's just being welcoming. It's the way he is. I'm not reading anything right, how can I when half the time it's all in a language I can't speak!

She felt, overwhelmingly, solitary. Even Grace was absorbed, drawing patterns in the sand and hopping through them, chanting, Joseph closing and opening the tent, demanding a password for entry, Ben still splashing about in the water with Huru.

She got up and moved away from the fire. She sat down

again, back turned firmly against the looming wall of forest trees and sands sweeping into gloom beyond reach of the firelight. She gazed out over the black sea.

In an instant Leli was in front of her, offering a drink from the can Lumbwi'd brought. She tried not to show the jolt of surprise, the nerves that shot through her. She took a sip, watched him jog down the beach to hand the can on, come back to drop onto the sand and lie back, propped on his elbows. He smiled up at her.

Did he avoid me only as long as Koffi and Eshe were around?

She became light with something like relief, and something else, headier and unfamiliar, that made everything she wanted to say well up and pour out in a torrent. 'I *really* wanted to come to Shanza yesterday, but we got back too late. I wanted – oh, to know what you think . . . you know, on Kisiri? It was strange, wasn't it, Leli? I didn't imagine it – Jack says I did, but I didn't . . .'

'It is what I tell you,' he said simply. 'It is Kisiri. Kisiri speaks.'

She tried to digest this. After a minute, she said, 'We went to some ruins.'

Leli rolled onto one elbow and pointed north beyond Shanza. 'That way?'

She nodded. 'There was an arch on a hill, and broken walls, lots of dunes . . . a long way – Carole took us in the car.'

'I have been to this place,' Leli murmured. 'When I was just very small, with my father and uncle, in the *ngalawa*. Teacher is saying she wants to take everyone there soon, but there is

120

no money to get a bus to go this way.' He paused, staring out at sea for a moment. 'It is a long time, but . . . I remember it . . . it was . . . very silent . . . it . . .' He seemed to run out of words.

He began again, 'You like this place? We must go in the *ngalawa* together, and look properly! This would be a very good thing to do, you and me?' She smiled happily at him, and he at her. 'I am thinking now,' he went on, still gazing at her, 'it is a bit like the story that Mzee Kitwana will tell you about Fumo and Zawati—'

'Yes! At the ruins there was an archaeologist who knew all about places like—'

Leli nodded enthusiastically. 'Makena! I know this lady. A good friend of Mzee Kitwana. She is in Shanza yesterday with the inspector policeman to ask about the visitor boats—'

Abruptly he sat up, staring at the water.

She looked where he looked. Saw nothing.

'*What?*' she said.

He pointed at Kisiri.

She saw the island, smudged by the darkness but its outline still visible: long and low nearest the mainland, rising to the high coral bluff facing the open sea.

Nothing else.

'I can't see—'

Then she can: movement, a quiver of shadow between the mainland and Kisiri, here, there, from left to right, merging with Kisiri's gloom. And again – a darker swirl, travelling across the black water.

Then a sliver of light from the rising moon slips through the

121

clouds and throws a pale path across the sea; clearly, crossing it, is a stroke of black *on the water*. Then a second, third, fourth, a long curving tail of them . . .

Now, her brain adjusting, she recognizes that other movements are more of these shapes – low, long, gliding at speed across the current, melting into Kisiri's shadow.

Her skin prickles. 'What *is* it?'

'*Hori* – canoes, many, many . . . I am counting thirty.'

'Canoes! Whose?'

For answer, he grips her arm to silence her, and she follows his gaze, beyond Kisiri, beyond the mangrove swamps, to the raw red glow that is seeping up through the night darkness from the land like a bilious sunset bleeding into the sky.

'Somewhere is burning,' he says.

His heart is thumping. All evening he's waited to talk to her without Eshe or Koffi. They'd turn everything to a joke and make his mouth clamp shut.

Now she is there, beside him.

And now, just as the old, old tales of Fumo and Zawati, the canoes are *here*! And the fire of a distant city burning.

But five hundred years have passed since Fumo! *Now* is the new band playing on the radio and the street boy Collins drumming with Lumbwi and Jack to their song. *Now* is a ship like a giant palace of lights on the horizon and a plane humming behind the clouds, leaving Ulima. Not canoes escaping in the night from a city's flames!

Moonlight has strengthened: he can see two lines of the dark strokes, each distinct and bold on the glint of the water.

They stretch from the mangrove swamps across the deep channel to Kisiri.

As it is always told. And the fire-glow in the sky – from the city on the distant islands of the north, destroyed by the men of the great ships – the massacre that Bwana Fumo and Mwana Zawati fled?

Foolish to think it! There is no city now on the northern islands. Only in the story does it live.

Foolish to think of Fumo!

He turns to Ally. Her gaze is following the dark shapes across the water.

'They've disappeared, Leli. The boats – look, they're gone!'

The sea is empty now, truly empty.

And the glow is gone – as swiftly as it came. The moon is submerging in clots of thick cloud.

'Like the strange light on the island, Leli!' Ally whispers. 'Isn't it? That glow over everything?'

Ben hears, demands, 'What strange light on the island?'

'We will ask Mzee Kitwana to say,' is the only answer Leli gives.

Which he knows is no answer at all.

Eleven

She threw her sleeping bag aside, the tent pinned wide to let in air, the night muggy with a damp, cloying stickiness. She could hear Jack moving about outside, his shadow against the glimmer of the dying campfire growing and shrinking on the canvas. Everyone else had drifted home, muttering about rain. All, that is, except Ben and the Boat Crew, curled up together beside the tent and fast asleep even before Jack and Ally stretched a tarpaulin over them as shelter from any downpour.

For a while she lay watching armies of transparent crabs scuttling like tiny ghosts across the sand. Her mind somersaulted and looped through everything. The way those canoes were there, then gone. The way the logical reason for the fiery light was a lightshow at the hotel or somewhere like that, or a bonfire. But she knew it wasn't. No one else saw it. How Leli had not really said anything at all, nothing that made *sense*, and then gone home, still in that closed-off mood of his. It left her with a peculiar sense of loss again, of the fragility of things, as if a door might close and never re-open, as if she should have stopped him going.

But she'd said nothing, and he'd not even said goodbye, or anything about meeting her again.

Lying here now, there was an edgy moaning in the wind, whipping her unease to a new sharpness.

Jack moved into view at the water's edge, his back to her, looking, or listening, for something. She gave in to her restlessness, and went out.

'Hear that, Ally?' he said, without turning.

She concentrated through the hiss of the surf and found the pulse of an engine. It grew rapidly louder – almost on them, though she couldn't see it. Swiftly Jack moved to kick sand over the embers of the fire.

'Why'd you do that? Maybe it's just night fishing,' she said, alarmed.

'Maybe. But in a large boat Huru says you'd go out beyond the reef – it's the season for big fish like marlin, or kingfish or billfish, he said, and also further out you wouldn't risk hitting coral banks. So *why* are they so close in?'

'Maybe they don't know.'

'But deep sea fishing's partly what tourists come for – and they'd be out with guides. Carole said.' After a minute more listening, 'Anyway, don't use a torch, Ally. We don't want them to see us here.'

'Maybe they have already, and don't care.'

'But it's like that boat going all along, close in, the other night, like they're checking things out. Like smuggling or something – I dunno, doesn't feel right.'

'It's getting further away now,' she pointed out. The engine note was accelerating.

'It is the big boat of the big hotel man,' came Collins' voice from the darkness.

'Can't tell that from here,' Jack said doubtfully.

'Dedan does engines extra good, he tells.' Collins emerged from under the tarpaulin.

Crawling out behind him, Dedan mumbled sleepily, 'Island now.' He rubbed his eyes, turned his head, listening. 'Going.' The engine was a moan, getting fainter.

'Tomorrow we see it in Tundani, I can tell you,' said Collins. 'For sure, for sure!'

'Well, Shanza people'll hear it, and if they haven't, let's tell them, hey?' Jack said decisively. 'Tell you what, Collins, do me a favour? If you see this boat in Tundani, have a really close look at it – *exactly* what it's like, and what it's called, and who's in it, and what they're doing. And come and tell us, so we can all keep an eye out. OK?'

Collins considered this soberly. Then he pulled one of his incomprehensible faces, winked, gave a thumbs-up, nudged Dedan towards the tarpaulin, and both disappeared underneath.

Jack linked arms with Ally. 'What's all this night stuff about, d'you reckon? That's what gets me, Ally, even with my rock-steady nerves.' He grinned at her, but underneath the joke, she could see he meant it.

*

I remember falling by the western gate, my sight blurred, skin burning. Arms lifted me, Goma's voice in my ear.

'Leave me, Goma, I die!' I said, but she held me firmer against her body as if her life would strengthen mine, calling for Diogo. They helped me to the shaded angle of the wall. Goma wiped my face with her cloth moistened in water, gave me drink, spoke in her language with Diogo.

'We have barred the gate against attack,' Diogo told me. 'You cannot open it.'

Did I try? I remember only that eight more died last night and I can do nothing!

I begged him, 'Disobey Fernando, take command, Diogo! You are the soldier. Courage deserts me! My ignorance shames—'

'My young friend, listen! Your father was next in rank to Fernando, but already dead when Fernando died. It falls now to we of Portugal still alive. Fernando appointed you. We others – I, Thomas, Paulo – are foot soldiers. We hold our discipline, we pledge our duty to you, we honour Fernando's wishes, and his wisdom.'

'Not wisdom! You cannot trust me!'

'Fernando knows we live – or die – together. Fernando, Theresa, your father, many other brave friends . . . are still with us.' His eyes held unshed tears. 'We will live to honour them. Hear me! Portuguese and slave are strong together against those who would slaughter us. Every man and woman here, Native and Portuguese! Together, all of us. And we will do it.'

For the first time, I fell asleep at Watch. In a nightmare I dreamed of Tomas dying. I woke, and Tomas, who was well not two hours since, is without warning in the grip of fever.

Yet Paulo, who seemed to become ill, has rallied; he is weak, but the fever touched him only briefly. Tiny Jorge is becoming ill, and

127

Neema tends him. Goma has taken the other children to the far side of the court and bars the door to others entering, to try to keep them safe.

I must cling to Hope! I have not dreamed the deaths of any of the children, nor Diogo's or Paulo's or Neema's or Winda's or Goma's or mine, or any others still with us.

Only Tomas.

He died within four hours. In some terrible way do I have true vision of what will come? Is it my soul, or my body, that travels these paths?

I fought to mask my terror, to shoulder my duties and find the courage of a true commander of this fort! I summoned strength deep in my shuddering muscles, and climbed with Diogo to the western bastion.

'Starvation feeds this fever,' Diogo told me. 'Before all else, we must try again to seek food. We must find some way.' He fell silent, thinking, and I could call up no wisdom, held icy, wordless, with my fear.

After a minute, Diogo spoke again. 'There is one of our number, a Native, Saaduma. I trust him as a brother – though he has no reason to love us. He had a ship plying this coast with cargos of mangrove wood before our dead captain, Dom Alvaro, seized and enslaved it to this fort. All the crew, save Saaduma, are now dead. But Saaduma has brought us a plan: we distract the enemy with marching from bastion to bastion at nightfall. He, by rope, will descend the walls above the sea cliff and down into the sheltered pool below – there he will fish and return before dawn.'

I see it is our only hope. Eleven nights ago three men left the fort by the hidden northern gate to try and trap some small animal for food and gather firewood. We heard their screams, and have not seen them since. Our enemy has help from Native troops much skilled in stealth and poisoned arrows, and a terrible hatred for all men of this deadly fort, and I cannot blame them.

We do as Saaduma urged: turn and turn about we march along the western battlements and make such noise! Let the enemy keep their eyes on us! Let them not see Saaduma descend to the rocks below!

We count the passing hours. I am most terribly afraid for him, for us all. Paulo bows his head in prayer. Winda pauses again and again above the parapet and stares into the dark below. No signal from Saaduma on the rope to say that he has climbed from the fishing pool again and we can haul him to safety.

Our besiegers' fires blaze across the water; the wind is westerly and we hear their voices. For days now they have done little but camp on the mainland shore before the forest and the town.

We wait for Saaduma's signal. We trace the flickering movements for any trail across the dividing water that shows our enemies come towards our shores.

Why have they not come for us already? They believe we are all nearly dead. What holds them back? They already have the force to take us: two large frigates drawn up near their camp. Five smaller ships traverse the channels between this island and the mainland. Ten of their dhows are here: surely more will arrive from their country in the north when the monsoon turns.

I watch the distant shadows of the ships, and as they move on the waters, I begin to feel the strangest certainty. As if Her spirit nears, as if courage flames anew, as if blood courses through my limbs again. My father's voice is in my ear: a great clarity comes over me.

I find myself speaking aloud to Diogo. 'They could attack at any hour, even tonight, Diogo. We must hold them back by seeming three times our real number!'

He turned sharply to look at me. Then he smiled and nodded. Without further word, we went to gather everyone strong enough to mount a show of arms along the battlements facing the enemy camp.

There are but five men able and Winda. Goma and Neema stay with the children.

At once Winda seized the fallen flag and brandished it high. She began a steady march, we found the rhythm and marched with her and there was no need for I or Diogo, or any other to lay out the plan and give orders.

We circled, split to other battlements, rejoined, on and on through the night, one taking rest, turn and turn about.

It gave such heart to all of us! Now I take up pen and ink again, my paper resting on the wall, my body upright as if I am at Watch. Paulo stands near, but secretly he leans against the wall and tries to snatch sleep, directing me to do the same.

The four others truly patrol, watching. In an hour Paulo and I will take their place, and give them rest.

'Why, at such a time, this need to write?' Paulo asked this even as his eyes glazed in sleep. 'I see your father in you, with his journals and letters! Writing, writing, writing.'

I have no answer. In life my father urged me to keep a journal. 'So will you draw wisdom from your past, enrich your future.'

I did not listen to him then. Now perhaps he sees the words pour from my pen.

They bind me to Life, to Hope, I think. I pray She hears them. Yet dread blurs the pages in front of me, for is it only my father's lost spirit who sees, and can do nothing?

Surely Her spirit surely burns anew! As the first sun on a cold dawn, She fired my bones and I looked across the strip of sea that divides us from our enemy, to their fires flickering below the forest. It is the forest of my dreams. Hope is there. I prayed She hears my pleas again. I prayed She calls me to Her, calls all our lives to Her life, every one of us, and we are saved, and in answer, sudden shouts came from the court below. Our faith in Saaduma is rewarded! Twelve fish he brings us, and a squid wrestled from the deep, still wound about him, dry wood and seaweed gathered from the upper rocks, that Paulo and Winda seized with cries of joy and carried off to prepare a cooking fire.

Enough to feed the children, a morsel to each of us, and a portion for the small ones again tomorrow! We clasped Saaduma's hands, clapped him on the shoulder, fell to embracing him, again, again, until he begged release!

He insists he will fish again tonight. And we will march along the walls and defy the vultures!

fifth day
warriors

Twelve

Leli scanned the shore impatiently. The rain had stopped: a sheen of raindrops glistened everywhere and the air steamed mistily golden in the early sun. Everyone was out, shaking and spreading the nets and baskets to dry. But only gulls hunting fish scraps peopled the storyteller's usual rock-seat.

Fumo and Zawati's tale must speak for me. Ally must understand the strange ideas – the ones he could not write to his brother Shaaban, the ones he wanted only to share with her. *Only Mzee Kitwana can tell Ally! Then I can tell her of the dreams, and she will see, she will know.*

Though if anyone looked him in the eye and said, *see what, know what?* he also knew he could not answer.

He spotted his mother with Eshe's mother. Both looking at Ally. She was watching Huru teach Ben to take the canoe across the currents in the bay, snaking and spinning the boat as he showed his skills and Ben tried to match them. When Leli arrived at the camp this morning to fetch Ally, he'd seen how she was light-hearted, as if some special happiness warmed her at seeing him. It had spread over him too, chasing away the gloom at his mother's waspish complaint as he left his house: '*You go to see this English girl!*'

He refused to be stung!

Ally waved at Jack sitting on the high ridge of Ras Chui, commanding a long view of both sides of the rock. There was still that watchfulness in the brother. This morning Leli'd found Jack standing in the rain to watch fishermen preparing to leave Shanza on the tide. Ally's brother was taut, closed-faced. A cold feeling had gone through Leli.

Have I caused offence? Can this brother stop Ally being my friend? Will he stop her coming with me to hear the storyteller?

The coldness became something hot and fierce, it was in him still, a preparation for battle, against mothers and brothers and anyone else—

But Jack said, 'We heard engines near Kisiri last night,' and Leli understood: tourist boats did pass by sometimes – it was not suspicious. But Jack's unease was a thread in the same cloth as his own dreams of Fumo, the strangeness of Kisiri he'd seen with Ally, the canoes in the darkness that only he and she saw.

He caught sight of the storyteller now. He was emerging between the houses with Mzee Shaibu. Both were gesturing at the village, the mangroves, out into the deep channel. Discussing, Leli guessed, strangers in cars and boats, road makers and bulldozers closing the school again today.

In a good mood the storyteller would relish recounting a tale to Ally. An audience pleased him. If his leg was hurting he would be irritable and put them off till another time and – Leli could not say why, but knew – it would somehow be *too late*.

He seized Ally's arm to hurry her, and with relief saw Mzee Kitwana cheerily signal a greeting with his walking stick.

'My son of the night! *Hujambo*, Leli! *Habari za asubuhi?* It is well with you this fine morning? It is well with your English friend? Sit! Sit!' Mzee Kitwana chased off the gulls and settled himself on the rock, prodding the space beside him. 'You come for Fumo and Zawati? You have time?' He chortled. 'Many months you have not listened to my stories, Leli! Must I hurry now? Nothing to delay your journey to busy places with your brother Shaaban?'

'Mzee Kitwana, I tell my friend Ally that you have the honour to tell the story at *Sherehe* and it is an honour to hear you,' Leli replied, cautiously. The old man's moods were dangerous – one minute merry, the next fierce like a raging goat.

'Hah! You are a flatterer!' Mzee Kitwana waggled a hand at him. But he drew breath as if sobering himself. He said to Ally, 'Once people came from far, perhaps it was from your England. They asked my father to tell the story. They wanted to put it in a book. I have never seen this book. But one gave me the story written in English on paper. This happened when I was a young man, and the paper has become old with me. But I have it here,' he tapped his head. 'I do not know how many years have gone. How many years do I have, Leli?' he challenged, spotting his distraction at the sight of his mother marching towards Mzee Shaibu.

She will not dare stop Ally's talk with the storyteller! She will not dare!

'Leli?' the storyteller insisted.

Hastily, Leli turned to him. 'Ninety-six years, you have, Mzee.'

Mzee Kitwana drew a wheezing breath. 'Certain it is, that when my breath did not creak like an old goat . . . yes, then, then . . .' He was suddenly dreamy, observing Kisiri island through half-closed lids.

The silence stretched. Leli willed him on. The old man was falling asleep! It had happened in recent years, even at the festival. Elders had murmured to him, music played, the little children allowed to run about and laugh to help him wake gently and remember what he was doing.

Mzee Kitwana cleared his throat. He drew himself up straight, folding his hands over the carved head of his walking stick. '*Zamani* . . .' he began softly, 'that is, you say – *long, long ago* . . .'

A chill touched Leli, like the hand of a ghost. He was small again, and something was being conjured by the rhythm of the old man's voice. Low and calm he always began, in that long night on Kisiri. Only the slow swell of the water beyond the shores, the trees' rustle, the firelight's flicker, his tone lifting, strengthening as the old, old story took his listeners and his words began to paint . . .

'Fumo and Zawati. Great warriors, wise leaders, to whom we owe our place, our good life here, the lives of our ancestors and the lives of our children yet to come.

'Many hundreds of years in the past, their tale begins. Five hundred years – perhaps more, perhaps less. Not far from here . . . a day or two's journey by the water, so they say.

'In those days, my young friends, many towns were on this coast, with many ships. To and fro, from city to city and far beyond, they carried the wealth of our land. And many ships from far away came on the ocean winds, bringing riches beyond dreams! Life was good, and the people prospered.

'But listen, now. One year, strange ships appeared. Great oceans they had crossed! Great dangers passed! They had dreams too, these strangers. To see new lands, to encounter wonders. But also – *also* – to take the good things of these lands for themselves and become rich with them.

'In one town, then another and another – the people felt the strangers' iron fist! Each day the strangers demanded more. Obedience to their king across the sea in Portugal! Taxes from every ship that passed!

'Sometimes, when the towns gave what they asked, the strangers sailed on quickly across the ocean to India and Arabia. But *sometimes* they were too late to catch the monsoon winds to carry them there. Ah, then, then . . . For many months these men had nothing to do, except feed their greed. And oh, what greed, my young friends! They wanted *everything*. Like pirates, they were. They wandered this coast. They captured ships. They took men and women and children as slaves. They stole cargos.

'Ah – sad, it was. Some towns tried to buy their peace. Sometimes, they paid a heavy, heavy price. Yet still those strangers took and took and took, and left nothing for the people of the towns, or for the inland people who traded with the towns.

'But *some* towns said, *No*! One of these cities was far, far, on the islands of the north, Utate, where the boy Fumo and the girl Zawati lived with their mothers and fathers. The King of Utate sent a message to the greedy strangers. *We have given you everything! Utate has no more to give.*

'How dare a king say no? In your most terrible dreams you cannot imagine the strangers' rage! *Trample him down! Destroy his people! All other cities must fear their punishment!*

'Oh, the power of those strangers' guns! The soldiers! Before the sun was high they captured brave Utate. They stole *everything*. From the king's palace and the people's houses, rich and poor. So much they loaded on their ships that one sank in the harbour and the soldiers drowned in their greed.

'All that grew, that fed the people, burned. The roar of flames and the pillars of smoke and the crashing of stone was like the end of the world itself, even the birds in the skies aflame. Only smouldering ash, and ruin, and death remained. Then the strangers went away, seeking another city to torment.

'But not everyone died. Some fled the flames. Some *lived*. And when the sails of the vengeful ships had vanished beyond the seas, they returned to the ruins of their city, to bury the dead, and to mourn.

'Ah, but was their torment ended?

'No. No, no, no. Their torment waited on the *Kusi* winds like a monster sniffing its next feast.

'The next year came; the *Kusi* monsoon blew. Dhows brought news of the strangers nearing. They told of how these

140

strangers had already murdered the sultan of another city and flogged his council.

'*We are too few to fight, we have no guns!* some of Utate's people said. *We must flee! Let us leave the strangers an empty town – at least we keep our lives!*

'But who can tell where courage lies, till it is tested? Some asked, *Why should these savage men threaten peaceful places again and again? Why should they snatch away what people have?* Among those who spoke was Fumo, who was of your age, Leli. And his friend, Zawati, who was of your age, Sunlight. Such anger in them! Such sorrow, for losing their mothers and fathers in the killing time before!

'And so, with some of the people, these two young ones remained. Others left in peace. Yet when they saw their neighbours prepare to defend Utate, they turned back, and peoples from inland places came to help, with archers and other fighting men, and even three men of Portugal. For in all peoples, all lands, *some* do great evil. *Others* fight evil wherever they find it. It is a choice a man or woman – or boy or girl – may make . . .

'These three Portuguese sailors hated the greed of their pirate countrymen. They had escaped the ships and hidden among Utate's people. They knew Utate had no guns: the ships had hundreds. These men of Portugal knew guns. So they took the many broken cannon from the sunken Portuguese vessel in Utate's harbour; from them they made three strong guns, and put them on the town walls. Then they stood ready, day and night, to defend their chosen home.

'*Three* guns against *hundreds*. But also the hearts and

souls of the people. Fumo and Zawati told each other, *there is no victory in fighting to the death. Thousands died when the soldiers came before. This must be a fight for Life.* Together they went to their king and said, *We must prepare our escape as wisely as we prepare our battle!* And the king and council heard their wisdom. Then, among the mangroves, in the sheltered waters, people hid boats with food and weapons ready. They prepared two dhows for sinking in the harbour, to make the enemy believe that everyone died in trying to escape, that no one lived to be hunted down and punished. Then this army of the people waited for the dreaded day.

'The strangers' ships sailed into sight. *Let the king swear loyalty to us!* the strangers ordered. *Let your king pay tribute!*

'The king refused.

'*Give us your king for punishment!* the strangers screamed.

'Only Utate's roaring cannon answered, and on the town walls, the marching men and women with bows and swords and spears held ready. For many hours they kept ships and invaders out. No boat could land, no enemy set foot on any shore.

'But Utate's people grew tired. Night fell. Unseen in the darkness, one ship surged in on the tide and threw a plank from ship to wall to make a bridge – and so the invaders broke into the town.

'Then, on the rooftops, in the alleys, on the stairways of the houses, the battle raged, and in the thick of it, Zawati and the other women. Stones and arrows hurled against the enemy's muskets and crossbows! Rocks rolled down the hills! Even driving the king's elephants around to terrify the enemy.

'With such courage all the people fought, and so fierce among them were the women and young Fumo and Zawati that for years their valour was sung and danced in places up and down the coast and in the inland villages too. Fame of that terrible battle spread everywhere.

'More and more soldiers poured in from the ships. Fumo and Zawati saw the tide was turning against their people. They sent some to harass the invaders and keep them busy, others to swim out in secret and sink the dhows to block the harbour so no Portuguese ship could leave. And in darkness, as Fumo and others held the invaders in battle, Zawati led the people from the town.

'But Fate waited to deal a heavy, heavy blow. As the people fled, a soldier trapped Zawati and raised his sword to kill her. A youth rushed in to take the blow upon himself, and was cut down. This is why Mwana Zawati never married, keeping this youth's love in her heart and for ever carrying the scars of that day. For in that moment, she lost her sight. Blind. And yet not blind. Do we see only with the eye?

'It was the time of *Kusi*, and the rain was heavy. The night was moonless. The last of the people entered the canoes. Together, they were led south by Fumo and Zawati, who was suffering greatly from her wounds but remained steadfast beside Fumo. Close to the shore the people travelled, hidden by the mangroves. On through the night and the next day, until, on the second night, the tides and currents brought them to an island.

'The island had many trees to shield them from enemy eyes. Thick sea mists rose about it. For the first time, they felt they could rest. During that long darkness, while others slept, Zawati rose. Something more was asked of her, she knew. She must open her mind and hear.

'She went up on to the hill of the island and turned her sightless eyes north, towards the dying flames of their distant, ruined city. They could never go back; no peace awaited them there. Only endless war, imprisonment to the strangers' greed. She wept for the deaths that would always come from it. She wept for their loss.

'Then she felt Fumo standing strong beside her. He too had woken and climbed the hill. She felt the spirits of the island gather round and hold her in their calm. The spirits told her that the people must cross the water and go into the forests of the land. Deep among the trees, they should build their home, for there the savage strangers would not venture, keeping to the sea they understood, afraid of the land they did not.

'Straightaway she went with Fumo and told the king and Elders of this vision. And so, in the place revealed to Zawati by the spirits of the forest and the spirits of the island, there the people settled.

'In time it was clear that Bwana Fumo, although he was very young, was a magnificent leader. They named him *Kwazi*, the Eagle of the Sea. And Mwana Zawati, our Gift, she who had great foresight, was a fine warrior and forever brave, a wise leader of the town beside Fumo, and a great poet. Everywhere, her all-seeing words were sung and danced!

'In time, when those savage invaders had long disappeared, the boundaries of the town spread from the deep forest to the sea. Fine stone houses it had, and palaces, and deep wells with fresh water. Many ships came to shelter in its creeks and trade with it. Peace reigned, and it flourished, and the people lived good lives.

'In time, when Mwana Zawati and Bwana Fumo were old and close to death, they asked to be taken to the island, to become one with the spirits who had led them to this place of refuge. The island came to be known as Kisiri, which means Secret, the secret place that had hidden the people, and the place from where the great leaders could watch over the people for ever.

'So it was. So it remained. Time went by. Sadly, new enemies from other lands came to challenge the freedom of the people in their great and peaceful city . . .

'But that, my young friends, is another story. And you would need much, much time to hear it . . .'

Are these stories calling me? In the forest. On the island? Is that what I'm hearing? The idea grew in Ally's mind, brought flickers of sound, trailing, chanting echoes.

She tried to drive the sensations away, to concentrate on Leli thanking the storyteller. She roused herself to do the same. Mzee Kitwana was already half-closing his eyes as if settling to a nap. She glanced round – at Shanza's thatched roofs among the palms, the earth yards, the narrow paths between the houses. At the small child leading a goat on a scrap of string, chattering shrilly to herself.

'You listen well, I see, Daughter of Sunlight,' Mzee Kitwana's voice came dreamily. 'You look at our simple place. You ask yourself, where are the fine stone houses of Fumo and Zawati's town?'

Astonished, she turned to him. *He knows? How?*

Eyes closed, he murmured, 'Our Shanza has been here many years. Before my life, Shanza was here, and I am very old. But this is not the place of Fumo and Zawati. That place was near. Perhaps it is all around us. This we believe. This we feel. This our stories tell us.'

He sat up suddenly, straight-backed, and waved a hand at Kisiri. 'There are other stories that my father knew, of a fort that was made, a great stone fort, on an island of these seas. Made by the men from the ships in the years after Fumo and Zawati died. And of the terrible deeds of the men who lived there, and the terrible death they suffered for their wickedness.'

Pure dread flooded Ally. And then shrill, strident voices, there, then gone. She fought back panic, dimly aware of Leli looking at her with worry in his face. *Did I say, do something?*

Only the storyteller's rhythmic voice continued. 'Some say the fort was built here, on our Kisiri, and the spirit of Fumo and Zawati brought the vengeance of the island on them for making a fort of war in our place of sanctuary. Me, I do not like such stories. I do not remember Fumo and Zawati as vengeful people! And you see there is no fort here on our island. Only the great Portuguese fort at Ulima, which is far, far. So perhaps the stories have twisted about each other like the strands of a rope, the way stories should, when they are made fresh and green by their teller.

'But I say this: the songs of Fumo and Zawati outlived the time beyond them. Even after these barbarous men in their ships no longer came to our shores, when others, not of the West, men of the *East* this time, who came as friends, came

146

to put their mark down and say, *this is my land now!* Then, others from the West came to take it back again! To and fro, to and fro! Like these strangers on boats who run roaring round us now as if they are the kings of everywhere—'

'Mzee,' Leli broke in, catching her eye with an urgent glance, 'we ask too,' he paused, as if marshalling his words, 'we want to know, if *you* saw canoes, in the night, many many canoes, travelling secretly like Fumo—'

The old man snapped his eyes very wide. He looked at Ally, then back at Leli. Then he threw back his head, laughing. 'I would think I had drunk too much *tembo*, Leli, and would perhaps not tell anyone! But,' he said softly, 'I would also know that knowledge is like a garden. If you do not cultivate it, it will not grow.'

He paused, reached into his pouch, and took out something small. He folded his fingers round it and put it to his forehead, then against his chest.

Then he held it out, palm upwards, opening his fingers.

'For you, Leli.'

Leli stared down at the small, round object, and then up into the old man's face.

'And I would hope,' came the deep voice again, 'that the spirit of Fumo is speaking to me, and that the message is worth hearing. *Is* the message worth hearing, Leli?'

'It is warnings,' Leli said fiercely to Ally, walking fast away – she could barely keep up. He halted suddenly. 'You will think I am very mad?'

She couldn't shake the images the storyteller had conjured.

Burning, slaughter, bodies, Zawati's blood running from her eyes. But it was not like seeing things in films, knowing it was only a film. Or even seeing it on TV news, knowing it was real but happening somewhere else and far away.

Mzee Kitwana's pictures dug deep inside her head, as if the stench of burning was in her nostrils. She saw the shadowy figures reaching Kisiri's hidden slopes in tiny boats, in the dead of night, in a storm, wounded, bleeding, battle weary, afraid.

'Not mad,' she said. 'No! Course not, Leli, I couldn't think that!' She tried to frame clear questions from the jumble of her head. 'Have you seen that kind of thing before?'

'What thing?'

'The canoes, the weirdness on Kisiri.'

For a moment he was silent. Then, 'Only when you came to here.'

'Me!' She stared into his face, trying to make sense of that. 'What do you mean?'

He held her eyes. 'I tell truth, Ally. I think, and think, and think about this, but truly, these things . . . only when you arrive at your auntie's house . . . when I know you are here.'

She tried to take this in. 'But—'

'It is so!' He looked down at his hand, and now he opened it, showing her what the storyteller had given him.

A circular piece of darkened, tarnished metal lay there, like a large coin.

'The Mzee carries it since always. He shows it at the festival when he tells the stories.'

He held it out, and she took it. It was warm from his hand,

and felt very old, burnished by many hands, the lines of an image almost worn away.

'What's the picture? An arch?'

'It is his wings. Against the sun,' said Leli. '*Kwazi*. The Eagle. He is flying against Zawati's light, and see—'

He turned it over in the palm of her hand. On the other side she could make out something like crossed sticks. She peered closer, and realized. 'Spears?'

'Fumo and Zawati. Two spears.'

With one finger, she traced the surface. 'So why's Mzee Kitwana given it to you? Is it a lucky charm?'

He was studying her face as if trying to make up his mind about something.

'I have dreams of Fumo – of this . . .' He wrinkled his nose and chewed his lip in concentration. He began again, 'I do not know why the Mzee gives this to me. But I have dreams. It is a trouble to me. I have not told Mzee Kitwana. The dreams come many time in the night. But I tell you, only when you are here! Truly, Ally! First, I tell you, the night you come to Dr Carole's house, before we greet you in the morning. Then next night, after you were in Shanza, and then the night after we went to Kisiri. After the camping, in the rain.' He counted on his fingers, showed her. 'Four nights.'

'All like we saw last night – like the canoes?'

'No, no. Sometimes I am . . . I am in the *hori* with Fumo. Sometimes . . .' his expression was at once self-conscious and defiant, 'sometimes I am Fumo. I look through his eyes. Sometimes Zawati is with me. But these are dreams, I know this! But it is warnings too! Kisiri is speaking. Fumo is speaking. I do not know why he speaks now. Why it is when you are here only. But we must now look for Mzee Shaibu, because Fumo is saying we must go to Kisiri. We must look what is the warnings for. I think this!' He thumped his chest with a clenched hand. 'I feel it here! Mzee Shaibu must say yes!' He pointed ahead: the Mzee stood under a canopy of thatch where men sat mending fish traps. An animated debate was going on.

'So . . . you're thinking what we saw last night, really *saw*, all those boats going to Kisiri, you really think that was like Fumo?'

'I am thinking,' he said, looking at her with that same slightly self-conscious wariness, before making up his mind. 'I am thinking it *is* Fumo.'

She digested this. Then she said in a rush, 'You know when I said your forest's strange, and then when it was odd on Kisiri too, well, I meant—'

'Fumo?'

Emphatically she shook her head. 'No . . .'

'Zawati?'

Again she shook her head. Though for a split second she was remembering the meaning of Zawati's name – Gift – and Mzee Kitwana's words to her, 'Leli's gift', and the image of the sun on the medallion and the strange thing about her own name . . .

'Ally?' Leli grabbed her hand anxiously, held it tight. 'What is it you mean?'

She clung to the power of his grip, thinking of the forest and the voices, and everything that flowed through her, 'It's like . . . like an echoey thing goes through my head. Like someone's calling. Like it's – desperate . . . helpless. Like I'm supposed to *do* something.'

'Do what? Who is calling?' His eyes searched her face, every inch of it, with a look of fright.

'Don't look like that, Leli! I don't know! I just don't know. But it's . . . it's . . . scaring me . . .'

He thought about this for a moment, locking both his hands over hers. Then he said vigorously, 'So, we go together, and together we will discover it?'

She nodded. He turned, and she laced her fingers through his, falling into step beside him, towards Mzee Shaibu.

Thirteen

We slept by turns. We watched and each in our own way prayed, and no one spoke their fear that the enemy will seize Saaduma and Winda as they fish for us.

Then, in the hour before dawn, the men Chane and Omar felt their signal on the rope and hauled them up. They spilled their catch from cloths tied to their backs, the beat of each fish falling on the stones a heartbeat of new life for us!

We lit a fire. Goma and Neema brought the children up. We turned the fish in the flames, and even the odour of the fire licking their flesh seemed to fill our bellies.

Winda portioned them to each of us in strict, small measure, and we ate, turn and turn about, some keeping the Watch while others took their food. Beside the fire, Goma sang a low chanting murmur that beat the rhythm of our march across the battlements.

I drew the memory of Her to me: dare I believe She hears?

Surely it is Her gift! I set it down here, each moment as it happened.
I can scarce believe.

At first dawn light, Chane spied a boat slide in towards the cliff. We stood alert, afraid. Some time passed. Then three men showed themselves at the forest edge. Each raised one hand with fingers spread to show them empty. The other hand laid a spear before them on the ground.

Then they took these up and moved quickly over open ground to come below the walls and call to us. We could barely hear their voices amid the shrieking of the gulls, but Omar knew them at once – two brothers, merchants from a far-distant town, a third man he did not know. He vowed no treachery would come with them.

We unbarred the gate and let them through. Disbelief and hope filled us in equal measure at their tale: the messenger we sent so long ago swam night and day to reach a village and secure a boat to travel onward. Six nights ago, he arrived at the brothers' city, Mwitu, and thus they learned of our plight. Now these three come whole and healthy into our midst, and in their boat, which they have hidden deep in the cave below, they have grain, and fruit, and chickens, and eggs and other such things we had forgotten we would ever see again.

All this I have learned since, for I barely heard their words. The single word, *Mwitu*, rang like a bell in my heart.

I looked at the third of these strangers entering of his own free will into our prison.

I saw a youth, my age, no more, in the stained garb of a fisherman of these parts. I saw how eagerly he searched the face of each of us as if he sought someone.

Then he reached me. His eyes came to rest. He studied my features. He smiled. Recognition stirred in me. Even before he spoke, I knew.

'You know me, my brother?' he asked. 'We are two sides of the

153

same coin, minted in the same year, the same month, the same day. Do you remember me?'

He asks, and ten years vanish! Like a bright spirit at his elbow, I conjure the child he was. Six years old, proud prince in his father's house. Jabari, Prince of Mwitu.

I could not speak. Jabari! He is here!

'My brother, it is my shame I have not come before,' I heard him saying. 'My father forbade me to sail into these waters to seek you. He grows old, and grows afraid. Your countrymen's price for passage along this coast is more than our city can pay. Great peril in travelling without permission that only they can give! My father fears they will seize and ransom me, and he will fail to buy my freedom. In his own land he fears this!

'But now we have learned of your father's death, and we mourn. We learned that you live, and rejoice. I come to you with my father's blessing. We will not stand by and do nothing! Take heart, my brother! There is Life beyond these walls, for all of you. Together we will seize it, as we once pledged we would!'

Surely She sends him? Her gift? Hope. Life.

He stepped towards me. 'Do you remember me?'

My words unlocked. 'Brother.'

He seized my hand and clasped it tight between his own. 'We will talk, my brother. How we will talk! We have years to cover! For now, food. We three will return to our boat and bring the supplies below your walls. Lower your ropes quickly, that we may haul them up! Then sleep, all of you. We three will maintain your Watch.'

I dreamed again, of striving to speak – again, again – and at last She turns, as if She hears and would answer. Her face is open. Sun flames in Her hair, and I know that if I touch Her hand it will have the pulse of flesh and blood, that She is real.

Then I am no longer with Her, above the sea, facing the sky. I am alone. The broken walls of the fort lie behind me, empty of our horrors, our lives. Only grass and the roots of trees bind its stones; animals burrow, birds nest in its crevices.

How do I know? It is in the scents of the air. The island slumbers. Empty shores, tranquil groves, seabirds crying on the wind. We are all gone.

I forced myself awake. Already Jabari and his friends patrol for us. They need what strength I have, and I must give it.

I climbed to the battlements. Jabari turned to greet me. I took courage and told him of the dreams. Of Her.

'She is the vision of hope your exhaustion brings, my brother. Feed your strength. Sleep again! So that together we may all escape this place and cheat the death that is planned for you. That is Hope!'

But there is another dream, of people thronging the darkness, a girl and boy walking among them. They are young, with power beyond their years. The boy is like Jabari, but not Jabari. And when I tell Jabari of this dream, he looks at me strangely and questions me deeply. For a brief moment I see he believes.

'You dream the birth of this place,' he says. 'You have heard it from the storytellers of these parts.'

I have not. 'The friendship of your father's court has never reached us here, in this fort, Jabari. We live afraid of everything beyond the walls. We know we risk our lives if we dare to venture abroad among people not of our kind. Such is the hatred against us!'

'Then you learned the story in my father's court,' Jabari said. 'Or your father heard it and told you. See, once a traveller brought this

155

gift for me.' He took from around his neck a small disc hung on a leather thread.

'He told me it is a talisman to bring the fortune of Fumo and Zawati on me. And so it has, for it has brought my brother back to me!' He passed it to me, and I saw the engraving of a bird in flight against the sun.

'See, it has the marks of the young warrior-leaders who once ruled the town we see there, on the mainland.' He took it again from my hand, and turned it, to show a cross of spears.

He looped the thread over my head, and pressed the medallion against my chest. 'Hold it fast, brother. Let us hear their call of hope, of power. Perhaps their voices will speak for us. Perhaps their power will reach us here. Seek and hold your Spirit of Hope, she who walks the forests and island shore for you. Perhaps she too is their hope, reaching for us. Keep your courage steady, for us all!'

Fourteen

'You *still* think you're picking up creepy stuff from the forest and the island?' Jack fixed Ally with a penetrating stare.

'*Leli* wants to go to Kisiri and see if people've been there,' she defended herself. 'He's asked Mzee Shaibu and we can go too, to help! *You've* been worrying about those boats—'

'But that's not all – you've just been listening to the story-teller . . .' He didn't finish, glancing at Leli, standing close beside her.

'We *can* help, Jack! You know, more people to look round.' She tried not to show urgency in her voice.

Jack looked from her to Leli and back again. The warmth of Leli's arm against hers was calming. It willed her on.

'We promised Carole to stick together – if you won't go, Jack, I can't!'

'But why right now? You're not telling me something. What's the whole story? Ally, what's really going on with you two?'

His eyes bored into her, sharp with suspicion. She refused to look away. 'That's not fair, Jack. I tell you things and you say I'm being stupid! You won't listen! We've got to look – we've got to *help*! Don't you want to help?' she challenged. You—'

'OK, OK!' he stopped her. 'We're going to help figure out these boats hanging about. But you're not going to make your big brother have to watch your back all the time, wandering off in search of legends and *spooky* stuff, are you? Not with all these other things going on. It's bad enough having to keep track of Benjy.'

She flushed hotly, 'Don't—'

'Just teasing,' he said, 'well, sort of. You've made your point, Ally. We'll all go, Benjy too.'

Jack insisted on dragging the canoes out of sight into a thicket above the beach. Huru had guided them to the only sandy bay on the rocky south shore of the island, the side they hadn't been before.

Leli led them all across low shelves of flat rock strewn with seaweed and shells, pushing inland. The ground rose, undulating through stands of palms, sandy banks laced with thorny creepers, grassy mounds and bushy hollows. It opened unexpectedly onto a broad, open plateau clothed in dense fern. Thick forest bordered its length on the far side.

'In this place they came on their journey.' Leli was low-voiced for Ally.

'Who came?' asked Jack, close enough to overhear.

'First people of Shanza,' said Leli. 'Festival story.'

Ally avoided Jack's eye. She could feel his scrutiny, always assessing her and Leli.

158

She followed Leli closely, pushing through the ferns, releasing a bruised, pungent fragrance. Two lone baobabs rose, gigantic, from the plateau's centre, their trunks broad enough to shield three people abreast, their branches dotted with crows. As they all neared, the birds broke into a shrieking argument, flapped off, swerved in a black cloud into the flanking forest.

Hysterical chirruping answered, and a violent shaking rippled along the high canopy. A lone dark shape soared from it, dwindling against the sky's white glare.

Ben squinted after it. 'Is that a fish eagle again?'

'*Kwazi*,' Huru confirmed. 'We saw in the mangrove waters.'

'How d'you know it's the same one?'

Huru rolled his eyes. 'And monkeys making the little birds angry, come, see,' the two of them pushing through ferns. To Ally's relief, Jack followed them.

Ally stayed where she was. The plateau was high enough for her to see the water on two sides – west towards Shanza on the mainland, south across Ras Chui's rock spine. Beyond it, the red peak of their tent just showed in the long bay. And beyond the bay, the white square of the Old Fisheries House on the distant headland. But on the north side, towards the mangrove creeks and Tundani, sight of the sea was blocked by the forest. *That's where we crossed in Saka's boat, the first time we came to Kisiri. That's where Fumo and Zawati came, to hide in the island's forest. It's where we saw the shadows of the canoes crossing.*

The hum of insects was loud, and the scent of crushed fern,

and she was suddenly overwhelmed by it all, by the sweat coursing down her back, by the bee buzzing at her, zigzagging away between fronds, droning back, by an unbearable sense of expectation, of alarm.

She shaded her eyes and looked for Leli. He'd moved on, heading for the seaward end of the plateau where the terrain sharpened to vertical rock slabs, lichen and creeper-covered. At the top, a twist of fallen tree. For a second it was a large bird looking down, then it wasn't.

Leli seemed to find an invisible path and leapt upwards easily. She chased after him, breathing hard, sweating hard, and caught up with him as he paused on a flat ridge to assess the route on up.

She turned to view the way they'd come. 'Can we see where they're buried from up here?'

He jutted his chin at the green rim of the forest. 'It is hidden. Usually we go only in the festival—'

She's listening, and then not. A sound has brushed her ear. Or is it sound? More as if a silence near them deepens, stirs, and settles in a new place.

She turns her head. Looks along the ridge. Both ways.

Nothing. Above. Nothing.

Below, only Huru and Ben scrambling up the rock path towards them, talking loudly over each other as they always do. And Jack following them.

Jack glanced up at her quizzically and then behind him at what she might be seeing.

Only the span of the island below, narrowing to the sand

bank jutting into Shanza's bay, where the heron always foraged. She turned back to Leli, and was surprised to see him already near the clifftop, edging up through a mesh of undergrowth. She set off in pursuit. She pushed through the tangle of bushes.

A buffeting breeze knocked her sideways, salty and fresh and wonderful. Sea glittered green on all sides, heaved in smooth, rolling swells against the cliff; birds wheeled in a slow dance. She was wrapped in incandescent sunlight. She breathed deep, her head clearing, her pulse slowing.

Ben burst through the bushes behind her, Huru and Jack on his heels. 'Cool! Are we on top of that cave?'

Leli pointed straight down. 'Just there. You go in when the sea is low. The cave is very long. It is not good to be there when the sea is high, like now.'

As if in answer, water boomed.

'*That's* what we felt last time,' Jack asserted. 'Water slamming in—'

And it's there again – that whisper she cannot hear. For a split second, in the gleam of the air, there's a warmth, not quite a touch, something apart, *separated*, yet close. She hears the intake of a breath.

'Ally?' Jack moved quickly to her, fracturing everything. 'You OK?'

She resisted looking beside or behind or around her, though every nerve twanged. 'Just . . . hot.' She glanced towards Leli – *did he see?* But he'd moved away, was gazing north.

I'm alone in this.

'Tundani is there,' Huru announced to them all, pointing

161

north up the coast. 'Not so long by water, more long on the road.'

She forced herself to concentrate. Far beyond the mangroves, pale shapes clustered along a flat coastline, vanishing into heat haze. 'The coral goes many miles after the mangroves far, far north, all up to Tundani,' Huru continued. 'And all round Kisiri – coral, coral. Just one big deep place for big dhows, there.' He pointed to the channel between the island and the mangroves.

'Well, one thing's certain,' Jack said, 'there's *nothing* that says anyone else's been *here*, is there? I mean, where we left the canoes there's just bird tracks. No other boats in sight now. Just those.' He meant Shanza's fishing boats, their sails making crescents of light on the water. 'So why've those powerboats been around here so much? And if there's coral reefs all along by Tundani like you're saying, Huru, that's dangerous for big boats, isn't it? So why come south, why not keep north of Tundani – safer for tourists, I mean? And what's all the stuff going on at night is what I *really* want to know,' he finished.

'When the D.O. comes to Shanza again, we will know why. For sure!' insisted Huru. 'The D.O. and Mzee Shaibu and the Elders will make them go away!'

'Hope it's that simple,' Jack muttered. Though no one but Ally seemed to hear.

Leli led them along the cliff towards the forest. In places the coral rim had crumbled and lush foliage hid treacherous crevices. It was even harder going as they turned inland, away from the water. Ally felt her way with feet and hands, shouldering through creepers that hung in dense curtains and sifted the light to a green twilight gloom. And Leli moved fast, Ben and Huru tracking close behind. Not a single private moment to tell him about the strange things happening to her again.

She was suddenly stranded, alone, in a stomach-fluttering foreboding. Every one of her senses was on red alert for the next weird happening, and when it came, she stopped so abruptly that Jack bumped hard into her.

'What's that?' she hissed.

A booming noise, deep below them. The ground almost drummed. To her relief, Jack heard it too.

'Echo? Waves?'

Sudden scrabbling above her head; foliage shivered. She met the hard stare of a gekko, throat palpitating. Waited, almost holding her breath.

Nothing else.

They went on cautiously, and for some minutes the noise stayed with them, a slow, steady drumbeat that to Ally's ears was more and more threatening the more muffled it became, here, out of sight of the water, cocooned by the web of trees.

The ground levelled off. Leli and Huru turned onto a narrow track and walked briskly along.

Trees thinned; needles of light warmed the gloom. A glimpse of greater brightness ahead. Leli speeded up, entered a sunlit clearing, turned, welcoming them in.

Purple flowers, long silky grass, butterflies in a yellow-white cloud above a tumble of bushes, a great pillar of rough black rock.

'It's here?' She meant Fumo and Zawati's place. She had a vision of them lying side by side underneath her. She felt compelled to whisper.

Leli was staring past her. She turned to look.

Clods of earth and grass, wrenched up, bushes flattened, branches splintered. Churned mud smeared the great rock of the warriors.

Leli felt it like a punch in his chest.

A long, hissing breath between clenched teeth came from Huru.

'Is it this place that's like a special graveyard or something?' Ben asked shrilly. 'Someone's messed it all up!'

Fumo, Zawati. Fumo, Zawati, drummed in Leli's head. *This place of their sleep. This place of their peace. Fumo's warning! Fumo's warning!*

He felt a touch on his arm: Ally – pointing at the path of devastation thrusting down through the trees towards the shore.

Anger was like a fist in his chest, strangling words.

Near the water, something had gouged long furrows in damp sand.

'It is something heavy, dragged,' Huru said. 'Two things, maybe.'

Ally trudged through the soft sand along the line of them sloping up the shore. 'Lots of footprints here.'

From the top of the shore, Ben yelled.

'Look, more marks!' he told them with an air of importance,

pointing. Another deep drag-groove merged into churned sand.

Ally's stomach heaved. She'd caught a stale, sour smell. Rancid. Sick-making. She'd smelt that before: one holiday, stumbling across a dead sheep, torn apart, half-eaten, on a hill in Wales.

The stench was there for a second, then gone, replaced by the salt-sea, seaweed, damp sands.

But among Kisiri's trees now, somewhere very near her, flies whined and buzzed, a fizzing, frantic, angry roar.

Fifteen

Leli fretted. For several minutes Mzee Shaibu had not said a word. He looked at the ground. His face told nothing. Was he listening, even?

'Mzee, they destroy Bwana Fumo and Mwana Zawati's place!' insisted Leli. 'The air is sick! There are dead things somewhere . . .'

'Nothing destroys Bwana Fumo and Mwana Zawati's place, Leli. It is strong in our hearts—'

'But—'

'Be still, Leli. I am thinking.'

It struck Leli that the lines and shadows of the old man's face had deepened. He had stooped to pass through the low door of his house, but now in his yard he was still bent at the shoulders. Suddenly he looked worn, smaller than Leli had ever seen him before.

A feeling rippled through Leli, like fear. *If Mzee Shaibu does not know what to do, who will?*

A further minute passed; Leli could barely contain himself.

Huru fidgeted impatiently beside him. Then the Mzee said quietly, 'And you have just come from there? The English friends saw this damage too?'

'Yes, yes, we saw and we come to you straight away now, now, just now leaving the boat!'

A decisive thump of Mzee Shaibu's stick on the ground and he straightened to his full height. 'Huru, you will go to Saka. If his foot is well enough, he may take us to Kisiri now, no need to wait for others to return from the fishing. Leli, you will come too.'

They needed no second instruction. 'Remember, Leli,' he called after him, 'it is not what these people have done now that matters, but what it tells us they may do in days to come. We do not look for punishment. That is a short victory, and it does not taste good. Victory will be if we keep our Kisiri and our Shanza safe for all of us.'

Ally sat astride the roof parapet and gazed out over the forest. In the windless afternoon it was hushed, weighted by a shimmering yellow heat haze that wrapped the house too. So did that sick-making stench she'd smelt on Kisiri. Memory of it had travelled with her since, stickily coating everything, seeming to infect the air even here, two miles from the island.

Is someone dead on the island?

And Leli's distress – edged with a kind of anger. *Is he angry with me too, with all outsiders? If only he'd come to the house, now, so we can talk about it!*

She felt helpless, just going with Jack and Ben to pack up the tent and come back to the house.

There'd be all the debates in the village. He'd be deep in all of that. *Not thinking of me. Why would he? Why should he?*

Fretfully, her eyes found focus on trees at the forest edge. Paler strokes against deeper gloom. A flicker of colour. Fusing, as she looked more carefully, to the shape of a person.

Her stomach lurched.

A person stepping out. Waving. With relief so overwhelming she felt silly, she recognized the archaeologist, Makena.

'Miss Curious Ally!' Makena called, walking quickly and arriving below the house. 'I may ascend and view the world?'

'Steps round the front.' Ally pointed the way, grateful for the prospect of company.

Makena leapt up them, two at a time, exuberantly flinging her arms wide, revolving to take in the scene on all sides. 'Magnificent vistas!' She followed the perimeter of the roof. 'Excellent site for a fort!'

'Oh! Was there one here?' Ally leaned over the wall to see where Makena was looking.

'Ah, well, some old Portuguese forts have never been found – records *name* them, but locations are very confused. Maps of that time left much to be desired! But no sign of anything *here* for us to uncover. Pity, eh? To make such an adventure would be a wonder, I think!'

'Mzee Kitwana in Shanza said there's a story about an island fort—'

'Oh, Mzee Kitwana has many stories. I am glad you are listening to them! I should live in Shanza to hear them all!' Makena settled herself on the wall with a long view towards Kisiri. 'But it is not just a story. Five years ago a storm washed

168

away soil from a hill. Underneath was the gate of a big stone building. It was on a land sticking out into the sea, fifty miles south of here. They learned it was an island once, even in the memory of one very old man still living! Sandbanks shifted and joined it to the mainland. We think *that* is all that is left of the island fort of the story. But, who knows, really? So many mysteries! For example, the rock below this house was once bombarded by Portuguese cannons. Why? What was here? Why would the invaders attack it? One day, I tell you, I will look carefully. In fact, Miss Curious, there is an interesting story – you will like it. Ninety years ago, the English Chief Fisheries Officer built this house, when this country was a colony of Britain. That is why people call it the Old Fisheries House, you see. He died here, very old, sixty years ago. In his last years he collected local people's stories, faithfully writing everything in his diary, perhaps a little mad, living here alone, scribbling. Everyone with a tale to tell visited him! But here's the thing: he wrote how one night he woke because the house was trembling. He recognized the sound of guns; he felt pounding, as if the cliff jumped—'

Ally's gaze, aimed at the headland and the sea as she listened, snapped to Makena's face. The cliff jumped? Like that jolting on Kisiri?

Makena saw her surprise. 'Strange eh? But here is the most strange thing. He went with his house-servant next morning, and in the coral they found a cannon ball embedded, deep. Then a second nearby. People said the old man had seen them before and forgotten! But who knows! His diary is in Ulima Museum, and the cannon balls, four hundred years old.'

Rapidly Ally sifted thoughts. 'Could old Shanza be some-where near? I mean the one that Fumo and Zawati built?'

'Ah, the great new city in the forest. Perhaps it is there! Or perhaps there never was an old Shanza! Perhaps it is the city of all peoples who fought the invaders, rolled into one legend. Shanza claims the story, but it has different forms in different places.' Then, more to herself than to Ally, 'Sad that the towns were so busy quarrelling with *each other*, they did not link arms to fight the common danger. Often so, yes?'

This last was unmistakably directed at Ally.

'I . . . never thought about it,' Ally said.

'So, think about it now! We say: *sticks in a bundle do not break*. What do you think Fumo and Zawati's story is about?'

'Oh! . . . Not giving in? Fighting bad things?'

'Yes, yes. And also more. The power of *unity* and *fore-sight* and *intelligence* among ordinary people – women, men, children – against enemies that seem so strong you think they are unbeatable. But they *can* be beaten if people join together with common purpose. The people survived. The *spirit of the people* survived. Rebirth, in a new city.' Makena sighed, elaborately. 'In truth, all the cities fell to the Portuguese greed. Their stories are only partly told – not much trace found in the *land*. Here and there little somethings come to light to make us look harder . . . I think, sometimes you feel the spirit of places, though my friend, the policeman Rutere, tells me I am a little mad!'

'I wouldn't be surprised if there was something in the forest here,' Ally said, 'it's strange. Kisiri too.'

'Well, Kisiri – in times past, a burial ground! A place of

final peace and sanctuary. You have instinct for these things? You have gift of foresight? Like our Zawati?'

She didn't seem to be teasing.

'Just . . .' Ally hesitated, then plunged, 'You'll think I'm being silly . . . But, well, bits feel really strange . . . it's frightening—'

'And this is different from the strangers on Kisiri who are worrying our friends in Shanza?'

'When we were walking round it, one time it felt like someone was right beside me, talking to me, but there was no one there. And it happened again on the cliff! I know it's stupid . . .'

Makena was listening. Intently. Ally became bolder. 'And last night we saw canoes, you know, the kind they call *hori*, there, out on the water – not just me, my friend Leli saw them first, then – gone! Like, *there – not there*!'

Makena sat tilting her head a little as if assessing the idea from all angles. Then she gave a start and looked at her watch. 'Oh, oh, I am to take tea with Mzee Kitwana!' She held out her hand and shook Ally's energetically. 'But I am thinking now that there is an interesting something I would like you to read. Very, very interesting! A friend in Portugal sent it to me. I will bring it when I come to Shanza again. I will look for you tomorrow and show you. I am eager to know what you think! But now I go. For now, please greet your auntie for me.'

At the bottom of the roof steps, she stopped and looked up at Ally. 'I forgot to ask – you were here when the visitors came looking for your aunt a few days ago?'

'Yes, and we don't know what they wanted.'

'I make a guess. They want this land, and I am thinking they will try to be very unpleasantly *persuasive*.' Makena clicked her tongue, frowning, muttering now to herself. 'New footsteps, haunting the old.'

'What do you mean?' Ally said. The phrase chilled her.

Makena focused on her. 'Invaders, Ally! Have we not been talking about them? Invaders, old, and now new!' She swung on her heel at the growl of Carole's car nearing. 'I think I will talk quickly to your auntie – she must be on guard, I think. Everyone must be On Guard!'

sixth day
vultures

Sixteen

Diogo and four others take this Watch. A canopy of cloud overhangs and Chane says the monsoon they call Kusi comes upon us early from the south. But it will bring no ships from Portugal to rescue us, for they have abandoned us.

We station one on each bastion, for the last four hours myself one of these. Pain in my bones fades. No fever. In two hours I will patrol again, and Jabari with me. Through all the hours of last night, every man and woman watched, for the food brought by Jabari and his friends gives such strength! The heartbeat of freedom comes with them. We had forgotten!

The merchant brothers from Mwitu, Badru and Rahidi, consider our defences, talk rapidly in their language with Saaduma, Omar, Chane, Winda, Goma. Prince Jabari roams the walls, restless as a caged lion. He observes our enemies' encampment across the water, below the mainland town.

I question him. 'Why do they hold back? Why do they not attack to take the fort? Do they wait for us to die, or is some other plan afoot?'

He studies the enemies' small craft moving across the bay and does not answer. Last night we watched them ever circling, beyond range of our guns, low-slung shadows, unlit, sliding silent on black water.

At last, he says, 'I cannot imagine the terrors of these months, my brother. Nor of the time before. Even in Mwitu, before we knew of the siege, people talked of the savagery and greed of your captain and his soldiers. Tell me the course of things. All. From first your besiegers' ships were seen.'

I drag the memories up, and am sick with horrors.

I write it here, as I told it to Jabari.

Seven months ago, it began. Those Arab ships from distant Oman swept down on the north-east monsoon and turned their guns on us.

We fired to stop their ships entering the channel between this island and the mainland town. Our shots fell short. Daily they taunted, holding their vessels beyond reach of our cannon; with cannon fire they raked the waters if we tried to reach our ships. Twenty men died of that alone. Four ships' boats sank beneath their volleys.

No need for them to turn their guns first on the mainland town to gain shelter along its shores, for the town opened arms to them as saviours from our evil. Weeks before, our captain, Dom Alvaro, had the town's king and council flogged near to death for slowness in paying taxes to him. He seized the town's ships and stole the cargos.

Five months ago, during darkness, the enemy cut the anchor cables of our ships. Helplessly we saw our vessels drift towards the mainland, triumphantly seized to swell the enemy fleet.

By night they crept onto the island and fired the houses outside the fort. They poisoned the wells, captured the last cannons outside the walls, put our own guns on ships and shores, and turned them against us.

We drew the families of the island natives, slaves and free, inside the fort. Outside, rats overran the blackened ruins, taking food stores not consumed by fire. Inside, our food stores dwindled.

They might have lasted months, but for Dom Alvaro's squandering. If he had listened to my father, half the dead might live and starvation never open the door to fever. Our own hands brought this death into our midst! Pestilence entered with supplies smuggled from Zanzibar. Five or six died every day; my father's skills could do nothing.

How the dead cluster round me, moving my pen!

Unrest brewed among the soldiers when Alvaro had the fever's first victims thrown into the ditch below our walls. It was, he said, to scare the enemy from coming closer. But the corpse-stench hung on the air and my father warned the disease would corrupt the wind.

Last night, it was the Muslims Saaduma and Winda who risked their lives to save us by bringing fish. But not two months since, three Muslim slaves tried to escape this siege, and with his own hand, Dom Alvaro slit their throats.

He ordered the statue of St Antonio, dressed in soldiers' clothes, to be placed on the parapet to defy the enemy. In the night it leapt into the ditch to join the corpses: some said it was a sign that God himself forsook us, and there was mutiny.

Alvaro hanged the leaders and left their bodies rotting before the chapel. Only Fernando and my father dared to cut them down and bury them with prayers. Alvaro dare not punish my father, the only physician in the fort. Or Fernando, for there was love for him among the garrison – Portuguese, Muslim and Native alike – for his small kindnesses to so many on this blighted island.

*

I relive that morning – the frigate *Santa Theresa* arriving from Portugal and anchoring in the outer roadsteads. With such eager hearts we awaited help from our countrymen aboard!

None came. No food. No medicines. No challenge to the enemy flaunting their ships and daring anyone to come near the island.

In darkness, we launched a rowing boat to the frigate, but our messenger was turned away for terror of the fever, fired on by the enemy and fell into the water sore wounded. He reached the fort and died hours later. We saw the frigate's sails fill and the *Santa Theresa* move on the winds, taking the last of our hope with her.

And I remember how, between one dawn and the next, the fever struck Alvaro down.

For a time after we buried him, a kind of peace reigned in these walls, if you can call it peace when Death looked each of us in the face.

There was talk he died with a secret on his lips that he seemed desperate to tell. Talk of that secret, rumour of a hidden thing, gave purpose to a few, and then that talk died with them.

All there, buried in my memory! Word by word I conjured it again for Jabari, each moment rising as if it lived again.

Jabari asked me if I knew the mainland town. I could tell him of dreams of walking there, of roaming its forests, of seeking Her. I told him only that in the last years I seldom set foot on mainland shores, for we Portuguese risked our lives by venturing there. Only Dom Alvaro went, and only with full guard.

'The townspeople have only hatred for us. They look for any chance to harm us. Such ills they suffered at the hands of Alvaro and

178

the soldiers of this fort! My father's journals rage against it, you can read it there. I rejoice that you are here, Jabari, but why throw your fate with ours? Those are your people, there – our enemies in the camp, on the ships, in the town! You too must hate us!'

'Brother, I *choose* my people. I will not have them forced on me by quarrels or alliances made by others. Deeds speak to me. Steady hearts. I did not ask Badru and Rahidi for help, yet when they knew I came to find you, they stood with me. Such are my people. Your besieging enemies are not.'

'But our besiegers are Muslim, as you!'

'True. Arabs from Oman, many, many weeks sailing north from here. They have their own quarrel with your countrymen, for deeds done by the ships and soldiers of Portugal in their own lands and seas. They come to avenge them. They promise the people of the mainland town here to rid this region and the seas of you.'

He seemed to think long and hard for some minutes, and then he went on, 'But think on this, my brother. What of Saaduma, Chane, Omar, Winda, Neema, Goma – Muslims all. Trapped here, with you. What of them?'

I thought of how, when the siege began, Alvaro barred them from leaving, on pain of instant death. Yet when Alvaro died, Fernando gave them freedom to surrender to our enemy and save their own lives.

They did not take that freedom. They did not leave.

I told Jabari this.

'And why?' Jabari answered. 'Because their bonds with men and women inside the fort were already tied. Saaduma loves Winda. Winda, Neema, Goma stayed for the children – orphaned, abandoned children of your people. Of Portugal.'

I had not seen that. The answer silenced me.

179

'But I see that your besiegers have truly slackened guard,' he said, 'as you have all remarked.'

Eight days they have not fired on us. Two nights Saaduma and Winda safely fished and returned; Jabari, Badru and Rahidi reached us in their boat unchallenged.

I spoke my fears to Jabari, that our enemies seek to persuade us they are careless and make us slacken Watch. Yet all the while they plot an attack now, when our defence is lowest.

We are now only twelve: six men, three women and three children. No more have died, though I am afraid: in the last hour, Neema, she who appointed herself guardian of the children since they lost their mothers, and so tenaciously clung to life for them, she coughs most dreadfully. Baby Jorge is very weak.

They number many hundreds, a thousand, if the numbers of their ships be counted.

'Jabari, if they attack, we cannot hold the fort against them! I truly fear the dark of night will bring—'

'These walls will not be your tomb. We will not wait for them to find you dead, or put you to the sword, my brother.' He clasped my hand in a gesture of promise. 'This we will do, now. Badru has travelled often to this mainland town; arriving there would cause no curiosity. He offers to go tonight and mingle with the townspeople. He will uncover any talk of attack! And we here will prepare. Brother, take heart! Call to your blessed Spirit of Hope and take heart!'

Badru left in the darkest hour, lowered by rope from the east parapet. We at once lost sight of him in shadow. He will retrieve the boat from the cave below, and travel north into the mangroves to reach the mainland, at dawn to walk into the town by the landward gate.

We wait, and in our different ways, we pray for him – for in the strangeness of these times locked here together, Muslim and Christian are bonded together against those who would slaughter us. I seem to hear my father's voice talking with Fernando. How often they condemned the diabolical ways of our dead captain, Dom Alvaro. 'We claim some God-given Christian right to enslave Muslim and Heathen thus! It is tyranny to attack these lands! Sorely will we be punished for it!'

I went to the chapel and prayed that no man or woman learns that Badru has chosen friendship with us, that he is a spy for us. There would be no hope for him.

Seventeen

A restless night, dream-wrecked, coiling, binding cobwebs of sound . . .

It left her wrung out, distracted. Everything ebbed and flowed through her: yesterday – the legend, Mzee Kitwana, Makena's talk, forts, cannons. Most of all, Leli, Kisiri.

Just one night since we landed on Kisiri again? It felt like a lifetime. *What did we find – what do those marks mean, that smell?*

She rested her head against the car seat. If only she could *be* with Leli. Now. Talk about it with him. Even just *see* him.

She caught a fragment of Ben's chatter, in the back seat. He was telling Carole, '. . . engines really early this morning, an' it was two boats in our creek, just sitting!'

For a minute Carole just guided the car across the narrow tarmac's bumpy cracks, splayed out like crooked spider's legs.

Then she remarked, 'Well, like I said, let's have a look at this Tundani place today. Shanza people think it's the root of all this. Maybe it is. Seize the time, eh? I've no chance of more time off for a week.'

'These boats are around all the time now. Like, everything's in secret!' Jack said.

Carole glanced at him in the rear-view mirror. 'Mmm . . . boats up our creek last night too, when you were sleeping—' She broke off as a crowded bus halted ahead of them. Two women clambered down: one balanced a suitcase on her head, the other, heavily pregnant, propped a cloth bundle on hers. They moved serenely off the road and turned onto a murrum track, walking up the middle, kicking up little puffs of red dust with their bare feet.

Ally watched them curiously.

Carole followed her gaze. 'They're heading for a village. That's also the track to the school, two miles up. All the children for ten miles round go there. The *new* tarmac road to the *new* Tundani hotel comes in the other side and goes right past. People've asked for something to be done about *this* old road for years – *nothing* happens. All of a sudden, a spanking new shiny two-lane highway all fifty miles from the airport to Tundani – straight there, no problem!'

Ally squinted through the glare at the red ribbon of track. It wound in snaking curves, rising slowly through maize plantations into the distant blue-green haze of low hills. Further away, the track was scattered with other walkers. Like Leli, Huru, Eshe, Koffi, Jina, she thought, and Lumbwi, Pili, Mosi, even the tiny ones just starting school – all of them walking all the way from Shanza, every day. Five miles there, five miles back.

'Bet they bunk off,' Jack commented. 'That kind of walk!'

'Actually, no,' came from Carole. 'Put you lot to shame, they do. Benjy, stop kneeling up! Sit down properly back there, and put your seat belt back on!'

The bus ahead rumbled on its way. Carole followed at a sedate distance. The dilapidated tarmac meandered on through scrubby bush.

Ben plumped down in the seat with a snort of frustration. 'So when're we going on safari like you said? See the lions and that?'

'We'll do it, promise! But we have to go fifty miles inland to the nearest game area. Lion, leopard, cheetah, elephant, rhino, hippo, impala, if we're lucky we'll see them all, and more. But it's very wild, very hot, and they're dangerous, we can't just stroll about there, Benjy.'

'I *know*. I've seen pictures. Hope there's *rhino*.' He grabbed the binoculars from Jack and scanned to and fro enthusiastically.

The dry grassland slid by, dotted with acacia trees, here and there a small cultivated patch. Another few miles on, the road curved closer to the coast and lush cashew and mango trees began to crowd in; glimpses of white dunes, the sea's gleam. A lot more people walking here, wandering randomly across the road, ignoring bus and car.

'All heading for Tundani, probably. We'll reach it in a moment,' Carole said. 'Oh!' She slowed suddenly. 'Look at that!'

They'd topped a rise. Ahead, a patchwork of brown shapes sprawled into the distance. The car rolled closer. Brown shapes became roofs – an assortment of cardboard boxes, corrugated iron, stretches of sacking. Motley partitions, propped, hung, tied together, broke up the crowded space between. A pall of smoke hung to one side, and a poisonous, sulphurous stink.

'I don't believe it! A month back it was a quiet little cross-roads!' The shock in Carole's voice made it hoarse. 'Tea shacks, a bus stop . . .'

Ally wrinkled her nose. 'What's that foul smell?'

'Sewage, I think. Burning rubbish.' Carole stopped the car and got out. 'In Ulima there's a whole valley like this, you know – where Collins and the others come from. Sticks, stones, metal tins stuck with mud, plastic sheets, anything to give shelter. But that's been there for years, evolving, putting down roots. This . . . *Already*!'

They pushed on at a snail's pace through goats and hawkers and curio sellers. Small boys jiggled wood carvings of animals across the windscreen and tapped at the windows. Ally looked for Collins, Dedan, but it was a sea of strangers, a sea of blankets spread with pots, baskets, necklaces, bracelets, shells . . .

Why does Collins think they'll sell anything here when everyone else is trying to do the same?

'Of course we've come in the *back* entrance,' Carole said sarcastically. 'Tourists are spared this view, and enter by the front door on the new road. When we get to the middle, there'll be fancy shops – bags, sandals, *kikois*, *kangas* bought for nothing from one of these local stalls, tagged with a price twenty times more! And Collins still won't have the price of a meal and Saka walks thirty miles to the nearest doctor!'

Ahead, a giant arch straddled the road and proclaimed WELCOME TO TUNDANI PARADISE VILLAGE; beside it, a large car park and a block of new pink-washed concrete shops, not yet open, and the Baobab Cafe, that was, under striped umbrellas.

'Collins!' Ben yelled, just as Ally spotted him too, lurking between two parked cars. He was watching something across the road. She leaned out of the window and called. He turned, but only to hiss, 'Do not make us seen! We are invisible,' flapping his hand urgently. Then he dodged through the traffic and joined another boy: Dedan, she guessed, but couldn't be sure. They'd melted away.

Carole eased the car into a parking space. 'Hope they're not up to something that'll land them in trouble.' She looked pointedly at Jack.

'Just asked them to scout about – see if the boats round Kisiri and our creek are from here,' he answered.

'Well, then I hope *you're* not getting them into trouble,' she countered. 'Are you?'

Jack raised an eyebrow at Ally. She got out of the car and checked all directions. No Collins or Dedan in sight.

'They're used to living in a *city*.' Jack joined her. 'They live on the streets, right? Probably ducking and diving out of trouble all day.'

That isn't the point, Ally thought. She pictured Collins' thin, earnest, too grown-up face, and eager Dedan following Collins' every instruction. And at the beach camp: Joseph and Grace eating remnants of the night's feast, chattering to Ben. Dedan and Collins pushing food into their pockets, slinging cloth bundles of shells over their shoulders. How they'd given the thumbs-up to Jack and set off for the forest path to the road.

'Let's hope they spot the boats that've been hanging about here,' Jack had said then. 'Then we can tell that policeman, Rutere, in case it's . . . well, *wrong*.'

Collins'll take his responsibilities to Shanza and Jack very seriously. He'll be so desperate to please everyone!

She had a quiver of apprehension. She surveyed the scene carefully once more. The two boys were nowhere.

'Drink first.' Carole ushered them pointedly away from the glossy Baobab Cafe and stopped by a cardboard sign in English: EXTRA EXTRA COLD DRINKS VERY SPECIAL EXTRA EXTRA. A handful of bottles floated in a small, water-filled oil drum, shaded by sheets of cardboard. A tiny boy jumped from his seat on a wooden crate. He doled out the drinks, counted the coins, fetched more crates and turned them upside down, motioning them to sit. Satisfied, he retired behind his oil drum and counted the coins again.

Their seat gave them a long view of the beach side of the roadway. A broad sweep of silk-smooth new tarmac flanked by gigantic peppermint-green concrete flower pots, all empty, the white and green block of the hotel at the end. On one side, scaffolding hid the construction, the other side was already open: arches led through potted palms and urns trailing scarlet bougainvillea and white frangipani. They were topped by a tower with a combination of minarets and crenellations, like some weird mix of mosque and castle.

'Looks like peppermint ice cream with blotches of raspberry jam!' Carole said.

'Or a stage-set for Sinbad the Sailor or the Arabian Nights,' Jack offered. 'Come on, Benjy, let's go in – you coming, Ally? Don't run off and leave us,' he told Carole.

'I'll be along in a minute,' Carole murmured. 'Can't face it yet.'

It was all air conditioning, polished stone floors, racks of glossy brochures: glass-bottom boats to see the coral, deep-sea fishing, scuba diving, water-skiing. Jack pocketed a handful under the disapproving eye of the receptionist.

Ally thought of Eshe's sister who wanted to work here. But this receptionist wasn't from Shanza or anywhere like that. She'd stepped out of a fashion magazine. Her heels clacked on the stone floor. Her nails clacked too – like purple claws when she handed over the price list Jack requested. Though only after she'd first snapped, 'Why do you want it?' then shut up when Carole pushed through the glass doors to join them.

'Thirty-two thousand shillings!' squawked Ben, inspecting it.

'That's two hundred and fifty pounds a night.' Jack showed Carole.

'It is less if you book many nights,' the receptionist said sweetly to Carole.

'How much of the hotel is open?' Carole attempted a retaliatory sweetness.

'In the Kaskazi wing, twenty rooms, madam. Very *luxurious*. Sixty rooms open soon in the Kusi wing. The swimming pool is beautiful. Non-residents welcome, madam.' She smiled encouragingly. 'Many interesting places to be. The Jahazi

188

bar. The Mtepe cocktail lounge. I will get you a plan.' With a flourish she produced a brochure.

'Our seafood is caught by our very own spear fishermen and served in the local manner. We have our own bank and hairdresser inside the hotel. We can also make very *special* arrangements for specially unusual expeditions. Tailor-made for just you!' She smiled brightly. 'We have other hotels, you can move from one to the other. We are very big! We are making new hotels everywhere!'

'Any near Shanza?' Jack demanded.

'Marisa!' came sharply from the back office. The woman who poked her head out of the door was no longer wearing the sunglasses she'd had in the car, and Ally remembered her hair differently. But it was the same one, Ally's certainty reinforced by the way the woman halted on seeing Ally and Jack, gave a rapid once-over for Carole and Ben, and withdrew sharply.

'It's *her*!' Ally kept her voice low. 'Carole, *she* came to the house with that man.'

'Excuse me,' Jack said pointedly. 'Can we speak to that person in there? She wanted to speak to my aunt. So, here's my aunt.'

The receptionist's expression changed from politely helpful to startled. She hesitated, and went into the office. There was an exchange of words, high-pitched and loud, then irate, and then she was propelled out again, the door slammed shut behind her. She came forward, pursing her mouth. 'You make a mistake. My colleague did not come to your house. My colleague is making an important telephone call and cannot speak to you. If you have questions you speak to the owner.'

189

'And he is?' demanded Carole.

The purple fingernails tapped a leaflet on the desk. 'Mr Heinrek. You must make an appointment. He is very busy.'

Ally picked up the leaflet. It advertised game trips to see 'the big five' – lion, leopard, elephant, rhino, buffalo. A picture of a man on the front, the face obscured by the brim of a white hat. Absurdly large, and definitely memorable. He posed – one foot on a rock, elbow on his knee. A familiar red Land Rover jutted into the picture behind.

She showed the others.

'It's the one who came to Shanza!' squeaked Ben.

'He'd have his gun in the picture too, if hunting wasn't illegal,' Jack muttered. 'Bet he's one the inspector's got his eye on.'

'I most certainly will see Mr Heinrek,' Carole announced to the receptionist. 'My name is Carole Seaton. Please make sure you pass it on. Mr Heinrek has sent people to my house. I want to know why.'

'It *was* her!' Ally insisted, outside. 'Why say it wasn't?'

'Doesn't want anyone knowing she's from the hotel,' Carole said.

They stood, ringed by petal-shaped swimming pools and sun beds sporting a few guests, lobster red and stupefied by the heat. Others lay under umbrellas. A few floated in the pools. No one on the beach below or in the sea – though three gleaming sharp-nosed powerboats bobbed by a bright-painted pontoon extending from the hotel. Ben squinted through binoculars and read the names. *Cool Running. Lucky Star. Blue Marlin.* In the distance a boat whined across the bay, a water skier rising onto skis, bouncing a few yards before collapsing in an arc of white spray.

Ally pictured the boat nosing past her, Joseph and Grace in the creek, the name on its bow. *'Blue Marlin!* That's the one we saw.'

A snip of conversation with Leli came to her. *Visitors from the hotel will like this?* he'd asked, steering the boat through the mangroves. *It is interesting for them, Ally?*

Brilliant! she'd said.

Magic! Ben had echoed.

Standing here, it was a ludicrous idea. Once, she'd have been so excited to stay in a hotel like this. All the luxury! Now all she saw was that none of these people had come to *look* at anything. They were in a bubble. The bubble could be anywhere. Even another planet. No idea of the ripples spreading out from their beautiful bubble like the aftershock of an explosion. She thought of the purple-clawed receptionist. Probably really just like Eshe's sister inside. But she'd found herself a job.

Ally pictured Leli's face, excited at new people coming. She wanted to fold him away, protect him from all this, appalled by an overwhelming, stark recognition of how huge was the juggernaut rolling inexorably towards his village, his life.

'What is this business with Kisiri, Leli?' his mother demanded. 'Why do you go there today? You go twice! I see you!'

'Mzee Shaibu said yes! Then we went again with him! It is not a problem, my mother! Huru was there. We are helping.' He turned away quickly, not trusting himself to further talk.

She caught his arm. 'And with all this going over there to Kisiri and walking about, what do you find? Eh? Eh, Leli?'

'Nothing, nothing!' The Mzee had sworn them to say no word about the damage on the island until he had consulted the other Elders.

But people had seen them going to Kisiri, and they wondered, and the talk went on and on, sometimes the stories wild and silly, sometimes angry that Mzee Shaibu did not explain. The air was becoming heavy with it, like a storm brewing. And it was in him too, something restless and unformed, made of frustration and uncertainty, and fury.

Warnings, warnings, beat like a pulse in Leli's head. The dreams of Fumo! The canoes. The *strangeness* of Kisiri! This damage that someone had done. The smell of death! *Warnings!*

He felt in his shirt pocket, and took out the metal disc given to him by the storyteller. His fingertips traced the faint, worn shape of the flying eagle against the arc of the rising sun.

Why does Mzee Kitwana give me this? Frustration welled up in him, and Shaaban jumped into his mind. Yesterday he finished the letter to Shaaban, and straight away gave it to Eshe to put in the post office at Lilongelewa. She was just leaving to visit her cousin there, and promised, on pain of banishment from further parties with Ally, Jack and Ben if she forgot.

Shaaban, you should be here now! You will know what to do; how to speak to our mother and father so they do not worry. He missed his brother's steady voice calming, helping them to think clearly.

192

His mother had followed him into the yard.

'You stop now, Leli! You listen to me! I do not like it, Leli! Listen! Why do you go with these *English* ones all the time? I do not like it, you hear?'

He rounded on her, astounded. '*These English ones!*' he mimicked her tone. 'Why do you say it like this? They are our friends!'

'It will come to bad things!'

'What will come to bad things?'

'Everything. This girl! This English girl!'

Heat seared through him. Hot then cold. Cold. Angry cold.

'What do you say?' She looked hard into his face.

'I say nothing. There is nothing to say. She is my friend!'

'Do not spend your time like this.'

'Like what?'

She glared at him. Yesterday he would have dropped his eyes. Today, his blood was boiling.

She sniffed with disapproval and turned her back.

With the tumult in his brain, he could not trust himself: he left the yard quickly before she could enrage him more. He went down to the shore, taking refuge in the darkness. He looked towards Dr Carole's house high on the distant headland.

No lights shone. *Everyone sleeps. Or perhaps they sit in darkness on the roof as Ally told me. And Ally looks towards me.*

A sense of her looking, knowing, hearing, filled him brimful.

He stood, trying to calm himself so that his return into

the house would not show anger. If his mother saw anger, it would provoke her more. *Why was she* – he searched for the word – *frightened . . . yes, frightened – by Ally and the other English? They are not the problem! They are not doing secret, bad things on Kisiri!*

But today was not the beginning. These days his mother provoked him too easily. Frustration turned to coldness again. Like fear, like fear. *If my mother forbids . . .*

It churned in him: Shanza, Kisiri, Fumo and Zawati, himself between everything. And Ally. *Ally.* Already in the weave of his life, torn if she left it.

The wind had dropped. He absorbed the strange, rare silence of the forest. The tide was low, the lip of the sands dark with the shadows of uncovered reef. Kisiri was cut in silver by the touch of the moon, hard and high behind it.

And for the first time, the shape of his fears surfaced through the seething disquiet. It went through him as a series of thoughts. That something big was breaking apart. That Kisiri would be *taken* from them. That this was not just the loss of the island, of the place, but the extinction of something. The thoughts came together: *if Kisiri is taken from us, does Shanza cease? Everything is changing. The young men angry at Mzee Shaibu; everyone argues about the hotel, my mother looks for quarrels. She scorns Ally and the others.*

If it falls apart, can it be put together again?

He heard the thrum of an engine on the water. But when he strained his ears, there was nothing. It was only his fears that thrummed, like the persistent beat of a warning drum in his head.

*

I dreamed again of walking shores I have never walked, to walls of a broken town. No fires smoke the sands, no person, goat or chicken inhabits the streets. The day is filled with such silence.

This death is our work, and the work of our enemies, come as saviours to the town, smuggling betrayal.

I woke, and in sudden terror fell to my knees and prayed to God, to Her: give us deliverance from this death, this fort, this death in life! I cannot shed the dreadful silence of the broken town. Is this the world we will leave when we are done?

I thought long of my conversation with Jabari, and took out my father's journal and papers again. Also Dom Alvaro's, which my father kept when Alvaro died.

I gave them to Jabari. He read in silence, and after said, 'Your father's anger truly fires every page, brother. He rages at your Captain Alvaro's pride at theft and murder and assassination of kings, his lists of every coin stolen from the townspeople, every tax, ransom, punishment, killing, every other town bombarded with ships' cannon because it is a place of Muslims, his pleasure at news of a ship's captain beheading a king and killing thousands of his subjects for "rebellion".

'I see why our fathers became dear friends. Muslim and Christian, joined. But what troubles my father too, is this. Now people welcome these men who besiege you, these Omani Arabs who sweep across the ocean with soldiers and weapons to rid the coasts and seas of you. Kings and people embrace them as saviours.

'But, my father says in truth it is merely one vulture competing with another for its prey. There is peril for any people caught between. It is true, they do not press the Christian way upon us, as your people do. They do not burst into our world with such contempt for our beliefs. They hail us as brothers in Islam. Their bonds with us are centuries old, tied by our ships trading across the oceans.

'But it is certain – my father says – we will come to feel their violence. First these Omanis will put to the sword all of you that have not already died. They will tear down your flag and plant their own. *Then* will this town, and others – even my own dear city of Mwitu – begin to know their true purpose. The day will come when they will seek to enslave us. My father is growing old; many dismiss his fears for our world, for the ever-circling violence of it. But he sees far.

'But we will escape this hell, my brother. We will see Mwitu and my father's house again, every one of us.' He put his arm about my shoulder. 'The power of the warriors and your Spirit of Hope will give this gift to us, I think!'

seventh day
attack

Eighteen

The hammering at the door came at five in the morning by Ally's watch. She'd been jolted awake by something minutes before. She lay in the dark, listening.

Thump of feet running on the veranda. She jolted upright.

The pounding shot her out of bed. Barefoot on the cold stone floor, she heard the urgent call of her aunt's name. She heaved open her bedroom shutters, and recognized Huru's cousin Saka.

'Hurry, hurry!' he urged. 'Small ones are hurt! Terrible! Terrible! Mzee Shaibu says *come*! I have the *ngalawa* for Dr Carole—'

'Who?' Carole burst out of the veranda doors looking as if she'd dressed in her sleep. 'How? The car's quicker, Saka. I'll bring you back to your boat after. Ally, where the hell did I put the car keys?'

'I'll find them, I'll come too.'

'These little children, Collins, Dedan,' panted Saka. 'They try to come to Shanza but they are hurt very bad! Jela and

Thimba see them when they are fishing for the lobster. They bring the children to Mzee Shaibu. They are in my house now! Hasina is with them. Her sister Aishia is helping.'

'Jack, find a torch?' Carole said as he appeared, struggling into a T-shirt. She threw things into a large bag. 'You'll be all right here?'

'Coming with you – Benjy, get a move on!' Jack yelled.

Minutes later they were bumping away from the house, slithering and jerking as Carole drove too fast over the alternating ruts and sand of the track. Ally had a vision of two small boys mown down in a car driving like this.

'Are they hurt really bad?' she whispered.

Saka sucked breath between his teeth. 'They are beaten. Very beaten. And thrown away in the mangroves.'

She felt the blood drain from her face. *It's our fault! We went on about snooping round the boats!*

She looked at Jack, sitting forward, gripping the back of Carole's seat; feeling his sister's gaze, he flicked her a glance and away again, staring blindly into the bouncing tunnel of headlights.

Grimly Carole said, 'We'll stop at Kitokwe and get Salim to ring Inspector Rutere.'

Dedan was cradling his arm, yelping when Carole fingered it, whimpering as she felt delicately around his chest, screaming at the slightest touch of his ankle, which lay at an odd, twisted angle.

Ally knelt beside her. 'What are you looking for?'

'Broken ribs, arm, ankle, dislocations . . . Here, shhhh,

200

Dedan, I know it hurts, but try to be still so I can look . . . Ally, calm him?'

Ally held his good hand and stroked it and murmured; he stared at her in terror and heard nothing. His shirt hung off, ripped from collar to hem. His jaw was swollen; dried blood matted mouth and chin, forehead grazed raw. A long, deep gash on his leg had bled freely and was crusted with mud.

If anything, Collins' face looked worse. His right eye had vanished inside a purple jelly of bruises and cuts; blood stained his face from brow to jaw; he was jittering with rage, muttering incoherently, Hasina said, though her sister insisted they were dark threats of revenge.

And there was a stench around them both. Carole sniffed, exchanged a look with Hasina, who nodded. To Ally it reeked of dung, though more overpowering than anything she'd ever smelled before.

'Right,' said her aunt, 'Jack, cut their clothes off, then help Hasina and Aishia wash every bit of sound skin – gently, mind – and keep changing the water. I'll deal with the open wounds. Then wrap them in something clean. Bibi Hasina, can you lend something? I'll replace—'

'I have, I have.' Hasina went quickly to a wooden box in the corner and sorted two *kangas* from it, shaking the lengths of bright cloth out and putting them ready.

'OK, Ally, once most of the mud's washed off, you give me a hand cleaning the wounds. I'll do the deep ones, you keep to the grazes and surface cuts? Only boiled water – one dab with the cotton wool and chuck it, see? Ben, pack up their clothes

201

carefully – we'll give them to Rutere to figure out what's on them that stinks so awful.'

She pushed herself off her knees and stood, thinking aloud. 'Tetanus shots, painkillers. Dedan – arm broken, ankle fractured, twisted; Collins – breaks, maybe. So, splints for Dedan. Then both into the car, hospital, x-ray.'

She turned and regarded Collins with a long, searching look. 'So, Mr Collins Karanga, time to tell us what's happened.'

He stared at her balefully.

Carole pressed her lips together, gave Ally a look that was unmistakably *find out*. 'I'll get bandages and stuff from the car,' she said pointedly.

For some minutes there was no sound except the *crump crump* of the scissors and the trickle of water. Ben busied himself collecting the debris and hauled buckets of water from the village tap for boiling. Hasina lit a second charcoal brazier outside, discussing something in emphatic tones with Saka. He went off and returned, ushering in Grace and Joseph. They stood, tiny, and wide-eyed at the tending of Collins and Dedan. And very close together, Ally saw, until Aishia persuaded them to help fetch food from her own home several houses away.

Jack watched them go. He had a look on his face that Ally couldn't read. 'They must have followed someone from the hotel! *I* got them into this,' he said.

'*We* did, Jack – not just you! I got worried – I should've said something! In Tundani we could've stopped—'

He shook his head wordlessly, abruptly stood up and went outside.

Ally knelt by Collins and began cleaning the grazes on his legs. Dedan drifted into fitful sleep. Collins, on the other hand, was restless, eyes roaming the room as if something might leap at him.

Then he stiffened, gaze fixed on the door behind her. Assuming it was Jack, Ally turned.

Leli's mother halted on the threshold: she held two large bowls. She eyed Ally. Then she came in and lowered the bowls.

'New hot water,' she said quietly.

'Thank you,' said Ally.

Silence, that stretched.

'Is Leli here?' Ally ventured. A pause. Then his mother jerked her head at the doorway. She retrieved the bowls Ally had been using.

Ally smiled at her. No answering smile, just another nod, a gesture towards Collins' battered leg.

Ally took a clean piece of cotton wool, dipped it in the water, dabbed gently at grazes on the boy's ankle.

I'll finish this, wash Dedan, then find Leli, ran through her head.

From the long shadow across the floor, she could see his mother had crossed to the doorway again, but not left. Ally continued, working methodically: clean cotton wool, dip, dab, chuck, new cotton wool . . . A minute more, and the shadow moved and faded.

'My mother says you are here.' Leli's voice, sudden, beside her. 'I—' He caught sight of Dedan's swollen face, then Collins. His mouth fixed in a grim, angry line.

'We have to clean the grazes,' Ally said, and held out the

203

cotton wool. He took it from her and knelt down, beginning work on the mosaic of scratches on Collins' arms.

The room was quiet. Collins seemed to doze off. They worked steadily – legs, arms, rolled him gently to start work on his back.

At the sight of the mess of black bruises and red welts, Leli pushed back onto his heels and stood up. 'I talk to Mzee Shaibu!' he said brusquely. 'I come back after, Ally.'

In the silence that followed, Collins stirred. His eyes fluttered open and fixed on Ally. He hissed – something unintelligible through swollen lips. Except the last word sounded like 'box'.

'*Box?*' Ally looked at Hasina's box for clothes.

Vehemently Collins shook his head. '*Box, box!*' shaping with his hands something square that came to the top of his head. 'Wire, *wire!*'

Light dawned. *Cage.* 'You were in a cage?' The stench of dung made sudden sense. 'An *animal* cage? There was an animal with you?'

'No! We would be died with this animal!' He winced as she dabbed his chin, jerking his head away.

'Keep still, Collins, it's got to be cleaned. I'll be really careful.'

He looked at her, his one good eye full of fury. But he obeyed.

After a minute, she ventured, 'I don't understand.'

'Cage, *cage!*' he said, as if repeating the word would force it through. 'They sleep inside, sick! *Simba*—'

Frustratingly, he stalled: Carole had come into the room.

204

'*Simba?*' Carole echoed in a tone of disbelief.

'*Simba,*' he spat. '*Chui.*'

His anger, Ally saw, was a way of holding back the tears. He glared at them both with one reddened eye. The other had closed completely with the swelling.

She looked questioningly at her aunt.

'Lion,' Carole responded grimly. 'Leopard. I hope this is a little flight of exotic fancy. OK, look, Collins, Inspector Rutere is coming, you tell *him* about this.'

Collins went rigid as if stung, springing to his feet. '*Askari?* We go!'

'Stay right there, Collins! Have you done anything wrong? *No.* Planning anything wrong? *No.* So you're not in trouble with the *askari.* No need to be frightened. Speak to Inspector Rutere. He will listen. Then you'll come to the hospital with me.'

'And then they will sleep in our house,' called Hasina forcefully from outside. 'Till he is better, and Dedan is better.' She entered and barred flight, hands on hips. 'Aishia will take Grace and Joseph and keep them safe in her house.'

Carole gave her a grateful look. 'It's good of you and your sister, Bibi Hasina.'

Hasina sniffed. 'I will be happy if the terrible clothes and the smell are going. And if the boy will stop arguing. He will get into more horrible trouble away from our eyes.' She bent over and fussed at tucking the *kanga* round Collins, pushing him back to lie down, more than a match for his protests with a few vigorous words of her own.

Ally went outside. She couldn't see Leli, just his mother

205

rinsing bowls, stacking them to drain. He must still be at Mzee Shaibu's house.

Less than an hour had passed, but it felt like a night. Everything in Ally was strung taut. A trickle of nerves ran up and down her stomach like an electric current. The commotion had woken the rest of the village. People were gathering. A murmur of question and answer filled the darkness. Rumours percolated along the paths from house to house. Two small boys battered and broken and dumped where they weren't meant to be found: her mouth went dry, picturing their thin, stick-legged little bodies submerging helplessly in the swamp.

She shut it out, found another: Collins dodging through cars in Tundani yesterday. *Something was happening right then, causing what happened later!*

The thought shot a new spike of anxiety through her. Jack was crouching by the charcoal stove, and got up as she went over. The look he gave her struck her as an appeal, but she couldn't think of anything useful to say.

She watched Carole leave Hasina and Saka's house and go along the path to Mzee Shaibu's. A greyness in the sky heralded first light; sea and sky merged in a shadowless flat gloom, only the palms standing out blackly above the roofs. And it was hot, oppressively hot, as if a storm brewed.

Sharply Jack said to her, 'Can't believe how stupid I've been! Getting little kids hurt. I never thought . . . It's all this *stuff*!' He made a gesture that took in the village, Kisiri, the bay.

Then they both swung round, because there was the rumble

of a heavy engine nearing. At the back of the village the engine shut off and car doors slammed. Voices neared. Inspector Rutere and another policeman came into view.

'I have received your aunt's telephone message quickly,' the inspector said, seeing them. 'Explain, please.'

Inspector Rutere regarded their circle of faces – moving from Ally to Ben beside her, to Jack, to Carole. A few villagers gathered a little way off, watching, listening, their murmurs an uneasy chorus to the policeman's interrogation.

The inspector removed his cap and mopped his forehead. The heat was building, even the stiffening breeze from the sea not helping.

To Ally he said crisply, 'So, now tell me fully. Exactly. What have these boys said to you? We must be clear if there are discrepancies with the story they told us.'

'They wouldn't lie!' Ally protested.

The inspector's face was impassive.

She tried to think clearly. 'Collins said they saw animals inside fences. Cages too. His English is muddled, and I don't know Swahili—'

'I know, I know! He also told me lots after!' Ben interrupted. 'They followed a car, and they walked for miles, and then they saw lions and things! But Carole said there aren't lions near here.'

'Indeed,' acknowledged Rutere. 'Any more?'

Ben screwed up his face with concentration.

'No-o-o . . .' Ally confirmed reluctantly.

Still Jack said nothing.

'*Haya*,' Inspector Rutere's glance swept over them all. 'This is what this boy says to *us*,' he tapped his notes. 'They saw something which made them curious. What it was, we cannot get clear. Collins is suspicious and resists giving any information. My sergeant gets only confusion from the younger one – truly, he is dumb with fright. We conclude that they followed a vehicle in Tundani which took a track inland. They asked a woman where this went and learned it leads to an empty place of hills and rocks. They followed the marks of the vehicles. They have no idea how far—'

'Walking for hours and hours,' Ben insisted.

Slowly, Ally made sense of something. 'Into a hole . . . a big hole.'

The inspector inclined his head. 'An area of rocky ravines some twelve miles from Tundani known as the Devil's Kitchen. I am concluding this is where. They followed the tyre marks to a crater—'

'Fences,' interrupted Ally. 'Collins said fences.'

'High wire fences, yes. Another vehicle, and guards. With guns. The boys hid and watched. Many hours. Nothing happened till after dark. Then what they describe as crates, or cages, were taken from one vehicle into another. They saw little, all was by vehicle lights. But they claim they saw lion, leopard, cheetah – which they insist were sick. Drugged, I think, is the truth. Unfortunately, as the vehicles left, the boys were seen in the headlights, chased, Dedan tripped and when Collins went to help him, they were seized, beaten with sticks to near unconsciousness, carried in the back of one of the vehicles, and emptied into the swamp where the fishermen found them.' He sighed. 'I have no way of knowing if the boys tell all the truth, or what part is truth—'

'But why would they lie?' Ally burst out.

The policeman eyed her shrewdly. 'It is an unhappy truth that children of the streets thieve and do many things to stay alive. Including telling elaborate lies if it will get them out of trouble! And they are often used to commit a crime for others. For the price of a meal, or shelter, or other benefit – to escape a beating, perhaps! Remember, not just ordinary people looking for work or honest hawkers come to places like the new Tundani *Paradise*. It is a magnet for anyone wanting to become rich from the tourists, also the more unpleasant people, with no conscience about using even the smallest and weakest and most vulnerable of children to help make a fat pot of money!'

'Ally's right, Inspector!' Carole spoke forcefully. 'These kids are not dishonest. Just destitute, and wary – understandably!'

The inspector looked from one to the other and made a ticking sound with his tongue against his teeth as if it helped him think. '*Haya.* Certainly it is strange for anyone to take the trouble to beat them so terribly. Indeed – even to worry about catching them – it would not be easy! So, it is not just a random assault on street children. And we have this story of big game animals where there should not be any! *Haya*, I will order a helicopter search. And what does any of this have to do with Shanza? Any ideas on *this*? Perhaps this connection is only in *their* minds . . .'

'No!' Jack broke in. 'It's our – I mean *my* fault. They went looking because we – *I* said to check out the hotel – the *boats* in the hotel – in case it's connected – you know, with all that . . .' He trailed off, waving a hand towards Kisiri.

'So! An interesting code of honour in our young Collins Karanga. He says nothing of your request!' The policeman tucked his notebook into his pocket. 'Be very careful what new suggestions you make to these boys, please. If this nastiness is anything to do with the hotel, we will find out. These people are dangerous. With secrets to hide. No more private investigation. Clear?'

Mutely, Jack nodded. In the pause, the sudden crackle and words on the police radio were shockingly loud and the sergeant's speed in handing it to the inspector gave Ally a sharp new twitch of alarm.

Inspector Rutere walked a little way off, alternately listening and speaking; then he halted, gave a rapid instruction to the sergeant, who charged off towards the voices raised in passionate discussion in Mzee Shaibu's yard.

In the slump of the inspector's shoulders, Ally saw his bleakness before he spoke. 'I have an unpleasant duty – to speak to the Shanza village council straightaway. I have disturbing news. The D.O. is very shocked. *I* am very shocked . . .'

He seemed for a moment lost in thought.

'What *is* it, Rutere? Please!' Carole prompted.

Rutere sighed. 'How do I tell them? How do I explain this? Someone has just bought Kisiri from the government! The new owners will take *exclusive* possession of the island within days!'

Into the appalled stillness that followed, he added, 'The D.O. has gone to Ulima to demand explanations from the Minister.'

Ally managed to whisper, 'Bought *Kisiri*? *Can* they?'

'Ha! When money can be made, many holes can be found in the rules! And many pockets some distance from these places will grow fat. The D.O. expects difficulty in learning who the purchasers are. He has already been told that it is no one's business except those who are part of the financial arrangements!' The policeman laughed, but it was a harsh sound, without a trace of humour. 'Clearly, there are some in high places who believe it is nothing whatsoever to do with those whose back yard is being stolen.'

Nineteen

'Something'll happen! I know it will!' Ally protested to Carole. Through the door of Hasina's house, she saw Inspector Rutere returning to the police vehicle from Mzee Shaibu's yard. 'Please, don't send me back to the house now, Carole! I'll just be hanging about wondering!'

'Ally, Ally, people have enough on their minds without us in the way. You should all go back to the house together.' Carole lowered her voice. 'You've been up for hours – what about breakfast? People here don't have enough food for you too.'

'It is good, good!' Hasina hurried towards them carrying a pan. 'See, here is *chakula* for them! I will be sure to know your family is comfortable. Do not worry your head. Go, go to the hospital with the small ones!' Her voice rose emphatically. 'You help, Dr Carole, I help. It is all the same things. Ally and Ben and Jack will take tea and *ugali*.' Pointedly she dumped the pot of maize porridge in Ally's hands and tossed her head towards the brazier. She pushed Carole's shoulder gently. 'You come back when it is finished, the hospital.'

'Bibi Hasina,' Carole grasped the woman's hand warmly, 'I'll bring in more supplies for you—'

'I should stay with those two,' Jack interrupted, white-faced, strained. 'Or they'll run away, or something . . .'

Ally glanced at Dedan, asleep, and Collins struggling to stay watchful. He looked shrunken. Exhausted fury had left behind only a very small boy enveloped in a purple *kanga* bearing the words *Kweli na asubuhi* . . . the rest wrapped out of sight behind his body. Carole had told her it meant *Truth and morning become light with time*. The word for truth – *kweli* – sat across Collins' chest like a banner. *What 'something' does Jack mean – whoever's beaten them coming for them if they find where the boys are?*

It hadn't crossed her mind before. Now she guessed that it crossed her aunt's too, for as they went out Carole checked for the sergeant. He was visible in Mzee Shaibu's yard, mug of tea in one hand, police radio in the other, listening to the debate amongst the Elders raging since Inspector Rutere broke the news of Kisiri's sale.

'At least there's instant contact with the outer world now,' Carole said. 'OK, Jack, let's get help carrying Dedan and Collins into the car? Ally, keep a firm eye on Ben, you know the way he is, he'll disappear somewhere. I'll let you know of any developments through the sergeant. We'll be back as fast as we can.'

'OK, and I'll look for Leli.'

A small frown creased her aunt's forehead. 'Ally . . .' She hesitated. 'Look . . . go easy?'

'I'll just help, won't get in the way, promise. Leli—'

'Ally . . .' Suddenly awkward, Carole began again, 'Look, I know I'm not your mother, but . . . well . . .'

Ally'd only been half concentrating, spotting Leli coming towards her. Her attention snapped to her aunt.

'. . . be careful,' Carole finished.

'About what?'

An imperceptible sigh. 'Leli,' Carole said flatly. 'Don't—'

Heat flooded Ally's face. All the sideways looks from her aunt bunched in her memory.

'Don't what?'

'Don't get me wrong, but . . .'

'But *what*?' Ally spoke tightly, clenched against what might come next.

'Just go easy.'

'What do you mean "go easy"?'

'Well—'

'Are you saying we can't be friends?'

'No! But friends is one thing . . .'

'And?' her heart beginning to hammer, her look at Carole deliberately obtuse.

'You're getting – well, too involved. It's . . . it's just not wise!'

'Why? What's *too involved*? You mean because he's African!'

'Course not, Ally! Just – there's so much room for misunderstandings. Different cultures – different signals. Expectations – you *know* what I mean! You're here for a few weeks, then off you go home. It's easy when you just visit a place – a wonderful place like this – to just see the magical moment and not think about when it's over. There's always . . . you know . . . consequences . . .'

214

'What consequences?' She was dangerously close to yelling – panic now, because she knew her aunt well enough to know that underneath her easy-going big-sister style there was a core of steel.

'Oh, I'm not dealing with this well, am I? Don't you see, Ally, people misread things—'

'You're saying something bad about Leli,' Ally persisted fiercely. 'There's nothing bad about him!'

'It's absolutely, absolutely, absolutely not what I'm saying. Unfortunately, I'm saying something much more complicated . . . Look, let me get the kids to the hospital . . . and maybe you *should* come back to the house for now, after all – I'll drop you off.'

'No, please!' Ally said, suddenly frantic. 'You don't understand. I need to stay—'

'I do understand, Ally. I'm not so far beyond remembering,' Carole said, obscurely. She looked away, looked around, looked back at Ally. 'There's so much going on, Ally, and people are worried about all kinds of things, and *they* might misunderstand. You won't know the way people are reading you, believe me.'

'You *are* talking about Leli!'

'Look, it's all too easy to sail into people's lives and then sail off again, not worrying about the wake you leave behind. Different worlds . . . you need to be very careful not to offend or hurt. Leli's mother, Mzee Shaibu . . . you may think that doesn't matter, but when you've gone, the fall-out is still with Leli, and that might not be very good for him—'

'I'm not going to offend anyone!'

'You might not know you have! Don't you see, all this stuff going on – it's making people frightened of – well, lots! The future – *change* can be frightening. You do come from very, very different worlds!'

The words dropped between them like ice. Ally couldn't look at Carole. She felt her aunt's gaze. She heard her say briskly, 'OK, Ally, later, we'll talk properly. I must get the kids to hospital first. Find Ben and stay together, then, stay with people, no wandering off, OK? No more unpleasant surprises, for anyone, hey? I'm trusting you, Ally, I know you're sensible— Oh, Makena!' she broke off, catching sight of someone behind Ally. 'Have you moved to Shanza now?'

'Oh, I am here by chance,' came the welcome sound of the archaeologist's voice. 'I come to continue an interesting conversation I am having with Mzee Kitwana. I did not know of these horrible events! The little boys are bad?' She looked through Hasina's door, and let out a whistle at the sight of them. 'This, and the bad, bad news about Kisiri! I will not detain you – to the hospital, quickly!'

She shook her head as Carole drove away, and turned to Ally. 'My young friend, I do not wish to intrude, but I detect sharp words from your auntie to you. Do not dwell too much on them. You have a good heart. Trust it. Trust it. You look very pale and very tired. I hear you have been here since early, early! Just go and rest. Things will look different, after, and you will know what to do.'

She put her hand lightly under Ally's chin and looked in her eyes. 'You will, you will! And I have not forgotten to bring that interesting thing for you. Here, read it in a peaceful

216

moment, when you are not troubled.' She took a folded paper from her pocket. 'It is from something recently come to light. In Portugal!' With a flourish, she handed it over. 'Only a little piece translated, but more to come! Very old. Very mysterious! Very, very! I am interested to have the view of your young mind brought to bear on it. I will look for you another day! Now is also no time for idle conversations with Mzee Kitwana.'

She turned away and clicked her tongue against her teeth, speaking almost to herself, observing the island. '*Now* the question for us is how to delay this *theft*! What ammunition against the new invaders? How, *how*?' She was still mumbling as she went, giving Ally no time to reply. Just the tumult Carole had left in her head and the paper Makena'd left in her hand.

She unfolded it. A typed printout – just three lines. English.
I walk the paths of the forest.
I seek Hope, a flame of life in the dark.
In my dream I find Her. In my dream I speak to Her.
'Ally?'

Leli's voice.

'You are not well? You are sick?'

But she was anchored in a different place: trees murmured, shadows rippled, clustered, words flowed and ebbed, unseen eyes touched . . .

She struggled to return.

Leli took the paper from her hands and framed the words silently with his lips.

'It is from a book?'

'Makena gave it to me – it's about the forest . . . See, Leli!'

'It is of a forest, yes. It is a poem?' When she didn't answer, 'Ally, what must I see?' He studied her face again, then the paper.

'I don't know how to explain, Leli, just . . . it's . . . oh, you know that first day, I said it was strange? The forest, the forest was strange—'

'This happened? You write of this?'

'No, no, it's someone else writing . . . But it's like . . .' *Remembering*, she wanted to say. 'Like . . .' She trailed off.

A flash of insight lit his face. 'It is this person you hear sometimes? Who is it?'

She held his eyes, wanted to say everything, and more. Said nothing.

From the shore came the sudden roar of many voices.

Boats were being rushed into the surging tide, fishermen chest high in the water, leaping aboard, paddling out swiftly, sails run up, whipping and snapping in the wind. Bellowed instructions from boat to boat rebounded off the beach, swelled by advice from the shorebound audience round Ally. Knee-deep in foaming surf, the inward tide thrust at her legs, knocking her off-balance. Koffi caught her before she fell. The tide-force heightened her alarm: she watched, hardly heard the ceaseless yells from Leli, Huru, Ben, others gathered with her.

The sails caught wind; the phalanx of boats veered to the south of Kisiri. In the distance beyond, something caught sunlight and sparkled.

'It's another motorboat,' Ben shouted. 'Coming this way. It's the baddies!'

218

'These bad people will have to stay away from Kisiri,' Huru declared. 'We will stop them!'

Leli's eyes didn't shift from the approaching powerboat. 'Not one stranger to put their foot on Kisiri! Mzee Shaibu is saying this.'

'There will be a fight, maybe,' Koffi spoke uneasily.

'There will not be fighting.' Mzee Shaibu had come up behind them; his tone held a warning and an instruction. 'Even young ones with impatient hearts must be wise today.' He watched the flotilla of Shanza boats draw away; for a minute he assessed the restless knots of people spread along the shallows. Then he strode towards them.

Ally could see the motorboat clearly now. It gleamed white, sharp-nosed, riding high on the water. Suddenly it slackened speed, arced a little towards Shanza. Then it stopped and sat there, rocking on the swell.

Steadily the twenty Shanza *ngalawa* headed towards it. They travelled in a line abreast. Behind them, canoes drew into a second line. Together, they left no direct unobstructed route to Kisiri.

But they were under paddle and sail, fighting a strong in-flowing tide. Effortlessly the motorboat could shoot wide round them under power of its engine, leaving the Shanza boats far behind. Even Ally knew that.

But for the moment it just sat there. The Shanza *ngalawa* and *hori* neared it. The hubbub of speculation on the shore fell tensely quiet. Then the motorboat shot into life and swerved away into open sea, passing out of sight some distance behind the island and emerging beyond, vanishing past the bulge of the mangroves to the north.

For a short while the mood in the village calmed. Some of the Shanza boats returned. Others lowered sail and sculled to and fro, or moved up into the shelter of the mangrove creeks in an apparently aimless course that failed to mask the fact that they were on patrol.

On shore Lumbwi and Koffi and Mosi and Pili settled to debating possibilities, including fights, keeping a wary eye on the listening ears of the Elders grouped at the highest point at the rim of the shore.

Everyone lapsed into continuous Swahili.

And Ally was more than ever reluctant to ask for a translation. She avoided looking at Leli too directly. Every pore of her skin traced each movement, each shift in his stance, each glance at her. But it was as if Carole had thrown a fence between them and she couldn't now quite find the gate. She saw how his face snapped taut when two more powerboats appeared from the north and then veered, accelerating, towards the island. Instantly Shanza boats holding the vigil north and south converged. Others put out from shore, making a beeline for Kisiri.

Again the powerboats changed course, swept wide into open sea behind Kisiri and sped away south past the high spine of Ras Chui.

It was going to go on like this for hours, all day, maybe all night, Ally saw, and she saw also that it was all that Leli was seeing now, and she understood why, and was frightened for him, for Shanza. Yet there was another fear too, at his absence from her, at Carole's words, at Makena's paper folded in her pocket that she couldn't explain to Leli, at the overwhelming

220

sense that what was between them was brittle, too easily ripped, and she might not know it was happening; and there was another sensation – that there was something she should *know*, should *do*.

It all lapped cold over her, like the fast rising tide around her.

*

Endlessly we scoured the darkness for Badru, yet told ourselves that many days must pass before he could return in safety. We did not voice our dread that he is lost to us – speaking it would give life to terror.

Then at dawn Goma saw his craft near the lee of the cliff. He climbed from the cave, unseen by our enemy. How we rejoiced as we hauled him to the fort!

But such news he brings – such strange, troubling news! We dare not slacken guard!

Something unseen gathers itself around us. It is in the air, in every part of me.

A rumour Badru heard, everywhere the whisper in markets and eating houses of the town, even among children playing in the streets. There is some hidden thing in the fort. A secret vast enough to hold our Omani enemies from attacking us, for the moment!

Badru found one man he knows well from former visits to the town. This man moves daily through the Omani camp carrying fresh water from the wells. He hears how they argue amongst themselves. Some say the fever has finished us already, an attack would take the fort in hours before the monsoon turns and winds bring Portuguese ships to rescue us.

Others say Portugal has already abandoned the fort. Just wait for our deaths. Do not bombard the fort, launch no attacks. Or you risk destroying *the fortune hidden here*.

Fortune? *Here?* We stared at Badru in confusion, every one of us. And then we laughed! Wildly and madly we laughed, till Badru became angry with us.

'Think! Your enemies believe! Riches beyond dreams are in this fort, they say! They will not let you live to fight them for it. They calculate land and sea assaults by night. They build ladders to scale these walls! Be certain, my friends! Is it really madness? Think! Think! Our lives may turn on this!'

Fortune? Where? Every inch have we scoured for food, weapons, firewood, blankets, clothes, even tools.

'A fantasy fed by our dead captain's pirate ways!' Diogo scorned. 'It is again that old talk of secrets on his dying lips, no more than this!'

'But *they* believe,' Jabari said. 'Think, my friends – this buys us a grain of time. They argue on the means to wrest your "riches" from you. They do nothing but keep their ships beyond range of your cannon. Eighty mighty cannon, you have: they fear that!'

My thought was that only twelve of us remain alive to fire them.

Twenty

Leli's thoughts were racing. *We must go to Kisiri. Why does Mzee Shaibu not listen to me? If we are there, they cannot be there. Even powerful men cannot steal Kisiri from us when all our feet are standing on it!*

In the afternoon haze the little mound of land was becoming a pale ghost of itself. It seemed to him as if some part of the island's life was draining from it. The line of boats paraded in front; others tacked to and fro from the mangroves across the bay. Their pattern imprinted itself on his mind: like the pattern of that strange procession two nights ago – the canoes of the first people of Shanza, of Mwana Zawati and Bwana Fumo.

His thoughts leapt again. *Why* do these strangers want Kisiri? Another hotel, another beach for another umbrella and another tourist to sit under? He watched a spiral of birds rise like a snake above the island's forest; then they fell against the sky and fled north in a shrill arrowhead of darkness like a shriek of fury.

He looked back at the tiny fleet of defending boats. His father was there with Huru's father, and Pili's and Mosi's and Eshe's. His mother was on the sands with the other mothers, their voices loud in discussion, swatting sandflies from their legs, lifting *kangas* across their mouths as gusts of wind flung little spirals of stinging sand around them.

Huru jabbed his shoulder, indicating the water's edge below them. Saka's friends Jela and Thimba were pointing at different parts of Kisiri while Saka held his boat in the shallows and Mzee Shaibu and Mzee Kitwana answered with sharp gestures of their own.

They are going to Kisiri! Leli set off at a run towards them. 'Mzee Shaibu, we must *all* be there on Kisiri!'

'Hear me, Leli! Thimba and Jela last night see a big black motorboat with no lights by Kisiri. These people do everything in secret. It is not honest. Saka, Jela, Thimba go to look again. You go to help, and Huru—'

'And the English friends!' Leli interrupted. 'Ally and Ben . . .'

'*Why* the English ones now?' Mzee asked quietly.

Leli glanced up the shore at Ally standing with the others in the shade of the houses. He felt her tautness. She'd taken the writing on the paper from her pocket several times. But not read it again, just put it back. Something was wrong. Why did she not say? Her silence made him afraid to be away from her.

I must keep her near. She must be on Kisiri, with me. She must not be away. And a clearer thought followed. *I must not lose her.*

'Ally and Ben have seen the marks and know what we look

for,' he told Mzee Shaibu truthfully, and untruthfully, and defied Mzee Shaibu to say no, signalling Ally to come down to the water at once.

Mzee looked hard at him. Then a glance at Mzee Kitwana. A brief nod passed between them. Mzee Shaibu moved away.

Leli felt the storyteller's gaze. The old man's eyes were narrowed, as if measuring him. He thought of yesterday, when Mzee Kitwana spoke of the spirit of Fumo, and he'd been annoyed at the teasing.

Steadily, he returned Mzee Kitwana's stare, and the hooded eyes gazed back. Leli was left to turn away and go down towards Saka and the boat with Ally and Ben and Huru, wondering in frustration what the unreadable expression of the old man's face was saying to him this time.

*

We obeyed Badru, and studied Dom Alvaro's papers. It falls to Jabari, Diogo, Paulo and me: only we are still alive who know the Portuguese language.

We looked at every page for signs of a secret, any hints of hidden fortunes. And we found one strange thing, a record of a frigate, *Nossa Senhora de Madre de Deos*, and how it sank. Alvaro writes that she had brought supplies to us and was standing off our shore, before unloading. At nightfall, two Arab ships appeared and fired on her. Without returning a single shot, she took hits to stern and bow, and foundered.

It is almost lost in my memory beyond all else, but Diogo and Paulo recall it well. It was in the first weeks of the siege; hunger and fever had not yet carved away our force.

225

'Each day the Arabs paraded ships along the channel between us and the mainland. Every hour they fired on us, and we on them,' Diogo told Jabari. 'But they feared our guns. Their ships' artillery was no match for ours.'

I began to remember. Weeks went by: by night the Arabs landed on the lower island with ladders to climb our walls. We sent raiding parties to burn the ladders. So it went, day to day, week to week: small skirmishes, the Arabs not yet able to stop us reaching the sea to smuggle supplies from passing vessels.

Then the Arabs sank the *Madre de Deos*. Some crew from the stricken ship swam to our shore. By dawn other Arab ships had arrived from the north, doubling their force against us. From that day, the battle changed.

Diogo pointed to a passage in Dom Alvaro's writing.

I read. I passed it to Jabari.

Dom Alvaro writes that during that first night of the sinking, he took a rescue party to the stricken *Madre de Deos* to retrieve the cargo.

There follows Alvaro's questioning of survivors from the *Madre de Deos*. One told of a sultan of a distant town complaining that his ships were seized by Portuguese vessels and his crews enslaved. The captain of the *Madre de Deos* took the sultan's messengers hostage, stripped naked, flogged, bound hand and foot and set in the burning sun in a drifting boat to die. As news of this reached the sultan's town, the crew of the *Madre de Deos* stormed in and razed it to rubble.

Then comes the lists of booty ripped from that sultan's town and loaded on the *Madre de Deos*. Gold, silver, ivory, ambergris, cotton, silk, ornaments of gold and silver, even rings and bracelets hacked from the limbs of women. Rice, millet, honey, butter, cattle, goats, and what they couldn't take, they burned including all orchards and ten thousand coconut palms. Each quantity, item, deed, noted by Alvaro.

We passed the list between us.

This bloody cargo has fed the rumours. It is here, within our walls. The wealth of that sultan's town bludgeoned from it and brought in secret *here*.

Where?

No man survives from that ship. The last died of fever with Alvaro. We can ask no one.

We searched again. Storerooms, dungeons, cells, passageways, Alvaro's quarters, the chapel, even the vacant animal pens, barracks, floors, roofs, walls, kitchens, guard rooms, gatehouses.

We found nothing.

The light thickens towards the south, and it is hot, beyond endurance. There will be storms. Saaduma warns that threat of these may hasten an attack on us before the monsoon turns.

No man or woman rested, even Neema left her sickbed and took a musket and stayed at Watch. But the children no longer cry, for the barrel of flour and other food that Badru secured in the town has stilled the ache in their bellies, for the moment, and that is hope for us.

I dreamed an eagle alighted on my hand. He turned, and looked at me, and I was not afraid. I woke suddenly and the shadow and the weight of him pressed on my flesh, and stayed with me for the next hours.

I could not sleep again. I rose and went to the battlements, and only the first rays of the rising sun on the parapet took the vast bird's presence from me.

Twenty-one

Ally's hands, deep in her pockets, touched Makena's paper. She didn't bring it out: when she'd looked at it before, she'd caught a frown from Leli. She longed to explain, *Makena said someone wrote it a long time ago, it's old, but I know it's new, too – it's now . . . I'm scared* – the word 'haunted' insinuated itself into her head again.

But she didn't say it. She couldn't bring herself to step on to the No Man's Land now stretching between them. Carole had conjured it up, this horrible awkwardness snarling her up. Everything about Leli filled with exaggerated significance, even the heat and strength of his hand as he steadied her leaving the boat just now, stepping onto Kisiri's shore. Did the others see it? Could they see how she felt about him?

Yesterday we shared things. Understood, knew things about each other, no need to explain . . .

But – it wormed its way in – *is that true? Really? Or did I make it up?*

It didn't feel true now. Leli was somewhere else. She was

alone in the tangle: Leli, Kisiri, Makena's paper. Leli prowled beside her through the forest, rigid with concentration. Not thinking of her. *Why would he, with everything else that's happening?* Carole had said it: *enough on their minds without you in the way, Ally.*

Trees roofed them in, trapped the stench of rotting flesh in their clothes, hair, skin. It seemed to crawl up Ally's nostrils, the forest a cage, trapping, she circling helpless, searching, searching, questions, questions, no closer . . .

He says we must be here, we're being told something, we must hear . . . He's right, I know, I know, but why me, why him? The body of some poor, dead person's here – I don't want to see—

Ignorance stalked her, confusion, like a creature sniffing her heels in the sultry gloom, and Mzee Kitwana's voice came suddenly to her – 'blind, and not blind, do we see only with the eye?'

What am I blind to?

Far to their right, Saka, Jela, Thimba moved quietly, steadily through the trees, searching for signs of intruders, lifting creepers with the blades of their *pangas*, looking for the source of the terrible smell. They'd passed where the drag marks in the sand had been, though several tides had pounded away all trace. To her left, Ben whispering to Huru, 'I feel really sick. It's something really big, that stinking thing, an' it's following!'

Huru pointing into the tree canopy high above. 'Over the leaves, the *koho* is flying – to eat dead things. They show us where is this dead one.'

'Vultures!' Ben wailed.

A sudden silence. Ally halted, listening: *Why no birdsong?* No trill, or warble or whistle, or single rustle. The island held its breath. The smell hung like a weight in the air.

A stark, shrill shout from the fishermen. Then a fast sing-song ululating chant. *Huru-Leli-Huru-Leli.*

They all plunged towards the sound . . .

The men were in a clearing torn by the fall of a tree. They were inspecting shapes camouflaged by the wreckage of branches. Closer, Ally saw two crates, wooden, both chest high, three sides solid, one side a lattice lined with thick wire mesh hanging open like a door.

Still several paces away, the reek of them hit her. Unmistakable. Wood soaked with urine and sweat and something glistening that fizzed with flies. She recoiled, and in a flare of recognition knew they were cages, thought of Collins, and understood the smell. Terror.

Saka, Jela and Thimba were arguing.

'What're they saying?' she appealed, stifling the urge to retch.

'The dead thing is from this box,' Huru informed her, 'but Jela says there are two boxes, so maybe—'

Too close, too loud, something crashed through foliage. There came a sequence of sounds – a rasping, grating hiss, rustling, crackling . . .

Then quiet.

'*Koho*,' grunted Jela. He moved cautiously towards the noises. A burst of new sound – wings, in a heavy, stuttering flutter. Then silence again.

Everyone followed, moving delicately, and Ally reluctantly, afraid to be left alone, dreading what they'd find. *Koho* – the bird that eats dead things, Huru'd said.

'Aren't we near Fumo and Zawati's place?' she whispered, but caught the alarmed flight of a large bird past a pillar of stone, and knew.

Jela and Saka and Thimba were bending over a glistening mound, an enormous reddish bulge on the ground that her brain recognized slowly, and with a deep, hot jolt of shock, as the bloody carcass of a very large animal.

But unrecognizable. It was skinned. Headless. It had no feet, no tail. And half its side was eaten away.

She helped slide the *ngalawa* into the water in an effort to erase the mutilated dead thing from her head. But it kept reclaiming space, and with it came the battered faces of Collins and Dedan and their talk of cages. And animals.

Jela hauled up sail and the boat took the wind, set course for Shanza out of sight beyond the curve of Kisiri's shore. Fighting the out-running tide, it would be more than a half-hour to reach it and give news of the dead animal, maybe an hour before anyone came back. Jela's voice carried across water, calling to patrolling canoes that responded and turned in to the island, Saka and Thimba wading to meet them. They hauled the boats up the beach and all disappeared into the forest towards the carcass.

Nothing to do but wait. Ally walked away fast. Anything to get distance from the stain of that poor animal's blood in Fumo and Zawati's place. She went towards Leli. He was

231

wading along the water's edge, kicking up spray angrily, drenching himself, didn't look at her.

Words blanked in her mind. She went past, hoping he would follow, say something, anything, somehow make things normal between them again. Then together they could face everything else.

He didn't. She skirted gulls squabbling over fish-bones; they circled and screamed at her and she ignored them and marched on along the shoreline, conscious only of the sea to her left and the forest to her right, and beyond it the deepening shadow of a high coral bluff.

She stopped, breath rasping. She'd been walking hunched, eyes on the ground, ploughing mindlessly ahead through soft sand. Now she took a deep breath, stretched arms above her head to ease the neck ache, and became aware that here no sickly stench of death had followed. And she'd left the forest behind, the beach narrowing sharply, fenced in by a tumble of rock from the cliff.

She glanced back: canoes on the beach still in view; the fishermen, Ben and Huru and Leli too.

She walked on. The wall of rock curved out of sight towards the bluffs that hid the cave. Only days ago she'd been high up there; anticipation of something unknown had filled her, frightened her. But she couldn't have imagined anything like this – this butchering of animals. Or Kisiri stolen from the village. Or the street kids' beating.

Or this bleakness, the door slamming shut between her and Leli.

She'd come up against a tongue of coral running out

from the cliff into water. It was high, steep, but ledges and crevices gave foot- and fingerholds. She picked her way up till she could see the water beyond. It slopped and sucked in channels and cavities in the coral. Beyond, open sea. Two large boats on the horizon – faint through heat shimmer.

She watched them, just in case. They didn't move: fishing, she guessed. And Shanza canoes sculled near the mangrove creeks, watchful, their meanderings marked by white frills on the green water. From this high she could even see underwater coral patterning the burnished sheen of the sea.

Though as she watched, it dulled. The sun was disappearing behind menacing cloud, the light yellowing, wind dropping, heat building.

She looked back. Leli was trailing the grooves of her footprints in the sand. He raised a hand.

Following her.

Sudden recklessness spiked her. Rapidly she crossed the shell crusts and treacherous slithery seaweed at the crest of the coral. It rose in a spine to the summit of the cliff. She began to climb, fast. A chance to be with him beyond everyone's eyes! Further up, further away – seize the moment before anything snatched it from her; even the rocks pulled her higher and further – when she got to the top, *everything would be all right.*

*

Storms fly towards us. A sulphurous light fills the clouds massing to south and west. I went and looked where the walls fall sheer to the spine of dark rock. Before my eyes the waves seemed to grow more frantic, hammering at the coral as if to wrestle it free, and a sudden hammering rose in my heart, as if there too something is wrenching free.

Dizziness overcame me. I gripped the parapet and closed my eyes. I heard the keening of birds, a chorus of warning. And then for one long, frozen moment I felt myself released from this place, at liberty, and at peace.

I knew beside me was the living presence of the One I have so often conjured. Certainty filled me: when I opened my eyes She would be there, real, of flesh and blood, signifying Life. I breathed the moment. I felt Her Life course through my blood.

I opened my eyes to speak to Her. I was alone.

Yet Her presence lingers. She is here.

As if in answer, the wind lifted and spun Jabari's talisman of the warriors hanging round my neck. I seized it and held it hard against me. There is a world beyond this place of death! I will find it, take it, take it for us all.

*

She scrambled the last few feet on hands and knees and stood up, heaving breath into her lungs. She was a very long way up. Beneath her was the echoing boom of water. She felt its thunder as if the cliff was a drum and was surprised at its power. She looked down. And was surprised too, her pulse quickening, that Leli's shadow darkened the grass at her feet, that he could climb so fast and already reach her.

Then she saw he was still on the sands below, not yet at the base of the cliff.

She went cold. The dark shadow still spread beside her. And for one brief, suspended moment, a word hung in the air:

234

the voice of a boy – not Leli or Jack or Huru or Ben, deeper, yet paler, as if flowing from a long way off, weaving round her, a whispering warmth, a breath.

Then the voice was gone, the shadow too, there was only the flat grass of the cliff-top, Leli climbing towards her, and a lightness in her as if she'd been lifted somewhere, somewhere airy and wind-whipped, and then set down again, her body reclaiming itself, reclaiming her hold on the ordinary solid land beneath her.

She stood frozen, half in fear, half in bewilderment.

Then she backed away from the cliff and glanced round for somewhere to sit and pull herself together, wait for Leli. She spotted a patch of shade in a gully and clambered down to it.

Only then did she realize that her eyes had passed something that jarred with the grey-pink of the rock and the green-yellow of grass and the blue pockets of flowers clinging to its rim.

She looked back.

The creature was in the gully. It was snarling and its head was turned so that for a split second she thought it was looking at her and fear jabbed – the cheetah was gathering itself to leap. Then she took in how its head was thrown back, the vicious twist in the torso, the peculiar angle of its legs, that the snarl was the fixed grimace of another dead thing. Its coat had not dulled, and there was no smell, no predatory *koho* near it. She saw this, and understood that the animal had not been dead long, that perhaps it had only just, only moments before, breathed its last.

I came down from the walls elated, filled with Her hope, to find Badru and Jabari calling us all urgently. I reached them, and Badru at once spoke.

He did not wish to raise our hopes, then shatter them. So he kept something from us until he could check his reckonings.

This is it: returning from the town at dawn and reaching the deeper recesses of the cave to hide the canoe, it had come to him that the space held more light than could be from rays of early sun through the distant cave-mouth. Being fixed on leaving the cavern and reaching the fort before enemy patrols might see him climb, he probed no further.

But he suspects two things: that there is a fracture in the roof of the cave, a hole or crack that allows some light to pass down from the surface of the rock above. And that the line of the cave brings those deeper regions, and perhaps this fracture, somewhere below this fort, below our *court*. With a meaningful look he glanced at Jabari and Rahidi.

I had no need of their sudden delight to remind me. I saw: myself, six years old, Jabari proudly showing me Mwitu's wonders, together running through the inner town and plunging between houses into a tiny stairway bored through rock. To my joy we emerged far below in the harbour. Mwitu's passage that affords the people *safe* and *secret* passage between the high town and the ships, in times of storm – or war!

It cannot be chance! I relived that moment on the parapet. It spoke of escape. It spoke of life beyond this place – and now we think what plans may be devised if Badru has truly seen a cleft in the roof of the cave below us, and if it be wide enough to take the shoulders of a man, or we can make it so!

eighth day
storm

Twenty-two

The storm came in with a shriek: rain billowed white across the house, trees whipped low, shutters banged like gunshots. As if the torrent was trying to rinse Kisiri clean.

Ally woke into the ceaseless, driving downpour and everything else poured into her head, all the ugliness of the animals' deaths, and Collins' and Dedan's beating, and the strangeness of that moment on the cliff, the certainty that someone stood beside her. Even the thrum of the rain against the house became the drumming she'd felt, and that sense of something swirling through her – moments before she saw the cheetah. Like a premonition – a signpost – to the creature's death.

Her frantic shouts to Leli, Leli racing up the rocks to reach her. Their headlong scramble down the cliff again to tell the fishermen. Leli stalking about stiff with fury till the police launch surged into sight carrying Jela. Leli sucked instantly into all the police said and did. The baffling clamour of discussion, Leli in the middle, she trapped outside because she

239

couldn't understand his language, and didn't want to be in the way.

She tossed fitfully in twisted sheets, at dawn falling asleep to dream of Leli striding away through towering dunes, so high and so soft that however hard she struggled, she sank, her legs like lead weights, and never reached him.

She woke to sudden silence. The deluge had ended as abruptly as it came – just high racing cloud and flickering sunlight. The lull only fuelled her sense of a void, away from Leli.

She went out, stepping across bruised litter of bougainvillea blossom and casuarina cones into air glittering with brittle clarity. Jack was on the roof checking Kisiri through binoculars. She rushed up to join him, away from Carole's voice inside the house. Last night's argument with her aunt was still raw. Carole emphatic, anxious: 'Ally, listen! To lots of people in the village, people like us cause these problems—'

'But we don't! They know we wouldn't!'

'Do they? Mzee Shaibu, Leli, your friends, Rutere . . . I'm sure *they* know that. But others? Why would they? How would they? We need to be cautious, not meddle in discussions and decisions that aren't our business. We can try to find a way to help, 'course we can – but only if Shanza wants us to! People need space to figure out what to do, not us plunging in to interfere!'

'I don't want to interfere, just help!'

Carole's sigh. 'You do understand, Ally, I know you do! You just don't want to hear it because it means staying away for now, not seeing Leli.'

And it was true. *I do understand. How could I not?* It

had shown in the heated tones all around Ally, the long discussions among Elders in Mzee Shaibu's yard, the rushing to and fro in the village, the young men already patrolling the boundaries of the village, families worrying when little kids couldn't be seen. In Leli's absorption with it all.

But I don't want to be here, looking through binoculars from Carole's roof! I want to be there, with him!

She couldn't tell if she was angry with her aunt or frightened by what she said. Or angry with herself, for her fear – the wedge hammering down between her and Leli.

'No police boats there now.' Jack offered the binoculars. She shook her head. She could feel his edgy mood, echoing her own, fed further by Ben's shrill, endless speculation about Kisiri, floating up from below.

'So they'll search everything for clues, Carole! You know, guns and people and stuff, so they know who did it. I saw it on telly. Maybe they're catching the killers now! What if rain washed all the clues away?'

'We'll go over to Shanza later and find out, Benjy.' Carole was trying to calm him. 'But they won't really want us around for a while—'

'Hey, look, Ally – smoke on the island!' Jack said sharply. 'Thought it was cloud, but it's smoke!'

She grabbed the binoculars from him. Spirals rose from several places. Rapidly, she scanned.

Below, out of sight, wheels squelched to a halt by the house. Then Inspector Rutere's voice. '*Hodi!* I am glad you are here!'

'I'm on late shift at the hospital,' Carole called. 'Come through, we're out front.'

Ally went swiftly down the roof steps, Jack close behind.

The policeman appeared on the veranda, took the offered cup of tea from Carole without noticing, and said quickly, 'I thought you would like to know developments. A motorboat near Kisiri in the night triggered . . . well, how can I say . . . Shanza has moved to the island! Everyone in residence on Kisiri!'

Ally stared at him. '*Everyone? Camping?* Is that why there's smoke?'

'Cooking fires. They build shelters. Just a few people left in Shanza to guard it—'

'Let's go too, Carole!' Ben shrieked. 'We can go now!'

'I regret,' the inspector went on to Carole, 'that I ordered my sergeant back to Tundani last night. My superiors are angry that I left the situation in Shanza untended. I did not prevent this crossing to the island. Now I am not their favourite person.'

Carole gave a snort. The policeman smiled faintly at her, and registering the tea in his hand, took several sips. 'Of course – young children and mothers there on Kisiri now, the police cannot move them off without a scandal. I am instructed that scandals are to be avoided.'

He's not regretful. He meant to let everyone go to Kisiri! Ally gazed through the binoculars. The plumes of smoke above the island, nothing more: the sea empty of the usual flotilla of boats heading to the fishing grounds, waves choppy, white-capped. They surged round Ras Chui and ran wild across the bay, restless beneath ominous ridges of cloud, even though shafts of misty sunshine still speared through.

'What if there's a storm again?' she appealed to the policeman.

'Their shelters are strong,' he replied. 'Do not worry . . .'

But they'll have to bring everything in boats from Shanza! On Kisiri there's no fresh water. The boats'll be tossed about by this kind of sea!

'Will it fix anything?' Anxiety made her voice sharp.

The policeman frowned. 'Sadly, the sale of Kisiri is in its final stage—'

'What about those dead animals?' Jack persisted.

'Huh!' the policeman snorted. 'I am instructed there is no evidence of *connections* between the killed animals on the island and the purchasers of the island. These events must not be allowed to delay the sale—'

'It can't happen!' Carole said. 'Shanza needs a lawyer, Rutere. Can we help get one? What can we do? Tell us what Mzee Shaibu's planning—'

'That chopped-up thing was a lion!' Ally burst out. 'Wasn't it? That's . . . horrible! Lions are protected! Cheetahs are protected.' Ridiculously, she was close to tears, which made her angry. She thrust the binoculars at Jack and turned away to hide it.

'Horrible, wrong, yes. Illegal, most definitely,' the policeman responded to her turned back. 'The cheetah you found, Ally – it bled to death from a gunshot wound. Only a short time before you came there. A slow, painful death – a very incompetent hunter, this one! All these motorboats around the island – probably to retrieve this animal. It escaped to die alone. Not allowed – no trophies for hunters!' He went quiet for a moment, drinking the tea.

He resumed, 'Yes, the first carcass was a lion. The poaching squad tells me a very nasty thing. Here is what happens. First, trap your animal – *illegal* – drug it – *illegal* – transport it somewhere else – *illegal* – some secret place where the animal cannot escape. An island is good! Give some rich person a big gun and 'professional' help to track the weakened animal. Kill it, cut off parts – head, feet, skin – as trophies. *Illegal*. Some visitors pay a fortune for the thrill of a "real" hunt and a "real" kill.'

'*Disgusting,*' Ben spluttered. 'Animals can't even try to fight back!'

'But much money for people who arrange it,' the policeman answered flatly.

'So that's why they want Kisiri . . .' Jack said. 'They think no one here's *important* enough to see them hunting big game animals there!'

'And no one to stop them,' said Rutere. 'Poaching, smuggling – we think linked with gangs, well-armed, indulging in piracy, capturing boats on the northern coast. Certainly *someone* is moving ivory, skins, animal parts that sell for much money, shipping them from isolated beaches north of Tundani. *Very* profitable—'

'So I was *hearing* them bring animal victims down through our creek the other night?' Carole muttered.

'Arrest them!' Ally cut across her. 'It's them, from the hotel, they called Kisiri "our island". I mean the people who came here the other day!'

'We have to catch them at it, Ally. Prove the connections. Or prove the buyers of Kisiri are breaking another law.' The inspector drained the cup, and got to his feet. 'In fact there is some help—'

'Did you go to the hotel and look?' Ally demanded.

'Ally, Ally,' Carole warned.

'It is fine, Carole, it is good to have people who care.' Rutere put his head on one side, regarding Ally thoughtfully. 'We have looked, yes. Owner and staff deny any connection with animals or Kisiri. They say no one from the hotel came here—'

'Ally and Jack saw the same woman in the office there, Rutere. They *are* interested in *this* place . . .' Carole indicated the house.

'*I* believe you. But the hotel manager insists she never came here. No link we could find. Unfortunately, we have not found the man who was with her. We keep trying! Our best chance is to find the vehicles or boats that carried these animals and the two beaten boys. These dead animals on Kisiri give *their* story a terrible ring of truth—'

'*Dedan!*' The idea leapt into Ally's head. '*He* remembers car numbers! It's like he sees pictures in his head!'

'The boy remembers nothing, sadly. He is in shock. However, I also came to say there is in fact something *you* can help us with, Jack. If you and your aunt are agreeable. Accompany Collins and Dedan to a place our helicopter has found? These boys insist you are with them.'

'Yes!' Jack looked quickly at Carole.

'Go, go! The sooner the better.'

'Good, good – these children will feel safer if you are with them. They do not trust us! My men have found signs of a temporary fence in that place, and many tyre marks. It may be where the boys saw cages.' The policeman consulted his watch. 'My men can fetch you in twenty minutes. I will radio them now.'

'If,' Carole was thinking aloud, '*if* there *is* even a small link between the Kisiri buyers and the Tundani hotel – and *if* you find the Tundani hotel is involved in this animal trafficking, Rutere . . . would that be enough connection? Could that stop the *buyers* actually getting Kisiri?'

'Ah, well . . . *if* is the big word! These buyers' groups – a giant octopus! One leg – local wealthy men, another leg – a politician or two, another leg – foreign businessmen. All trying to get rich! Possibly the hotel is in there, or some individuals from the hotel. When the octopus is threatened, it sends a cloud of inky darkness to hide itself.' He turned to go. 'Have no fear, we do our best.'

The glossy Tundani hotel, its smell of money, washed over Ally. And the mess rippling out from it like the aftershock of an explosion. That could be Kisiri and Shanza in no time; Leli, Huru, Eshe, Koffi, Mosi, Pili, Lumbwi, Saka, Thimba, Jela, Hasina, Mzee Kitwana – all the people she knew, all their lives – vanished under it.

To the policeman's retreating back, she appealed, 'We've got to find *something* to stop them getting Kisiri!'

He flicked a sharp warning glance at her. '*Shanza* needs to find something!'

'But—'

'Violent men – I cannot say this too much. Shanza—' He turned at the distant chatter of the police radio. He went through the house to the car.

He reappeared almost as fast, a distinct change in his step.

'Well! We have found a line that may, how do you say, join a few dots? Some distance from here, surprisingly, at Breezy Point Garage in Kinyangata!'

Ally frowned. 'That's where Leli's brother Shaaban works!'

'Ah-ha!' The policeman beamed at her. 'Then in truth it is this Leli and his brother Shaaban who have found it for us!'

'Leli, do not idle!' his mother said sharply. 'If we all walk about on Kisiri like you, nothing is done. It will storm! We must build more shelters!'

'He is not idling, Tabia.' His father's voice was mild and he gave Leli a small smile. But his tone was firm. 'The boy has done enough already. Let him alone! He must be clear in his head for the policeman.'

Leli returned his father's smile. But he went to help his mother arrange containers of water and heave up the palm fronds to be laid over canes. He could not be angry with her today. She was the first to be ready with food and blankets and water, yelling encouragement to her friends. '*Do not dig potatoes with a blunt stick!*' she scolded one who brought only a single bottle of water. '*What will you drink when this bottle is empty? We stay on Kisiri till these bad people leave us in peace! Many days. Many weeks!*'

And the shelters were going up fast, palm thatch tied in firmly against the storms. Hard sun was forcing through the cloud and drying the ground, but rain would come before night – a few hours only to become truly prepared.

He looked through the trees at the water and Shanza beyond.

Where is the inspector? He takes too long! His thoughts fizzed in a thousand different directions. The inspector must see how it all fitted together!

He ran through it, in his head. Last night, Mzee Shaibu calling people in the village together to hear the D.O.'s assistant.

'*Three things happen, just in the last three weeks,*' the assistant explained, opening a big map and pointing to it as he spoke. '*First, someone buys land on the Tundani road – there. A big piece – only sand dunes and birds. Then another one takes land to the south, a few miles from here – there. Now someone buys Kisiri.*'

'*And they look in our forest!*' Leli had flared up, '*and they go to Dr Carole's house, it is all the same thing! They will join everything together and swallow Shanza,*' and he'd braced himself for a rebuke for interrupting the visitor. But Mzee Shaibu just drew his finger from the bottom of the map, through Shanza, to the top at Tundani to show people what Leli meant.

For a long time everyone went quiet, thinking, before the arguing began.

Then Mzee Issa held up his hand for silence. '*We must hold our place. We must walk the thorny path, even though it tears our legs,*' going three times round in his words the way he always did – and Leli could not stop himself from shouting, '*We must be there, on Kisiri!*' and others agreed, Mzee Issa, Mzee Kitwana, Mzee Shaibu, his father, his mother, many, many others.

He looked across the water again, this time towards Ally's house. She would not know he was here. He itched to tell her all that had happened since finding the dead animals on the island, since their late, tired arrival back in the village last night. Fumo had warned, and Leli had heard. Fumo understood this. Leli knew, because Fumo had not come again.

A mad thought! I cannot say this to anyone else, but I can say it to Ally.

He felt bold. He would tell Inspector Rutere, *Ally found the cheetah. Ally is important. Ally must be here on Kisiri with us now. You must fetch her!*

He saw that a police boat was leaving Shanza and crossing the bay towards Kisiri. He jumped at his father's voice. 'No tangled paths in your mind to waste the policeman's time, Leli?'

In truth his thoughts were as tangled as the branches of the fig tree overhead; Shaaban, Kisiri, the dead animals, Fumo, Ally – they all quarrelled in his head for attention. He stuck his chin in the air and squinted into the tree for inspiration.

What must I report to the policeman, so he understands everything?

One – Eshe decides to take my letter quickly to Shaaban herself and goes on the bus from her cousin's house to Kinyangata.

Two – Shaaban reads, and questions Eshe about the strangers in their boats. Eshe tells him what she knows, but . . .

Three – Eshe has already travelled to Lilongelewa a day before the dead animals and the street boys' beating and someone buying Kisiri, so she does not know, and cannot plant ideas in my brother's head. But . . .

Four – Shaaban telephones Salim at Kitokwe, and Lumbwi

is there telling Salim everything. Lumbwi takes Salim's bicycle to ride quickly to Mzee Shaibu and fetch Leli to the telephone.

In his head, Leli could still hear his brother's words. '*Show Mzee Shaibu my letter, so he can put all the parts together. There is a truck here in the garage right now. It fell in a ravine last night and broke. The driver is angry, shouting all the time into a satellite phone till another man arrives. Hear this, it is important, Leli: this new one is the man I told about in my letter, who is maybe a poacher or soldier. These two men quarrel about a map, throw it in the truck and leave. I have just looked at this map.*

'*Leli, there is Kitokwe, Shanza, Kisiri, Tundani! Many marks, red, purple – near Shanza and on Kisiri. More even forty miles away. A thick blue line makes a big shape round Tundani and Kisiri and Shanza. It is like a boundary—*'

'Leli!' With a nudge, his father broke Leli's train of thought.

The police boat had reached the island. Leli took Shaaban's letter from his shirt pocket and went down the sands to meet the inspector.

Inspector Rutere finished reading.

'So your brother works at this garage—' he began to Leli.

'He is a clever mechanic,' Leli's mother intervened. 'He is young but he is a bird that flies with his own wings.'

'Tabia speaks the truth, sir,' his father put in quietly. 'Shaaban has a good head. If he puts one and one together it will always come to be two.'

Urgently Leli held out a scrap of paper. 'Shaaban gives the

number of the broken truck in his garage, and also the car that he talks about in that letter to me – the one that belongs to the same man. I gave the numbers to the sergeant and here they are for you, sir.'

The inspector took them and smiled. 'This is very good, very good. We will see if Dedan or Collins have memory yet of vehicle numbers they followed or saw in the ravine. Or the one that carried them. We can look in the hotel and its records . . . Let us pray there is a match between these things. Let us pray that when our officer gets to Kinyangata garage this map is still in this truck where your brother saw it. And if we are lucky, the forensic team will find traces of animals, even of Collins' and Dedan being carried . . .'

As he spoke, he was looking round at the shelters, the running children, everyone busy and shouting across to each other, the air thick with woodsmoke from the cooking fires. On the high ground, above the steep cliff, men stood as lookouts. Canoes were drawn up in ranks on the beach, ready.

'I am very grateful!' he said. 'I am thinking everyone will have reason to be grateful.'

Leli felt suddenly immensely lighter. And determined. He said, 'Sir, Dr Carole, and Jack and Ben, and Ally . . .' he steeled himself to ignore the look his mother would throw, '. . . they must hear that we are staying here on Kisiri. They must come—' He could not bear the thought of Ally not being *here*.

'My sergeant brings them. Mzee Shaibu has asked for Dr Carole. A doctor may be needed here. See – already.'

Another police boat was crossing. Eagerly, Leli watched.

'Leli!' His mother spoke sharply. 'You will—'

'The boy does not need instructions, Tabia,' his father intervened. He put a hand on Leli's arm, just a fleeting touch, and catching his eyes. 'Be steady, Leli. And be patient. The sun never sets without fresh news.'

Twenty-three

Badru has measured the cave – it is six hundred paces from the mouth to its innermost wall. The cave's deeper reaches curve out of sight of the mouth, into a large cavern.

We tested the distance above, on the cliff. From the fort's outer wall, above the cave-mouth, six hundred paces brings us beside the chapel in the court. Goat and cattle pens were there. The animals now all dead: only a well remains, abandoned when it became rapidly and strangely dry, filled with broken stone to prevent any creature falling into it.

The centre is solid, the stones wedged firm, but we saw narrow cracks.

We waited till the westering sun was low enough to put our eastern walls in shadow and the enemy patrol passed far out on the ebb-tide. Then we lowered Badru again outside the walls to the cave entrance, waiting for his returning signal on the rope to haul him up.

He saw light glowing in the cave-depths, the colour of the dipping sun in the west! It could not come from the cave mouth to the east, at this hour deep shadowed by the high cliff. Some other source is lighting the cave.

We set to prising out the wedged stones from the abandoned well, and were an arm's reach down before we saw the lower stones have shifted and opened a broad channel plunging deeper.

Jabari went to the store below Alvaro's house to fetch the mason's chisels and hammers. We removed the stones to the height of a man. We lowered Badru into the well. He hung there, holding up a hand for silence. Then signalled wildly for us to bring him up again.

From within, he heard the surge and suck of tide below!

We dig more urgently, and yet more carefully, lest we send stones tumbling to block the space below. We work into full darkness, for the Arabs are moving three ships closer. Diogo calculates they have forty cannon and prepare ships as firing platforms to send against us.

The treasure draws them. Badru's friend in the town said that scores have joined this Arab fleet since the talk of riches – tales born of a siege held month after month by men kept far from their homes, to do nothing but wait for other men's deaths.

Alvaro's records show that the *Madre de Deos* carried the booty plundered from that hapless distant city and its sultan, also a cargo of gold from Sofala, and ivory from a captured Indian ship bound for Cambay. A fortune indeed!

But we have not found it, and with fire in her eyes, Winda scorns any talk of fortunes. Our only prize is that every woman, man and child may fly this desolate place and *live*, forever free of it.

Neema is stronger again, and baby Jorge rallies. Hunger has weakened him dreadfully, yet he has a spirit that will not succumb. All gives us hope. I took my turn at Watch and felt my limbs stronger, all trembling gone. I drew into my heart that moment of freedom on the wall. I felt again Her presence, real, and strong, my Spirit of Hope who will save us.

It began this night. We heard movement among the ruined houses outside the western gate. We feared the worst and stood at arms. Chane and Diogo stayed to widen the channel through the well into the cave.

At first light we saw their ships nearer, that some hundred men have landed and with utmost speed and cunning thrown up earthworks among the broken buildings. Paulo says they will have brought up guns from the ships and lodged them behind. Our time runs out with increasing speed.

But with Badru I descended our new-cut channel, and saw there is a second cavern, high above the cave. It cuts into the coral as a deep shelf, invisible from below. It has space to take us all, affords safety to stow our preparations and to hide and wait.

We are still twelve in number, and three children. The fever has claimed no other.

Chane and Neema prepare ropes and slings for carrying things. We have the canoe brought by Badru, Rahidi and Jabari. Paulo has repaired another. Omar and Saaduma build a raft from remnants of damaged boats. We will lower it in sections through the channel, to be roped together in the cave below.

Again and again, Jabari stalks through the captain's house, paces and views from every angle. The house is built against the fort's outer wall; a stone staircase climbs outside from the courtyard to the living floor above. Beneath is the storeroom, empty now of all but the scuttle of spiders. Broad doors lead to the store from the open court, also a narrow wooden stairway goes up inside to the captain's chamber above, closed by a trapdoor that—

I could not finish – Jabari called me and Diogo to the captain's house!

He was moving through the empty storeroom, counting his steps for us to hear. Then paced its walls outside, counting again. 'You see?' he demanded.

Inside the store, the span of walls is shorter from rear to front, than the measurement outside. *Three whole paces shorter.*

We fell to inspecting the wall along the back, but detected nothing. Yet something fills the rear of the storeroom and there is no doorway into it.

A large hidden space between the store and the fort's outer wall.

We climbed the stairway to the captain's rooms above and examined the floor, its empty hollow sound ringing beneath our tramping feet. Long ago we burned every stick of furniture for firewood, except the bed, pushed hard against the wall. A broad stone ledge protrudes there and two legs of the bed rest on it. We drew them off, and with our newly suspicious eyes, we saw.

Four blocks of stone with fine cracks between the joints, no mortar sealing them.

We fetched the tools and levered one stone up and the black damp of the place below breathed in our faces. Our lamp illuminated the dulled wood of many chests, packed close, and when Jabari prised one open, the sheen of metals: gold, silver, copper – goblets, plates, bracelets, rings. In another, coins – more than any man could imagine.

Here is the poisoned treasure that sucks our enemy towards us.

It sets a fire amongst us, igniting a plan!

Goma and Neema brought the children into our midst so they could see our hope. We embraced, one and all, each making the promise to each other.

Without time pressing dangerously against us, how we might dance!

Now will we escape this place of hell, in such a way that no one will know we have gone, or follow us.

We believe they will attack from their earthworks outside the western gate. They will cross the coral ditch and throw ladders against the wall, believing few of us alive to throw them off.

This we will do: pack the guardrooms above that gate with gunpowder *salted with items of treasure*. At an appointed time, ignite the gunpowder, by slow fuses devised by Diogo and Paulo. Chane and Omar prepare the cannon to follow – to fire in quick succession as if many men are poised to fight.

In such a way we will set a great diversion, and, with the treasure, so tempting a distraction, that they will not think to look at what we do on the distant side of the fort!

Winda and I have strewn clothes in the gatehouse. In the heat of forcing entry to the fort, and the explosions, they may think we have in error blown ourselves up with the treasure. Only later will they find no bodies there, only the poor souls buried beneath the court, long dead from pestilence and hunger.

Badru, Rahidi, Saaduma and Jabari have moved the remaining chests of treasure from their hiding place beneath the captain's house and lowered them through the well, to stow them deep in the cavern above the cave.

'If the town survives these new Arab rulers,' Jabari said, 'if we live and it be within our power, we will find ways to tell the townspeople of it hidden there, and how it came there. It may be some recompense for years spent suffering the thievery of your Captain Alvaro and this cursed fort.'

Already Goma and Neema have taken the children and the food we have left down into the cavern. Badru and Rahidi fashion a way to close the head of the well above us by dropping a stone and setting a fire and small explosions to burn by slow fuse, so to blacken and appear to age the stone and mask our route.

So may the dusk approach, and as the last light fades, the guns will fire, the gatehouse blow, and we, in the cave, will hold ready for that moment. Thence, in the night's chaos, to freedom.

Thunder rumbles, and flocks of birds flee before the coming storm. We must leave this place before it breaks, crossing to refuge among the mangroves. Jabari says we trace the journey of Bwana Fumo and Mwana Zawati, they who first came with their people to this island. Now we travel the self-same course to freedom.

'Our next birthday we will celebrate together in my father's house,' he says. 'For the rest . . .' He lifts the talisman of the warrior leaders where it hangs still around my neck. 'For the rest, we trust to the spirits of Fumo and Zawati, and to God, and to your Spirit of Hope, my dear brother.'

All is now ready. A spiral of black cloud stands like an anvil above the mainland, fired at the base where the sun does battle with it. Waves thunder against the cliff. As the wind rises they boil and pound and suck, and I think of them sucking our poor weak craft into their depths.

But I must hold fast to Hope. I lift the talisman, and send my prayer for the gift of Life from Her, and know now that She hears it.

Twenty-four

Ally tried not to watch Leli. He'd rushed to greet her off the boat.

'Fumo warns us – now he knows we have heard!' His face eager, excited: 'You see!'

He'd taken something from his pocket and held it towards her. She saw it was the little silver medallion Mzee Kitwana gave him. And she was about to ask what he meant, what she should *see*, but Mosi called, Leli put the medallion into her hand, folded her fingers over it, and then rushed off again.

Now he was locked in discussion with Mosi over something, she hadn't the faintest idea what.

She stood uncertainly. *Does he want me to look after the medallion? Is it a secret I've got it – will Mzee Kitwana be angry if he sees?* It didn't seem right it was in her hand, it was a gift to Leli. Would she offend Leli if she gave it back? It seemed important to know, and she was stricken by not knowing, by Carole's words about not understanding.

And she still hadn't explained anything to Leli, about how

frightened she was for them all, or how angry Carole had made her, about what Carole had said.

Or about the other fear – from the words on the paper Makena'd given her.

For perhaps the hundredth time, she took it from her pocket.

I walk the paths of the forest.

I seek Hope, a flame of life in the dark.

In my dream I find Her. In my dream I speak to Her.

Waiting in the village for the police boat to the island, she'd looked in vain for the archaeologist. How could she just give her this and not explain! Who wrote it? And the real fear, lurking below all that – *is it about* me *in the forest?*

Is any of this weird stuff really happening, in the forest, on the cliff? She couldn't get out of her head another thought. *Maybe I'm a bit mad. Maybe I'm just rolling everything into a scary tangle because of the trouble on Kisiri, and because of Leli – what Carole's planted in my head, meant to cut me off from him.*

'Be sensible, Ally,' her aunt had said just now, quietly, so no one else could hear. 'Remember what I said. Please.' Then just left her on the village shore, and gone to find the Elders.

Ally didn't answer, angry.

In three weeks nothing'll matter. I'll be gone again. Home. If I'm inventing things, I can stop.

But the words on the paper circled in her head, and Makena's words about ammunition. Ammunition against invaders. What ammunition? What can anyone do?

She sidestepped a collision with Ben. He was rushing along

with Huru and Pili, lugging a heavy basket between them. Others streamed past, answering a warning shout from the cliff. Every minute brought new alarms like this: boats sighted, alerts in case someone was coming to seize the island.

She shivered, despite the heat. Crossing from the village in the boat, voices, an undersong surged in the tide, fluting echoes, drumbeats on the wind. It all lurked at the edge of her racing mind.

She tried to steady herself, saying to Koffi, who'd stopped nearby, 'The inspector said we'll know something soon! The police are taking Dedan and Collins and Jack to that ravine—'

Koffi tossed her head, not listening. 'Yesterday, the ones who want to take Kisiri are *trespassers*. Tomorrow, they make *us* trespassers! *In our own place!* Eh, there is Eshe arriving!' She launched into a run – Eshe was just reaching the island in a *hori*, exchanging shouts across the shallows with Leli, being told everything she'd missed.

Ally turned away. From the hullabaloo in the camp, that she couldn't understand because she didn't speak his language; from the helplessness; from Leli. From the horrible distance opening between them.

She went down, away, through the lines of beached boats, and out on to open sands marked only by the long, looping tracks of the birds.

Tiny waves curl inwards and cream softly up the beach. The tide is falling; a starfish – fiery orange – lies stranded. She scoops it up gently on a mat of seaweed and lowers it into the next wave. It moves with an exuberant twist into the twirl of water. She waits in case it surges back, needs rescue.

How still everything is! Hot, still, and ominous. The sea olive green. The litter of shells, coconut husks, mangrove pods, the flaccid hanks of some sea plant heaved up by the tide. Everything stands out so boldly – as if demanding attention.

A white shell like a miniature skull: a fleeting image: arched trees, a baobab where water booms.

Near where the cheetah died? She looks for the place, into the high rocks far off, seeing a flock of birds take flight in a vast, undulating crescent, dipping and rising till they dwindle to nothing.

Looking up like this burns. Tight bands grip her forehead, as if she's not slept for weeks, her eyeballs like hot coals. Sunstroke, maybe. Dehydration. *I should drink something.*

She lifts her hand to shield her eyes and presses the medallion against her forehead, its sudden coolness soothing against the heat of her skin.

She closes her eyes.

Without sight, sounds are stark. The rustle of breaking surf; strident cries of the birds; no silence—

Then in the centre, like a door opening, silence. She feels it like a presence.

It *is*. Someone. Speaking. Though no words she understands.

A boy's voice. Leli. In relief she opens her eyes. He's dark in the white blast of the sun.

'Leli!'

Then sees it isn't. Gaunt. White-skinned. Dark hair straggles long across his shoulders. Clothes hang about him in shreds. Blackened, as if he's burst through a fire. His eyes hold hers. They lock hers. An extraordinary intensity: she recognizes it as yearning – it fizzes through her like her own need for Leli.

His lips move. A whisper . . . *speranza*? He lifts his hand towards her face, towards her eyes.

But a lance of light blinds her, she blinks against the needle of pain, and he's gone.

*

You. The talisman on your brow, your gaze warm as the sun. Life's light flowing.

You see me.

Hope quickens my blood, bone, heart.

I am strong,

Awake.

Life beckons in the white heat of this coming day.

*

She was racing away from him, climbing too fast, clutching with hands when her feet slid back in the mudslides from the storm. He clambered behind and was terrified she would fall and he would not catch her.

Leli'd turned from greeting Eshe. He'd looked for Ally and seen her standing alone on the beach. Even the angle of her body spoke to him. *Something is wrong.* She no longer let him see into her eyes. She was looking away from him always, except when the terrible thing of the cheetah happened yesterday.

Except for once, today, she had seemed to search his face, and it was like a touch that stopped his breath.

But then she'd closed a door – quietly – as if she didn't want anyone to hear it closing. And she was going away, the space between them stretching, stretching.

It is Makena's paper, he thought.

It is not *Makena's paper* – the new thought entered him like the twist of a little knife. *I have caused offence. I have made Ally unhappy.*

How? What have I done?

He'd halted at the top of the beach, overcome by a cold feeling, and Mzee Kitwana was sitting by a tree, saying something strange. It seemed to be, '*Your friend asks, Leli – you must find your answer,*' – and something about the eagle. But the old man muttered always to himself, perhaps it was not what he said at all – *it is my worries making up stories.*

Then Ally was running to him. She was holding out the disc of Fumo and Zawati that he had given her to keep her safe, and she'd looked back at the sands, then up at the cliff, then back at him, it was a wild, wild look on her face, and it frightened him. She'd said, 'It's not just Fumo, Leli! Warnings, like you said, like in the forest, and down there! I can't explain, Leli! It's like he's calling, really, just listen, please, just come, he's up there, we have to look, we have to, it's what it all means!'

'Who? Who is calling? What means?' Studying her face, trying to understand. Mzee Kitwana's voice again, in his head, '*Your friend asks, you must find your answer,*' and Fumo, and the dreams.

He had studied the rockface where she looked, his skin prickling as he saw the fish eagle swoop down, and vanish.

The storm has brought down a tree. Roots have wrenched off a chunk of the cliff. The torrent of rain has done the rest, a slew of mud and stones barring Ally's path.

There's a distant call. Lumbwi above, on lookout, waving.

Below, climbing fast behind her, Leli's answer echoes.

She turns along a ridge. It steepens to her right, sharp and rocky.

Swirls, flickers on the cliff above.

Flames.

Burning.

Heatstroke, tricks of light, blinding.

No. The boy's voice stays with her. His word: *speranza?* Speransa? She can barely remember, except its urgency.

There's a turret of rock, she has a prickle of memory, of looking up and seeing a bird looking down, a twist of tree above.

She struggles up a gully towards it. Pebbles dislodge with a dull rattle.

Out of sight of the camp here, among scattered trees.

Is it here – the thunder of water in the cave we heard before? She listens.

A hush descends, a cocoon around her. Her own breathing, deafening.

A tremor in the ground. Twigs snap. She whirls, sees a shimmer of movement, steps towards it, the earth seems to shunt aside and she slips, slithers, skids, scrabbles for a hold, hits a nobble of rock. Jerks to a stop, painfully.

Swings there, one-handed.

Soil scrapes her cheek. Threaded with roots.

In a hole. Not dark, not far down.

She tries not to panic. *Think. Think.* Feels for a toehold. Nothing. She can just brace herself, one foot, then the other, pressed on each side, teetering.

A downward glance. The hole doesn't seem to go any deeper, and the soil trickling has stopped. She's covered in the fine reddish stickiness of it, in her nose and mouth, she can taste it on her tongue – she's had her mouth open in a yell. She clamps it shut.

Gingerly, holding tight to the nobble of rock, she ventures her foot on the mush at the bottom of the hole. Tests it.

With a soft, tearing sound it drops away and the world fills with a low rumbling, then a louder creaking, then a crashing avalanche of noise and she's toppling, one hand clutching the rock, the other flailing for a hold – the medallion spinning wildly from her grasp.

She hangs, swinging, above a gaping hole that goes down and down and down. Rocks and bits of tree tumble and bump past, following the medallion down, how far she can't see, doesn't look, because if she does she'll go faint and lose her precarious, slipping grasp on the rock.

Leli hurled himself forward as the ground dropped away and took Ally.

He lay, gathering his wits. He tingled with shock. When the world steadied, he was on a ledge bound to the cliff by the roots of a baobab still stubbornly upright.

He grasped a looping root to anchor himself firmly.

'Ally?' His call sounded pale, frail. He took a deep breath to send his voice further: '*Ally! Ally!*' and with a flooding relief so complete it almost paralysed him, heard her answer.

He edged forward. He dared to peep into the hole. She was beyond reach, dangling precariously by one hand. Below, a sheer drop into gloom.

Her face turned up to him, white with terror through its coating of smeared mud.

He heard the ululating cries from the fishermen on lookout, knew they were coming. But the rock she'd grasped was tipping, any moment would come loose from the soil and she'd plunge.

'*Hold, hold!*' he urged frantically, and swung his feet round to hook them into the baobab root. He tested his weight. He released his hands and unfolded his body again.

He slithered over the rim of the hole, head down, arms reaching.

Her eyes shot wide in alarm. 'Don't, don't, Leli! You'll fall!'

He locked his eyes on hers. He willed her to keep firm. Reached for her outstretched free hand, missed. Edged a little further, reached again, and again. Felt her fingertips. He stretched till he was coming apart. She gave a little twist and a lurch towards him and he grabbed and caught and held, feeling their hands slipping, sweat made them slippery, mud made them slippery, blood pounded in his head, arms throbbed, eyes glued to hers, if he let go with his eyes she'd fall, only the eyes mattered, his eyes and hers, his life and hers, fused. Cramp in his legs dulled, the wrenching pains – arms, feet chained in the roots, numbed.

He heard cries; twigs snapping, rustling. He was dimly aware when arms reached past and her weight was suddenly not his to carry. When a rope passed round his body and tightened, and someone unpeeled him from his tangle with her hands, with the tree, turned him the right way up, cleared the soil from his upside-down face.

He was promptly, violently, sick.

Twenty-five

They sat on the bank, shivering despite the heat. She gave him a quivery smile. 'I heard . . . saw . . . someone – really – I did – near me on the cliff!'

'Ghosts!' he said with a little laugh. 'You, me, ghosts, ghosts of Kisiri!' He was light-headed, immensely happy, everything else had gone away. He was anchored firmly in somewhere very calm and very warm. He could stay here for ever, just sitting and being safe with Ally. Just Ally. He wanted to wrap his arms round her, fold all of himself round her, to make sure. But he just smiled and smiled into her face, and she gave him that look, deep-eyed and dark in the blue of her eyes, the look that left him without breath.

He said, after a minute, because all other words vanished, 'Mzee Kitwana will not mind.' He meant the loss of Fumo and Zawati's disc. 'He will care that it has kept you safe. He will be happy. Now we stay still.' The lookouts, Lumbwi, his father, Jela, would not let them move till the route to descend to the camp was judged safe. More rock might fall: chunks were dropping away from the collapsed cliff now as the sun dried exposed slabs. Lumbwi and his father had gone back to fetch ropes . . .

I am the stupid one! Leli thought. To let her climb when the storm makes everything loose. Lumbwi told how lucky she was. A miracle Leli reached her, just in time, Lumbwi said. A miracle Leli held her till they could reach him!

He leaned a little to look into the hole, at where she might have plunged. Ally leaned too: the warmth of her against him was a glow on his skin, and he was drifting into thinking about that when he heard her make a small, startled sound. Her gaze was fixed on something – the rock she'd gripped with her hand. It was picked out by the strong shaft of the sun. More soil had seeped away. The rock was bared. It was balanced on another. A flat thing. A platform. And another thing was above, smooth – like a cut shape.

Cut! Fat, smooth, round. And poking out of the mud behind like the mast of a ship half-sunk, a cross shape. In the hard shadows, marks showed . . .

Carved marks. Other shapes were emerging from the dribbling soil. Marks on them too.

Words. Words cut in stone.

He said, in sharp, stark recognition, 'Like Ulima Fort – Teacher showed us in a book!'

'Fort?' Ally stared at him, wide-eyed. 'Like a Portuguese fort?'

'I do not know Portuguese. But in the book of Ulima Fort, the words on the stones are like that.'

*

270

'*Chini, chini!*' Tensely Leli motioned Jela to go lower.

The fisherman, roped securely to a tree some distance back, obediently moved down over the broken wall of the hole. He paused at the peculiar bared stones, peered without touching. He played out the rope and lowered himself to other protruding nobbles and lumps.

He teased mud aside. Damply sticky, it fell away, and he said something, rapid, excited.

The edge of something dark showed, straight, different from the stones above.

Tentatively, he scraped more, yelled as the shape slid suddenly forwards so that he had to dance out of its way on the rope. And they watched it roll in a slow, bounce, bounce, bounce against the sides of the hole, reach the bottom, come to rest on end, topple, and subside in soft, crumbled soil, settle, and ever so slowly split, and they were all looking down at a gentle cascade, a soft gleaming yellow river, trickling silently into the beam of the hard midday sun.

'It is *dhahabu*! I mean gold!' Makena jerked the binoculars from place to place. 'Coins there, and at the back, ingots. Other chests in the soil behind! Wedged on rock, I think, but we will have to investigate properly, and contain our impatience.'

From her dancing from foot to foot, Ally could see this was difficult. Since arriving, Makena had not stopped talking. 'Rutere telephones, *come this minute*, he instructs, *tell no one why, bring a trusted journalist and photographer*!'

The photographer was feverishly taking picture after picture: Ally, Leli, Jela, Lumbwi, his father, the ropes still tied

271

to the tree, the ledge where Leli'd lain, the stone she'd held, the chest at the bottom of the hole. The journalist was scribbling down every word spoken by anyone about anything.

'Ally, Leli, it is the biggest, biggest adventure, and you give it to us! Over there, look,' she thrust the binoculars at Leli, 'you see? A stone platform. The curve below . . . it is a drinking well, I am guessing.' She pointed to the stone with the marks, 'That, *very* interesting. Very, very! Inscription above a door or gate maybe . . . Fractured in some violent way. The experts will have to say, but I think an explosion, fire—'

Ally stared down at it. She was seeing the figure of the boy on the beach. Blackened clothes, in shreds . . . *As if he'd burst through a fire.*

The way his eyes locked hers, *telling* her. Imploring.

She looked up, into Makena's face. 'It's the gate of a fort, isn't it?' she said, but knowing. 'It's the lost one, on the island, like Mzee Kitwana says . . .'

Makena's grin was wider than ever. 'And see, this top thing, this thing you so luckily found to hold till brave Leli could save you, Miss Very Special Extra Clever, this is a bit of a stone cross. It is called a *padrão*. When the Portuguese ships claimed land for their king, they planted these to mark—'

'Never mind the detail!' Inspector Rutere broke in brusquely. 'Be clear! What does it mean for *Shanza*?'

'Rutere! The details must be savoured! Even by an impatient policeman! But OK, OK, I make a guess for you. We are definitely in the ruins of a very, very, very old Portuguese construction. It is built above the cave in the cliff – and the roof of the cave has fallen, *whoosh!* in the storms. Quickly we make it strong or everything will drop to the sea before we learn more! And those chests? They contain items of immense value! *In-com-par-able* value! So much that you and I and other ordinary people cannot possibly imagine!'

The broken chest splaying its extraordinary contents seemed to Ally to bask in their silent gaze.

She glanced at Leli, who seemed transfixed, unable to find any words. He met her gaze, a world of meaning in his face.

'Is it enough?' she asked Makena, phrasing the question for Leli. 'I mean, is it the ammunition, like you said? To stop Kisiri being sold?'

'Ho! Is it enough, she asks! Is it *enough*! I will stake my reputation on it, Ally! No government could risk allowing a site like this to pass to private owners before further investigation! So what it *means*, Rutere my friend,' she clapped the policeman exuberantly on the shoulder, 'is that I doubt this island can be sold for some time. Till we get to the bottom of this, so to speak! The very, very bottom!' Her eyes shone. 'Oh, there will be dancing! Even Mzee Kitwana, we will have dancing!'

Leli reached out and gripped Ally's hand, very tight. 'Miss Makena, do you know a word – Ally, it was *speranza*, you told me, yes? *S-p-e-r-a-n-z-a*? Do you know this thing?'

Makena pursed her lips. 'No, no, no, I do not think . . . Oh! It is perhaps a bit like one Portuguese word. *Esperança*. See,' she pronounced it slowly, 'a little bit the same?'

Esperança. Ally savoured the sounds, repeated them slowly inside her head, recognizing. She asked aloud, 'What does it mean?'

'Eh!' Makena said in delight. 'A good word for us all! A very, very, very good word! *Hope!* Hope! It means *hope*! Let us all descend, and let us inform Mzee Shaibu and Mzee Kitwana and all our friends of *hope*!' She flung her arms out, enjoying herself. 'Ah-ha, let us broadcast to the world that Shanza has received the Gift of Hope! Shanza has found a most powerful weapon! The legacy of the old thieves who plundered these places, to use against the new thieves who wish to plunder her again. Truly, it is all in the secrets of the island!'

one month later, London
dancing

Twenty-six

Words floated in her mind: *esperança . . . ghosts . . . you, me, ghosts of Kisiri . . . secrets of the island.*

And faces – the boy's, ragged, fire-scorched; Leli's eyes willing her not to fall. Nothing else quite penetrated the half-world of muted sound and paled colour that seemed to have closed over her since she stepped off the plane in London. Like being suspended here, while everything in that distant place paused, and waited for her, and she for it.

She stood looking at the large padded envelope on the kitchen table. Still sealed, though the postman had delivered it an hour ago.

Her aunt's writing: *To Jack, Benjy, Ally.*

Upstairs, she heard Ben's voice on the landing, then Jack's door flung open. The bathroom door slammed and the shower ran. Ten minutes, they'd be rushing down, heading for Saturday football, spotting the envelope, opening it.

Any minute her parents would emerge too, full of curiosity.

She needed to know what was in the envelope. Alone, privately, in case—

Suddenly decisive, she tore it open and emptied it on the table. Several sheets of Carole's writing; a green plastic folder of typed pages; a wad of photos . . . She upended the envelope. A handful of other photos flopped out. Nothing else.

Disappointment rolled over her like the darkening morning outside, light rain becoming a swiftly murkier downpour. And something deeper and more lasting settled in her, a bleakness, a greyness, that not even Carole's letter and the photos could lift from her.

Truth was, nothing waited for her. It all raced on without her, she no longer part of it, and a bit of her seemed cut away.

What did I expect? the other part said. *I went away. Just got on a plane and went away. Why expect him to share his life with me now?*

You could write to him, a bit of her answered back. You had to come home. It was just a holiday.

Write about what? Not the truth – that she was just sleepwalking here. That the *awake* Ally, the *alive* Ally was still there, left behind, with him. And that the sleepwalking bit trapped here was afraid *he*'d moved beyond and away from her.

Of course he has.

Then she was angry at the wallowing self-pity, and made herself sit down and splay out the photos and go through them properly, one by one.

There they all were – Ben, Jack, Leli, Huru, her, sitting

on Saka's *ngalawa*; then one of her and Leli walking by Mzee Shaibu's house and looking back over their shoulders, laughing.

She remembered that. Eshe took it. It was the afternoon after the discoveries on Kisiri, Makena donating the camera. 'Record everything! Who knows what is important and what is not?' She'd instructed everyone clustering to learn to work the camera, and Eshe was first to have a go, following Ally and Leli along the path. 'I record the founders of everything: Fumo and Zawati born again,' she'd yelled, and Leli'd attempted a withering look, 'old joke, Eshe!' because it was the joke Mzee Kitwana made on that very first day, that very first walk through Shanza with Leli. She remembered saying then, 'It's a nice joke! I quite like being called a warrior and a leader!' and Leli'd given her his narrow-eyed look, suspicious she was teasing.

The memory warmed her. She sorted quickly through other pictures, imagining explaining who was who to Zoe and other friends, where things happened, how they happened, what it *meant*.

But not about Leli, not even to Zoe, folding him away just for herself. And how could she really explain Kisiri, strangeness, beauty, the horror of those slaughtered animals, the way everything about that place – *his place* – *him* – woke her up? Or the boy on the beach and the cliffs, whoever he was, who'd somehow made everything happen, sent her scrambling for the cliff, drawn them to the treasure, pulled her and Leli together again.

She'd only ever told Leli about him. It wasn't something

feverish and invented, the way people might think. Distance – four thousand miles between them, all the days since, made her certain. Sometimes she saw those moments again with a stark sunlit precision, like watching a film – the look in the boy's eyes, his voice, the burst of flame on the cliff that sent her clambering up, the shimmer of movement that she *knew* was him.

How could you tell anyone here any of that? Impossible even to say it to Jack or Ben or Carole, who'd *been* there. Only Leli.

Misery surged up again, making her cold. She focused hard on picking through the other pictures: a shot of the Boat Crew, four little figures standing to attention, luminous in matching orange T-shirts, like a uniform; Dedan in plaster, arm and leg, brandishing a crutch proudly, another of Collins – all smiles on his still battered face – drumming on the little drum just after Makena gave it to him. 'My Ghana friend has given me this,' Makena'd said. 'Special! A Talking Drum! You will make it speak for us, Collins. *I* cannot . . . you can make it tell our story!'

Picture after picture – the celebration dancing on Shanza's beach every night in those following weeks, among the fishing boats, the radio singing out, Collins on his drum; everyone canoeing to Kisiri as Makena brought people to see the discoveries and assembled her team to excavate and uncover more of the ruins.

The last picture she recalled clearly. Lumbwi took it. Mzee Kitwana in the middle with Ally on one side, Leli on the other, on the storyteller's rock-seat where he'd told them the Fumo and Zawati legend. They were all three lit by one of those basking streams of light that always came after the squally bursts of rain those last weeks. Mzee Kitwana's eyes fixed sternly forward, but she and Leli were turned to look at him, because out of nowhere, in his bewildering way, he'd declared, '*Bwana Fumo, eagle of the sea, Mwana Zawati, our Gift! You see, my children – beginnings and life, not endings and death!*' And then looked at them both with his head on one side, and flapped his hand to make them go.

Leli'd linked arms with her as they walked away.

Now, she stacked the photos together and picked up her aunt's letter, sheets and sheets of large, scrawly writing. Headings underlined with fat purple highlighter.

Update, (it began) – **everything's moving so fast, faster since you left, I can barely keep up!**

KISIRI
They've finished shoring up the roof of the cave, and now Makena's begun excavating. The ruins are buried much, much deeper than she expected. She thinks it'll turn out they were covered by the tidal wave that hit this coast several hundred years ago.

But they've already located the one bastion of the fort! So far just the parapet, just above the mouth of the cave on the edge of the cliff.

Makena came by the house last night to report about that inscription on the stone you found, Ally. They've matched it to official records in Portugal, so now they know exactly which fort it is! The

inscription celebrates the opening of the fort in 1648 – nearly three hundred and seventy years ago.

Makena has also started to poke about in the forest very near our house – she says she was curious about a mound near the path. Wishful thinking, I thought, concentrate on Kisiri! But then she uncovered the tip of a stone pillar from an old Swahili tomb – much older than the fort on Kisiri, at least five hundred years old. It's held in the soil almost upright, and there's a bit of wall near it. So now Makena thinks there may be an old Swahili city under the forest, and under this house – one of the 'lost' ones.

Of course Mzee Kitwana announced he'll die happy now because it's Fumo and Zawati's city. Makena just says cryptically that YOU made her look in the forest, Ally! If so, even I will start believing you've got a sixth sense. I still wake up in a nightmare sweat about what might have happened to you up there on the cliff. And the other thing – what it would be like on Kisiri and in Shanza now, with the new buyers in control, if the storm hadn't loosened everything and some piece of lunacy hadn't sent you charging up there with Leli. What if you'd never found the fort and its treasure? Doesn't bear thinking about.

I just had tea with Mzee Kitwana and Makena. Arguing, as ever! Mzee Kitwana declares, 'Before. Now. Again, again, they try to take Kisiri from us. They fail! The land and the sea – greater than everything, good friends we must never betray. When everything else is gone, the land and the sea are there, to give us life!'

'Not if the hotel got its way,' Makena grumbled, but only to prod Mzee further. I sort of understood Mzee – it's like Kisiri's a refuge, a salvation – in the legend, and now; it gave everyone back their courage to fight against impossible odds, didn't it?

LIONS AND CHEETAHS ETC

V v good news: Rutere told me police have seized ivory and skins on a boat on the north coast, AND they've managed to link it forensically with things here, including (Rutere's delighted), Collins' and Dedan's clothes (the ones you packed up, Benjy). Also to the vehicles Leli's brother reported. There's evidence of animals in the boats and cars, and even traces of soil from the ravine you went to with them, Jack! Ten arrests so far, SOME AT TUNDANI HOTEL. Of course the Kisiri buyers denied it was anything to do with them and tried to rush through the purchase. But the newspapers jumped on the story and there was a big public outcry.

Buried forts, treasure, ruins in Shanza forest – it really has stopped everything! Just think, Ally – you, Leli, Lumbwi and his father, Jela – you did that by falling smack in that hole!

Tundani 'Paradise' goes on, of course, with 'new management', and tourists flock in. But – some really good news – Shanza gets a Finders' Reward for the treasure – more than enough to pay for a lawyer, and then some! The D.O. and Mzee Shaibu, Rutere and Makena between them have found one. He's fierce about people's control over places like Kisiri. He made Mzee Shaibu get up and speak at the public hearing last week. I thought Mzee would be very nervous! But he was immensely calm.

Here's what he said: 'We are not backward–looking. We welcome change and development. But we have a right to control this change in our lives and our land, to be guardians of its past and its future.'

The newspapers loved it. They keep quoting him, so Kisiri and Shanza are becoming test cases for how tourism should work in places like this, and what happens to the people caught in the middle.

Makena of course mutters dark warnings about archaeological

pirates who'll loot the ruins (thieves, just like the Portuguese in the fort, she points out). Let's hope the lawyer can work his magic and keep Shanza and Kisiri safe.

WHAT'S NEXT . . . ?

A lot! Some of the reward is going to an Education Fund to pay school fees for everyone (including the Boat Crew). Makena's also plotting a little museum in Shanza, and I predict those four will wangle their way in as guides. The village now runs a ferry service for the archaeologists going to Kisiri, and Collins and Dedan have taken charge. Dedan organizes who and when, Collins collects fares and delivers them to Mzee Shaibu. He demanded a uniform (there's a photo of them wearing it). But Makena tells me Collins also finds excuses to ride the boats to Kisiri and hang about asking questions. So Makena thinks he's secretly fascinated by the finds. A budding Makena? And other big changes afoot: the women, led by Leli's mother and Halima, have asked for a voice or two on the village council 'so they can look after everything properly'. Some of the Elders are squirming, but it's going to happen!

At one point there was a plan for the four kids to live with Hasina and Aishia, Grace and Joseph with one, Collins and Dedan with the other. But they refused to be separated, and stayed in the abandoned boat. So now everyone's helping build a room for them next to Mzee Shaibu. The four kids inspect it daily, v impressed with the real bed the carpenter is making for them.

FINALLY – I can hardly believe it myself – A HEALTH CLINIC! Impossible for the government to ignore the clamour now – the area is too much in the news.

It's to be right here, on the main road at Kitokwe. Salim's very excited and is going to paint the shop and put chairs and tables under a shelter for people to sit while they wait. Mosi and Pili are organizing everyone to draw pictures on the walls – of Kisiri and the fort (looking like Ulima Fort, we don't know yet how it really looks) and decorate the tables and chairs to make it welcoming.

So – you won't be surprised – I'm staying on in the Old Fisheries House after all! I'm going to help my friend Dr Kuanga run the Kitokwe clinic. We're thinking of starting a temporary weekly one in a tent, just for minor treatment, until the building is finished. Rutere insists it's the seed of the North Coast General Hospital. We're going to prove him right!

Next thing is 'Sherehe ya Kwazi' on Kisiri, once the rains finish. First, a big boat procession round the island. My guess is that the festival this year will go on for weeks and weeks. And oh, will there be dancing now!

One last thing – but v important: Makena just gave me the enclosed folder to read myself first, and then send on to you. Also she's written to you, Ally, because she showed you some lines from this document when you were in Shanza, and she wants to tell you more now.

I've just finished reading – v startling and puzzling! I'll say no more, let it speak for itself!

More news soonest,

C xxxxxxx

Ally reread the last few paragraphs. She pictured the hundred expressions that would colour Leli's face as they debated all this together. Then she firmly blocked them out, and opened Makena's folder, taking out the envelope tucked in the front, her name scribbled slantwise across it.

Makena wrote:

Dear Ally,
You kept asking me to explain about the writing I gave you and I promised I would when I could. Here at last is that explanation! I am sorry to be so secretive!

This folder contains a translation of papers donated to a museum in Portugal just two months ago. The three lines I gave you in Shanza come from the very beginning of it.

An old friend of mine at the museum is studying the papers: as soon as she realized what they are, she began to translate them from Portuguese into English for me to see. When I showed you those lines, I had only received a few pages. The rest arrived just today!

The original papers were wrapped in several layers of leather. They were found in the belongings of a very old lady who died in Lisbon nearly one hundred years ago. Her name was CATERINA JORGE PEREIRA.

Remember that name, while you read!

Till now, her relatives have not investigated the contents properly. They do not know of any definite family connections with Africa. But there is one very vague family story of an ancestor who arrived in Portugal, as a tiny girl. This was (they think) some time in the 1600s. This little girl was orphaned, possibly in Africa. Some suggestion too that she was in the company of another small child, a boy, and also a much older youth.

You will see these papers are a kind of diary, though the entries are not dated and seem to record only a few days. The writer says he has just turned sixteen.

Also in the Lisbon woman's belongings when she died were letters (in a different writing), addressed to 'My Brother' and talking of events described in the diary. I have not seen translations of these yet, but my friend says the letters are in Portuguese, though it is clearly not the writer's native language. He is a person of some rank, possibly royal – he refers to 'my father's court' and signs himself, 'Your Brother, J'. These letters are dated 1667 and 1670 so we conclude the diary probably dates from before.

When you have read, you will make your own guess who wrote the letters! And what happened to the writer of the diary too!

Ally, some of these pages are strange, strange! This diary person was having big, strange hallucinations. He sees visions. He believes he encounters the Spirit of Hope. This spirit appears to him as a person, a girl. He believes he travels to places on the mainland he would not, in truth, be able to reach if he is trapped in the circumstances of siege and imprisonment and illness he describes.

My museum friend says the handwriting begins unsteady, broken. It wanders about the page. Then it becomes firmer. Towards the end it is very bold, and as if made at great speed.

Ally, in my bones I know this was all written in Kisiri's fort! This diary never names it, though the captain, Dom Alvaro, is named. We are trying to trace records of the fort commanders, to see if we can prove it.

Of course, from the inscription on that stone you found, we know which fort it was. There are documents in the museum here in Ulima that say it had a garrison of about one hundred and ninety.

There were twenty Portuguese with one hundred and seventy African slaves and soldiers. It was a half-way port for Portuguese ships travelling up the east coast of Africa to the Persian Gulf and India.

There is also a reference to a very long siege by an Omani Arab force. They sailed down from the Persian Gulf to help the African coastal cities fight the Portuguese invaders. It is recorded that these Arabs blockaded the fort till some terrible sickness killed everyone inside. Possibly it was the bubonic plague – of course we cannot definitely know now.

The thing is, Ally, you will see that the diary talks of such events!

Think how terrible – at first they feel a duty to defend the fort for Portugal. Then they understand that Portugal has abandoned them! The chance to escape has gone – they have no ships, no help from outside, until . . . well, read for yourself!

The diary even speaks of what I think is the treasure you found! And other, FAR STRANGER things.

The last page is most exceptionally odd. It is clear to me that the writer is no longer in his state of feverish, delirious dreaming. He is stronger, excited, alert, intent on escape. And yet . . . and yet!!

And I remember another thing. That you asked me about the Portuguese word for hope. I thought you had seen it in the inscription on the stone, and did not enquire. Now, when I read this diary, I wonder, and wonder . . . !

And I wonder also about something your auntie has told me. We were discussing the shortening of names in your country – it is not often done here – and she says your given name is not Ally, but Elidi. People called you Elly, and as a little child you insisted you were not Elly, but Ally, and so it became, for ever more!

288

Somewhere in the untidy jumble of my head, a little bell of memory rings, and so I went and checked. Ally, you never told me you share a part of your name with our warrior sister, Zawati! I find that Elidi – your full name – it is an old Greek name meaning 'Gift of the Sun'! And I am struck again by how things, the strangest things, have bound us all, one way and another, to Kisiri and its fate!

If anything more arises, I will send news through your dear auntie!

Go well, my young friend.

Your friend,

Makena

P.S. Read the papers WITH GREAT CARE. Most particularly read the last page!

Twenty-seven

The last page, Makena said. Ally turned to it.

She didn't see the lines of neat, impersonal typing in front of her. She imagined them as they were found in Portugal – bold, hand-written at great speed. The writer was sixteen, Makena said – like Jack. Only a year older than Leli, two years older than her.

Trapped, maybe dying, in an ancient fort, on Kisiri.

She was afraid to look.

But in the end he was no longer in his state of feverish dreaming, Makena said. Stronger, excited, intent on escape . . .

Escape.

She made herself see.

Short sentences, one below the other. Like little stabs.

Am I robbed of my reason?
My heart knows truth.
Not dream.

Not fever.

Not madness.

No fort or ship or cannon here.

Calm waves, empty sands.

You. Your hair like the rising sun. On your brow the talisman of Jabari, the mark of Fumo and Zawati, the founders of this place, that I hold against my heart now.

I know that in some place I too inhabit, is your life.

Hear me. Carry my words with you.

I write to fill the waiting time, and for you.

I pray that you know of our hope.

That you know that in the darkest of hours you gave this gift.

That you know all is not lost, that we are not in vain – I, Rubairo de Brita, and my friends, Bwana Jabari, Prince of Mwitu, Badru, Rahidi, who chose to share this destiny, my countrymen, Diogo and Paulo, and those of this land whom Fate brought to this place, Saaduma, Chane, Winda, Omar, Goma, Neema, with the children, Caterina, Jorge, Sefi. All.

In the refuge of this cave we wait together now for the shelter of the night, from which we *will* take the tide to our true freedom.

I, Rubairo de Brita, know this.

Line by line, word by word, line by line again, she read it. Then she tried out his name: *Rubairo*. And with it the word Makena had taught her. Esperança. Hope.

Ghost?

No. He's there, she thought. *Really there! On the island. Still.*

I saw you. You spoke to me.

You are there, and also you're long free of it. And you're in the forest, the village, on Kisiri's cliffs and beaches.

It couldn't make any kind of sense. But it did.

She replayed his words: *in the darkest of hours you gave this gift. We will take the tide to our true freedom.*

She wanted to say to him, do you know you gave freedom back? Not just the ammunition, as Makena called it – the fort and the treasure that could save Shanza and Kisiri from being wiped away. It was how all that ripped away the barriers people tried to throw between Leli and me.

Even if it's over now, it was real then.

The day before she left for London, they went alone to Fumo and Zawati's clearing. It was rinsed by days of rain. The black pillar gleamed. New grass speared through the mud. Butterflies flickered through purple flowers. As if every live thing worked busily to erase the horrors of what had been there.

She saw it so clearly, reliving it, moment by moment. Leli walking the boundaries, making sure, listening for Fumo. Then he grinned, as if apologizing for being 'foolish' as he called it, and came to sit beside her. They leaned against each other and breathed the solitary, warm peace of the place.

'It comes to my head, Ally,' he said, 'that in Kisiri there are many roads that cross, and many journeys and many lives that meet? I am thinking that maybe this is what is Kisiri's life.' And that was strange, because she was busy hunting down an elusive thought; as he spoke, it came sharp into focus. About *time* – that on Kisiri it was like the tides around the island, ebbing and flowing. And looping, like the tracks of the birds, so that Fumo and Zawati's time, and the time of the fort, had ebbed and flowed and looped through theirs – hers, and Leli's.

Or was that just foolish too? It didn't feel so, now, sitting in the kitchen with the words of the Portuguese boy in her hands; she had a name for him and a name for the time of the fort – *Rubairo's time*, and she was meandering through another memory, too. Just before she saw Rubairo, as she went down to the sands from the camp on Kisiri, she passed Mzee Kitwana.

'*Sherehe ya Kwazi*,' he murmured, though like a little sigh to himself, not to her. 'Bwana Fumo, Mwana Zawati.'

She'd glanced back to see where he was gazing. She saw the bustling excitement, the air wisping blue with woodsmoke as it might be for festival cooking. She heard the women's gales of laughter, as if the chance to shout advice to each other across the camp was enormously funny, as if some weight pressing down on them yesterday in Shanza was tossed aside by coming to Kisiri.

'*The soul of Shanza flies to Kisiri to be safe*,' Kitwana said, and this time it was to her. Then he threw her a glance full of questions – the kind that said there was more to be said and more to be asked. But he only moved away among the shelters, slowly, seeming smaller and older than ever before, and not once looked back.

It *was* all true, Leli and me. It was, it was. *I mustn't let it be not true, just because it's over.*

She looked down at Makena's folder. In a minute she'd read it all, from the beginning. But there was a rattle at the

293

letterbox – leaflets probably, and she got up to go and look. Then, she thought, breakfast, and after I've read, I'll begin a letter to Makena and Carole, and – a new, firm thought – I'll just write, even if *he* doesn't answer. A card, a picture of London he could put in his room. Happy wishes for his future. No room for bleakness – throw off the bleakness! Not fair to him for me to be bleak—

Envelope on the doormat. Small, blue, stripey coloured border. Airmail. Her name, and above, postman's scribble. *Sorted it to wrong bundle, sorry!*

No sender's name or address on the back. Just fat and crackly with paper: she ripped it open – newspaper cuttings – and tissuey blue paper – writing crammed into every space, even sideways up the page and curling over the top—

My dear very good friend Ally!!!!!

I greet you from the high place where the land fell down and we saw the old stones and the treasure. They have finished putting wood into the hill to hold it safe and now they look inside to see what is hiding there. They make a strong roof in the cave, which is difficult because of the sea underneath, but now nothing will fall down if rain wants to wash it away.

Is it well with you and Jack and Ben? Huru greets you. Today he is going with Saka to the lobster fishing place. Every person in Shanza sends greeting. My mother says she will very welcome you in our house every time. She has specially given the money to buy the paper and the stamp for this letter, and I am very happy she has done this!

I send you the newspapers about our island and our forest which will be a Protected Site of National Heritage. It is very exciting for us all! It is very exciting that we did this, Ally, you and me! I am proud! We all did this, even my brother, Shaaban. He is just now taking his first mechanic's tests, which is very important for him. When he is finished, in four days he will be here for a holiday and I will tell him how it all was, everything, and all the village will thank him!

I am content because we can do many things in Shanza now and not let these people take our island. We will welcome all visitors who do not spoil it. We have many friends who are working with us. Perhaps I will not be a doctor but an archaeologist! That is a joke, I will be a doctor, but truly, Eshe says she will be an archaeologist. She takes all her time to help them there. She is running about, below where I am sitting, and Collins also. They are putting the big ropes to mark the next place to look into. Eshe says I must become a lawyer to keep Shanza and Kisiri safe. But Lumbwi will be the lawyer – he is very impressed with this man who is helping us, Mr Kamusi. Maybe he is only impressed with his good suits! Lumbwi is a chameleon, like his name. But he is a good person. Sometimes I am angry with him that his brain jumps about with big ideas, but now I thank him with everything in my heart that he came to fetch me so fast to speak on the telephone and I thank Eshe with all my heart that she took my letter fast to my brother, so we learned about these cars quickly and we did 'make a join of the dots' as Inspector Rutere calls it.

The newspaper and radio and television came here. They made pictures of Collins and Dedan, also me and Huru, Jela, Lumbwi and his father, and Saka, and Thimba too, in the place of Fumo and

Zawati, and the killed lion and cheetah. I told them about you and Ben and Jack, and that you nearly died when the cliff fell down, Ally. Maybe they telephone you there in London City and ask about it.

Mr Kamusi has won that Fumo and Zawati's place is sacred. It will be allowed to stay always the way it is now. Soon it will be *Sherehe ya Kwazi* there. We will say thank you for all things! There will be Makena and Inspector Rutere and Dr Carole and Mr Kamusi in the festival. They will come on the journey in the boats round Kisiri too. All Shanza made a vote about this. Inspector Rutere sometimes has gloom because of the feet tramping about Kisiri, but it is only because he does not want it to be spoiled.

We will stop it being spoiled, this we will do!

Today there is even a new thing! There are some students at the university where Makena works. They like to dive to look for old wrecks. They have been here this week to dive round Kisiri. Today they came in from the water very excited! They think they have maybe seen a part of a Portuguese ship sticking from the sand. Makena says this is maybe very important, and I must specially tell you.

Now, Ally, Makena has shown us strange things about Kisiri. It is like that writing she gave you, before. She is sending the writing to your auntie for you to read. She says your given name is Elidi. It is like Zawati's – it means Gift. You did not tell me! Gift of the Sun, like the sun of your beautiful hair. And I remember all the strangeness about Kisiri. I remember Fumo's warnings and now I think it is Zawati who speaks to you too! I remember the silver thing of Fumo and Zawati that Mzee Kitwana gave to me and I gave to you and that is now under the earths of Kisiri when the cliff fell down. I remember what you said to me when you go climbing there! I think and think and do not know what to believe. It is even more what I said to you before. Many paths go across each other on Kisiri. Why do they cross? When you receive this writing, tell me what YOU think. You must read it very quickly and tell me quickly.

Today I made a promise. It is to myself. I will visit you one day, in your place, Ally. I will see you! Perhaps you will visit us again in our place, and we may dance together in Shanza to celebrate! I hope you will maybe think of this. I am hoping and hoping and hoping. I am very very very happy if our journeys will meet again.

Go well, my very good friend. Write to me soon, if you can find the time.

Your friend for ever, Leli.

P.S. You do not have a free choice! Write to me STRAIGHT AWAY about what Makena sends, and about everything about you. Makena says she thinks a little door opens in your soul when you came here. I hear her say this and I see that a door is open in my soul when you are here. It is in my soul and my heart. It is painful if you do not write and the door is closed. It will burn me away. Write quickly! Write to me about what Makena says. I must understand what happened to you on Kisiri. It is the thing that makes me unhappy, that I do not really understand what you had there. You must tell me. Read everything quickly, Ally. Tell me everything, everything, everything about your life! You are not allowed to be too busy!

Leli

As if he'd simply strolled into the house; she saw him with the same clarity she'd seen Rubairo in the glare of the sun on

Kisiri. The angle of Leli's head when he tilted it and studied her face. The way he had the last day in Shanza, walking along the beach together, the looming departure bristling with misery. She'd looked away at the boat traffic that constantly moved about Kisiri since the discoveries, and a dhow coasting south, and she'd tried not to think of the call that would come any moment from Carole – *time to go.*

'I am thinking now to say goodbye, quickly,' he'd said abruptly. And he'd held out his hand in a formal, strangely awkward way. As if they were strangers again, meeting and parting after nothing. She'd wanted to fling herself at him, hang on, never ever let go. But she'd just mumbled something, shaken his hand and dropped it, the threatening distance, awkward and cold and immense, wedged between them.

Now, she could hear him say, 'tell me everything about your life.' Just as he said 'sacred' to sound like 'secret', he'd pronounce 'life' so it sounded like 'love'.

She laughed. And didn't care that Jack and Ben, coming down the stairs, would hear and want to know why.

I am very happy if our journeys will meet again, Ally, Leli said.

She threw all caution to the winds.

'They will, Leli,' she vowed. And though they were more than four thousand miles and two continents apart, she thought he probably heard.

Inspirations, experiences, echoes

When I was twelve, I used to wander around the ruins of an ancient Swahili town nestling in a primeval forest. It wasn't far from a long white beach curling round expanses of coral reef where we camped. I remember the strange moods and sudden silences that shrouded the ruin – birds, monkeys, animal scuttlings in the undergrowth, all ceasing abruptly, then tentatively beginning again. I still recall my first glimpse of a great fig tree, its aerial roots forming a twisty door through, shafts of sunlight beyond, as if from another world. Years later I took that idea from my twelve-year-old self and wrote my first novel, *The Keeper of the Gate*.

You can visit this place now: Gede (sometimes spelled Gedi) a city dating from the twelfth century, its ruins buried in beautiful, unique Arabuko Sokoke Forest in Kenya.

Song Beneath the Tides draws on these memories and all the friendships and places of my childhood and teenage life in East Africa. I was fascinated by other ruins I saw, so many up and down that coast: I began finding out about their birth, life, and death. It all fuelled this story.

The events revealed in the Portuguese boy's diary, and the legend of Bwana Fumo and Mwana Zawati, centre on the savage two-hundred-year Portuguese pursuit of the trade in African gold, ivory, ambergris and slaves. The ships of the Portuguese explorers and invaders – the first from Europe – arrived on the east coast of Africa in 1498. They found vibrant Swahili city-states each with their own Kings or Sultans, trading across the ocean with the Red Sea, the Persian Gulf, Arabia and India. At once the Portuguese set about trying to subjugate these communities to seize their trade. The people of the coast and inland tried to survive this onslaught of massacre and plundering by juggling outright resistance and shifting alliances amongst themselves, against the Portuguese, and with them. Disillusioned Portuguese sailors and soldiers deserted and were welcomed into African settlements. Punishment if caught by the Portuguese was horrific. After two hundred years, the Portuguese left behind – as Makena says in the story – only destruction, and a few forts.

All this is shown in vivid Swahili and Portuguese records from that period now housed in museums and universities in Portugal, East Africa and London. In all this I found anecdotes, eye-witness accounts, diaries, letters, official reports from Portuguese commanders and chroniclers. Many of the Portuguese records comment in repulsion and disapproval on the antics of their own countryman. Archaeological evidence from hundreds of scattered ruins is another rich mine of inspiration.

The events of my story, and the characters in the fort, all have some small original thread here.

My fort is inspired by many real ones, particularly the long siege of Fort Jesus in Mombasa by Arabs who came down the coast from Oman to help the Swahili cities. There really was a sixteen-year-old Swahili prince commanding the fort for the Portuguese for a time, though rather different to my invented Jabari. The sickness that killed many in the fort may have been a strain of the plague. One tiny reference to a few survivors in the fort being a handful of African men and women, a Portuguese youth and some children, set me off on my journey to create Rubairo.

Fumo and Zawati, the Songs of Zawati, are inspired partly by, as a child, hearing drums echoing nightly from places along the coast, and wondering what people were celebrating, what story they were telling; also by Fumo Liyongo, legendary hero, warrior and poet, reputed to be eight feet tall, who is celebrated in ballads and stories. Even Mwana Zawati entered my head because of the real Swahili poet Mwana Kupona, who, although very different, lived on the Kenyan island of Pate two centuries later.

Animal trafficking and poaching is of course, all too real. I witnessed the horror of skinned, headless cheetah, and dead elephants with tusks wrenched out by poachers. News reports of this continuing onslaught on wildlife across the world are all too frequent. But so are the efforts to combat it, and advice on how we can all play our part in stopping it.

For the effects of uncontrolled tourism on people and places, I've drawn on what I saw: peaceful, purposeful communities, unspoiled beaches and reefs overrun by massive hotel building projects designed exclusively for the wealthy.

Places I knew became unrecognisable within months. Land-grabbing by business interests is often part of this, ignoring the rights of people whose territory is seized and livelihoods threatened. It's happening all over the world. I've tried to portray the eye-view of people buffeted by these winds of change and fighting the distortion to their lives that too often follows.

The island of Kisiri is inspired by many islands off the coast of East Africa, including those around Lamu, Kenya. Some have ancient Swahili ruins on them. Some are privately owned now, with hotels on them.

All over the world there are court cases brought by people fighting to protect sacred sites from seizure for tourism, mining or other business interest, just as in my story of Shanza and Kisiri.

I've drawn Leli, his family and his community of Shanza from my own friendships then and now, and from the many narratives from African writers and poets across the continent that I've been reading since my teenage years.

In the end, however, this is a made-up place and made-up people – I've threaded all this through the weave of my imagined story. If you want to know more about the realities behind it all, and see pictures of the places that inspired me, visit my website **www.beverleybirch.co.uk**.

Acknowledgements

First and foremost, profound thanks and gratitude to Bella Pearson for your steady guiding hand, understanding and nurturing this book with such wisdom and insight, insisting I meet your very high standards! And for launching your wonderful Guppy Books. Thank you to all your superb team. I'm honoured and grateful to be published by you: you are the editor and publisher of my dreams.

Thank you Salvador Lavado for this beautiful, apt, resonant cover. I couldn't have imagined it before; now it feels as if it was born with the story.

Thank you Catherine Alport and Fritha Lindqvist for your energy, experience and enthusiasm in launching this book out on its journey to readers.

Enormous thanks to my wonderful agent, Ben Illis, for your unstinting encouragement and inspirational conversations as I developed this story, from its early beginnings.

Gratitude to writer friends, Sarah Mussi, Jamie Buxton (J.P. Buxton), Sam Hawksmoor, Margaret Bateson-Hill.

I inflicted a very early draft on you: your enthusiasm and incisive comment was invaluable and egged me on when I might have flagged. To Jon Appleton, author and former editorial colleague and friend: for important editorial comment and a firm push forward. I remember you standing over me, rejecting my nerves, insisting I press the send button when I first approached agent Ben Illis. How important that was!

Thanks to all CWISL (Children's Writers and Illustrators for Stories and Literacy), for friendship and all the shared experiences in meeting young readers to talk about books and writing. To the librarians and teachers who foster these encounters and work so hard to bring books to young people. To all the other writers and illustrators out there, your work and talent is a continuing inspiration and you are such a committed and supportive community.

To Ann Cloke, Jayne Gould, Shirley Imlach, and all the Ipswich Children's Book Group – thank you for welcoming me into your midst, providing so many opportunities to get to know other local writers and their books, and for your interest in mine. I'm so glad I've found you!

To Adamma Oti Okonkwo: your editor's eye, your wise comments on the nuances of this story, its characters and voices, have all been profoundly helpful and encouraging. The book is all the better for it. A special thank you.

To Sofia Burnay, for your invaluable and timely help with the Portuguese language, thank you.

To my daughters Rachel and Kate, thank you for always being my first readers, giving me an essential critical (never any punches pulled) overview on the chasm between the raw ambitions in my head and what is actually reaching the reader. To Rachel a big thanks too for a detailed, knowledgeable comment on a late draft, and for many midnight conversations which led to the title.

Thanks to others (you know who you are), who absolutely refuse to be named, who have put up with me while I write this, and for many conversations about Life, the Universe and Everything.

To young readers everywhere, so open, curious, eager, and honest: you're the most exciting audience to write for, and hard task masters! You tell it how it is and keep all of us on our toes. I wouldn't have it any other way.

BEVERLEY BIRCH spent her childhood roaming vast plains and deep forests near her home in East Africa, dreaming of becoming an intrepid explorer in fantastic, far-away places. Instead she became a writer, and explores people and places through her books. She travels widely, and says, 'Wherever I go, I'm fascinated by the way people and events of the past seem to me to leave a gleam, or a shadow, or a resonating murmur of sound in a place. In a way, that's where all my stories begin.' Critically acclaimed, and translated into more than a dozen languages, she has been nominated for the Carnegie medal, and shortlisted for awards here and abroad.

Beverley worked in children's publishing, on both sides of the fence, for many years, running her prolific writing life alongside commissioning and editing children's fiction. She first joined Penguin in 1975 to edit adult nonfiction, but moved immediately to the children's list, and there found her true home. Three times shortlisted for the Branford Boase Award in recognition of the editor's role in nurturing new talent, she continued to commission until 2013, working with many outstanding and award-winning writers.

She lives on the east coast of England with her husband.

www.beverleybirch.co.uk

Praise for *RIFT*:

'Rift is that delightful thing, a book which holds you from the first page. It's a fine book, with heroes to cheer and baddies to hiss at, with a satisfying ending and yet resisting the desire to tie up every single detail – readers are allowed to finish some of the jigsaw puzzle for themselves'
MARCUS SEDGWICK, GUARDIAN

'Set in Africa, this is a fragmented enigma, the story of a school trip gone mysteriously wrong, with not only several students but also a journalist gone missing in a wild, rocky region . . . stylised, sophisticated and richly atmospheric'
DAILY TELEGRAPH

'A tightly written, highly entertaining novel. Vibrant and haunting, Rift will hold readers' attention well after they've finished reading the last page.'
SCHOOL LIBRARIAN